FARRAH NOORZAD

NOORZAD

AND THE
RING OF FATE

FARRAH NOORZAD

AND THE
RING OF FATE

BOOK 1

DEEBA ZARGARPUR

 LABYRINTH ROAD | NEW YORK

Text copyright © 2024 by Deeba Zargarpur
Jacket art copyright © 2024 by Alessia Trunfio
Map illustration copyright © 2024 by Deeba Zargarpur
Map illustration by Virginia Allyn

Visit us on the Web! rhcbooks.com

Educators and librarians, for a variety of teaching tools,
visit us at RHTeachersLibrarians.com

Library of Congress Cataloging-in-Publication Data is available upon request.
ISBN 978-0-593-56441-7 (trade) — ISBN 978-0-593-56442-4 (lib. bdg.) —
ISBN 978-0-593-56443-1 (ebook)

The text of this book is set in 11-point Scala Pro.

Editors: Liesa Abrams and Emily Shapiro
Cover Designer: Katrina Damkoehler
Interior Designer: Michelle Crowe
Copy Editor: Barbara Bakowski
Managing Editor: Rebecca Vitkus
Production Manager: Natalia Dextre

Printed in the United States of America
10 9 8 7 6 5 4 3 2 1
First Edition

FOR ARZU—

for then, for now, and for always,
everything is for you

DEAR READER,

When I was a little girl, I often found myself lost in daydreams, in tales of make-believe, of fairy tales hidden beneath rugs and lands trapped in glossy mirror reflections. I believed in the mystical unseen, the mischievous jinn, the delicate pari, the simurghs of the sky, and so much more. In my heart of hearts, I knew that one day magic would come for me. One day I'd open the door and a grand adventure would take me away from my real life— a life where I felt split in two after my parents' divorce. Because at least in that magical world, I could find a true home where I finally belonged.

So while I waited for my grand adventure, I decided to write it all down. I wrote what it would be like to be a part of the mystical, magical place where the seen world ends and the unseen world begins. I got lost listening to stories about impossible things—like phoenixes and faeries and dragons and jinn. And then I let my imagination fly. Year by year, I built pieces of that world on paper. I wrote a place where a kid from a single-parent home could be exceptional and where the pieces of my mixed identity just *fit*. A world without explanation, where I could simply *be*. Little did I know that this place would spark the world of Farrah Noorzad.

Writing Farrah's story was the door that led me to the grandest adventure of my life. In many ways, Farrah saved me. She reached deep into my heart and found twelve-year-old me. In her own way, she taught me how to leap without looking, to learn the real meaning of strength, and to realize it's okay to ask for help when you need it. *Especially* when you need it.

But most of all, she taught me the true meaning of the *chosen* one and to hold on to the people who choose you.

My hope for you, dear reader, wherever you are on your chosen-one journey, is to always look for the stories that save you. Whether in Farrah's tale or another's, never stop searching for the place where you belong and, most importantly, where you are *chosen*.

And remember: you're only one door away from your grandest adventure.

With love and magic,

DEEBA ZARGARPUR

CHAPTER ONE

THE WORST BIRTHDAY E V E R

The first couple of times Padar took me climbing, he'd always say something cheesy like *To be truly free, we must face the things that scare us.*

I'm not sure *freedom* is what I felt when he tripped over a tangle of rope and let me drop twenty feet before saving me from imminent death at the Go Vertical climbing gym.

I was only six then, so what did I know about metaphors anyway? Or gym rules, like *Parents shall not let go of rope when belaying child climber, otherwise risk being banned forever.*

It's safe to say we never went back there again. It's fine, though, because now I don't need my dad to belay me. Now I hold my *own* rope. And I haven't been afraid of falling since.

Which is good on a day like today. My fingers are crimped into the crack of a large boulder, my toes are wedged into a crevice, and there's nothing stopping me from plummeting to the ground except my own strength and expertly placed clips. I like to think that gravity and I are in a never-ending fight that I *always* win. I push myself higher and smile when I'm eye level with the treetops. Up here, I can imagine that impossible things could be real, like little flying pari with their wings fluttering in between leaves, or tricky forest spirits waiting for lost travelers to confuse. Or impressing barely-there dads.

I sneak a quick glance at the ground of Wissahickon Valley Park—one of my favorite places in Pennsylvania to climb. My dad and I have a birthday tradition to try different climbing spots (even though December can get pretty chilly, but I don't let a little wind and dry skin stop me). In between our yearly trips, I practice anywhere I can—up the side of my rowhome, dynoing between one fire escape and another, improving my grip strength by hanging off my school's roof by my fingers *and* toes (because you never know).

From up here, my dad resembles a burly ant with his thick brows pinched together (breaching into unibrow territory). He smiles encouragingly. I can't help but shyly grin back. I feel like a bottle of freshly shaken soda when my dad gets to see me climb. The excitement convinces me I can do anything.

Get ready to be impressed, Padar. I want to show him a trick I've been practicing since our last trip. I keep one hand on my rope and push out hard with my feet, so for a moment I'm flying like the mythical simurgh—the fabled Persian phoenix that's way cooler than regular phoenixes. I pretend I have wings and arc with the rope as it swings. The periwinkle sky shimmers around me while I wave at Padar. I swing and pivot, ready to catch the rock when it nears again. Clumps of chalk flutter from my bag—and land directly on my dad's face.

"Sorry!" I frantically wave, causing more chalk to fall from my pouch. My body veers to the left, and I miss the catch. My shoulder crunches into the edge of the rock, causing little stars to dance in front of my eyes. "Oh no no *no.*" Something goes slack above me.

Suddenly, I don't feel as great as a mythical phoenix. To make the whole situation worse, Padar loses his grin. "Stop goofing around and focus, Farrah," he chastises. "Remember our lessons! Check your rope and clips."

The fizz I had goes completely flat. My cheeks are hot and sweaty. *Lessons.* My entire life was a lesson. Why couldn't he see past my mess-ups for once? I can imagine his voice now. *You're doing awesome, Farrah. You've gotten so much stronger since last year. I wish I could see you more too.*

The last thought slips out before I get a chance to squash it. *Get a grip, Farrah.* I pump myself up. *You're twelve now. No one needs their dad anymore at twelve.*

I climb higher, ignoring Padar's shouts to come back down. Climb, clip, climb, clip. The farther I go, the taller I feel, and the bad feelings fall away until there's nothing but sun and sky and air. My best friend and sister-in-crime, Arzu Ahmadi, thinks if I started a social media account to show off my doodles and calligraphy (with some ASMR sound effects), then Padar would be so impressed, he'd start coming around more often. *Nobody likes to feel like they're missing out!* she always says, before jumping into a roundoff back handspring full twist.

Maybe she's right. If Padar could only see how much I can do now, things will change. I just know it. He'll stop hiding me. And maybe it'll be *me* getting on an airplane and visiting his house in Abu Dhabi.

I'm reaching up when a bird flies right at me with a piercing squawk.

"Don't let go!" Padar hollers, but it's too late.

I mess up my clip, and my rope gets super loose. The ache in my shoulder shoots up, and I lose my grip. I can't hold on—I start dropping fast. As I fall backward, the worst thing in all climbing history happens: my rope slips out of my clips, one by one by one.

Oh nooooooooooooooooo.

I scream as I tumble faster and faster. My hair slaps against my face as I plummet—ten, twenty, thirty feet and counting—to the ground. "Heeeeeeelllllllp!" I squeeze my eyes shut and start praying for the next five seconds. *I promise to do all my homework ahead of time. I'll help Madar clean up in the kitchen. I'll stop farting next to Baba Haji and blaming the smell on him—*

Someone must have been listening because the last clip holds, jerking me to a stop two feet above the ground. Stars dazzle in my eyes, and I feel like someone sucker punched my entire body. I unbuckle and collapse into the dirt, flat on my back, breathing a mile a minute.

"What were you *thinking?*" Padar's angry face blocks out the sun. "Why don't you ever listen to me? That was dangerous. Reckless. You could have gotten hurt. Or God forbid—"

The fizz is back when I jump to my feet, but this time it's different.

So much for being impressed.

"I'm fine. I've had worse falls." Like that one time a fourth-story fire escape suddenly broke off midjump and I fell into a dumpster. "And I've never broken a bone from a fall." *Or ever,* I want to say, but I keep that to myself because that's pretty weird. I like to think it's my special superpower, being indestructible (that is, if superpowers existed). It helps with getting through the tough stuff anyway, like having to deal with a disappointed dad. I wipe dirt from my pants and nervously tug on my ponytail. "Can I have my phone back, please?"

"You nearly smash into the ground, and the first thing you ask for is your phone?" Padar looks like he's about to blow a gasket. "How about we discuss how you went past your limits!"

I bristle. "I practice in the gym all the time—"

"Apparently not enough to know you clipped in backward."

Red alert. The warning signs are flashing little red and

blue lights in my eyes, but I can't stop it. The fizz bubbles up and pushes the words right out of my mouth.

"How would you know what I can do when you're never around?" I say loudly. "If you were here, you'd know I'm stronger than you think." I stalk off. My favorite blue chalk bag crashes against my legs as I stumble up, up, up on the uneven path.

Padar outpaces me and catches me in his arms. "I'm sorry. You're right." He falters. His bushy brows crinkle together the way they always do when he's about to say something unpleasant. "I wish I could change things, but you know the rules."

Rules. Another word like *lessons.* I'd rather drink lemon juice mixed with unsweetened almond milk (or warm, week-old doogh) than hear another one. The glare of the sunset hides my frown. "I just don't know why I have to be punished for something that's not my fault." I break away from his hug, even though I really don't want to. "Anyway, we're wasting daylight. We don't have much time to get to the best part of the hike."

Padar's relief is a little too obvious when I change the subject. He doesn't miss a beat and switches back to his annual updates on what's been going on with him. He's a judge in the UAE, so he doesn't really have that much free time. The same old *work never ends* and *time flies so fast* and *wish I knew the secret to slow it down* and *I promise things will be different when you're older* and *you know how it is.*

"Right." I kick rocks out of my way. "I know."

In my community, people like to keep it traditional. We don't like to stray from the OG way. So when Padar and Madar had me, a *harami*—an out-of-wedlock kid—when they were younger, well . . . that just wasn't something good Muslims did.

Because of that, I've lived with Madar and my grandparents my whole life, which is fine, minus the old-people smell. And Padar was married off before I was born to someone who didn't break the rules, so we've lived separately since forever. I guess Padar's family is really into rules (which is probably where he gets it from), but sometimes I wonder if there was something *else* that happened the adults won't tell me. It's not like I'm saying this because I want anyone to feel sorry for me, though. I'm still lucky because I have Arzu, and she only lives ten blocks away, plus she's Muslim and Afghan American too. So she *gets* it.

And it's really not all that bad. I mean, at least I get to see Padar on my birthday. It could be worse. I could not get to see him at all.

"Can you stop looking like you've sucked on a lemon? Or do I need to tickle a smile out of you?" Padar creeps up from behind, and I dart out of the way just as he swipes for me. I can't help the grin that breaks across my face. Padar knows I can't resist a good challenge.

"Only if you can catch me first!" I take off, full speed, through the worn trail, keeping an ear out for the sound of

Padar's laughs and stomping feet as I push vines and branches out of my face. For a second I pretend we're running from a small army of elves and I'm the one leading the way to safety. The burn in my legs encourages me to go faster, push harder until I finally reach the clearing and stop at the edge of a cliff.

"Beat you!" I throw my pack on the ground and whoop in triumph.

"That's not fair. I'm the one carrying all our supplies." Padar drops heaps of rope, shoes, and his own pack. He stretches out his back, twisting left and right. "I'm getting too old for this."

"Didn't anyone tell you, excuses aren't a good look?" I tip-toe toward the ledge. The cliff juts fifteen feet over a massive drop. Wind hums in my ears and dances with my hair. The forest marches out, just begging us to come explore and discover all its whispering secrets.

The sun makes itself comfy on the horizon as it gets ready to switch places with the moon in preparation for the longest night of the year. Which means our day is almost done. I go home to Madar to finish Yalda night celebrations, and Padar just . . . leaves for another three hundred and sixty-four days with his real family.

I hunch over and hug my knees to my chest. My stomach always starts to hurt when I think of the rest of Padar's life. I wonder what it would be like to see what my dad's *real* family looks like. What it would feel like to have a dad at home. Or to know if he had other kids besides me. No matter how hard

I try, I can't imagine it. It's hard to picture a family you've never seen. And I don't want to ask my dad if I do have any siblings in case he says *no* or *that's not for you to know.*

"Figured we'd need something extra warm for the sunset." Padar drapes a gray-and-white blanket around me. He sits and pulls me in. "I can't believe Yalda night is here again." The Night of Birth is the longest night of the year, where darkness roams for as long as it can. My grandmother likes to say it's the night where magical jinn lurk in the shadows, waiting to create havoc and mischief. It's also officially the start of winter. Even if it wasn't my birthday, it's still my favorite night of the year for this reason.

I lean into Padar's shoulder and listen to the steady *whoosh* of his breathing and hang on tight. With my eyes screwed shut, I make myself *remember* this moment. Remember the way Padar always smells like vanilla and soap. Remember the way his left eye squints when he smiles. Remember the way it feels to have a dad. Even if it's just for a day. And then I slip it away, into a tiny little box inside my head for safekeeping, so I can focus on the happy feelings instead of the sad.

"Maybe now is a good time for a picture." Padar fiddles with my phone, angles it high, and says, "Paneer!" before snapping a photo. I laugh when his eyes cross. "Okay, less goofy one now."

"Let me see." I grab the phone from his hands and swipe through. "I need to approve it, you know? Make sure it's good enough."

"Yes, ma'am," says Padar through a mock salute.

"It's serious business. If you don't take the right picture, how could anyone know we went hiking?" Not like I'd ever show anyone these photos (well, maybe Arzu, since she bugs me every time), but it's important to make sure there's one that's just right. I erase all the mess-ups until there's one perfect picture left. Padar and me, bathed in a dewy glow of golds and violets—the in-between of night and day. We look happy, like we have all the time in the world.

After a moment of gazing at the sunset, Padar asks, "Do you want to know why this night is so important?"

"Yes," I say, because it's the last part of our birthday tradition before we head back to the car. I already know the answer, but I still wait to hear it.

He holds me a little too tight when he says, "It's the only night where we must feel the weight of darkness and fight against it, knowing light is waiting for us at the very end." He hesitates and stares at the sky again, like he really doesn't want to keep talking. His dark eyes mirror back the violets from the sunset. "Waiting for us to make the right choices."

I nod and wait for the next part of his story. Padar usually goes on to tell me about mystical beings, creatures that exist beyond our wildest imaginations, like phoenixes and faeries and dragons and jinn made of smokeless fire, all living slightly out of our reach. Invisible to the human eye, but just as real as the light that warms my skin.

Magic, in the realest sense of the word. I'd never admit it to Arzu, but I'd like to think it's all real.

"What do you know about fate?" Padar asks while fiddling with something in his pocket. The ground rumbles a little. A spark of lightning slashes the sky in half.

My face scrunches when a clap of thunder follows. "Like destiny?" I mean, I've heard those words thrown around a lot, especially during Friday prayer at the masjid, but it's hard to focus when there's a storm coming. "Like things turn out the way they're supposed to?"

Padar smiles a sad little smile. "Something like that. All of us are bound by what is prewritten in our destinies. Everything that you are meant to be is predestined. From the moment you were born, fate has lived in you, has wrapped its threads around your heart, around all our hearts." At this, Padar looks even sadder.

I get a little sad too. Because if that's true, then that means we were always meant to live apart. . . .

Padar grips a small box tightly in his hands. His knuckles turn white as he clears his throat. He blinks a little too fast. The purple glow hasn't left his eyes. Little shadows dance behind him. "Though what if I told you there was an item so powerful, it could break your threads of fate if you wished on it? A power long ago lost to the depths of the sea and drowned in an enchanted box." He drops the box into my hands. His voice gets strained. "Would you . . . wish on it?"

"I thought we didn't do birthday gifts." I shake the box (a little too aggressively). There's no latch or keyhole to open it, but I feel a buzzing in my fingers and head, like a whisper or a voice. "How do I get it open?" I try prying the lid with my fingers, but nothing works. Something tinkles softly inside.

"Don't . . . focus on that," Padar says with a pained look on his face. "Don't . . . think about it." Padar shakes his head, like he's changing his mind. "Don't—" Padar gets tongue-tied and stands up abruptly. I've never seen my dad have a hard time expressing himself before. Normally, it's hard to get him to *stop* lecturing. A light rain sprinkles on us. "I should get you home before your mother worries." He starts to pack our belongings while muttering to himself.

I look at the box in my hands and wonder if he's acting so weird because of the gift. Maybe he didn't want to give it to me, or maybe he felt he had to. My stomach twists, and I find my heart wishing I had the guts to ask why this is bothering him so much. If the day didn't have to end, maybe I could try to ask why he never sticks around, why he always has to go, why we can't do normal things like exchange gifts for birthdays without it feeling weird or forced.

Maybe it doesn't have to, a little whisper, like static, rumbles in my head. *If that is your heart's truest request.*

A louder, more furious crack of thunder shakes the sky just as the box opens. Lightning follows. The rain is falling heavier now as I finally get to see what was hidden inside: a glowing golden ring. My eyes get as round as coins. I gasp.

"Do you see this?" I call to Padar, who is too busy throwing packs on his back to get out of the rain. The soft glow from the ring lights up my face. I can't help but stare. How is it glowing?

"The lightning? Yeah, looks like it's going to be a bad storm. We should get out of here."

But that's not what you want, is it? The voice startles me. It sounds like it's coming from the ring, but that can't be. So then why do I feel something pulling at my heart as I hold the ring tight to my chest, squeeze my eyes shut, and wish for one of Padar's stories to be true?

"If this isn't some silly bedtime story," I whisper with all my heart, "then I wish to be hidden no longer. I wish to find a place in Padar's world. I wish my fate to be rewritten."

Nothing happens.

"Please," I add, just in case. The blanket clings to me like wet plastic wrap as a bright bolt of light illuminates the sky.

Padar jumps back in shock and finally looks at me. When he sees the ring in my hands, it's like he's woken up from a long dream.

A wish is a wish is a wish, the whisper roars loud in my head. *And now your fate is mine.*

Light erupts from the ring as it swirls around me, louder than the storm. The rain comes down in sheets. Harder.

Little bolts of lightning crackle, pinching my arms and legs. It really hurts. "Padar! Help, what's happening?" I run and try to get away from the energy around me, but it ties itself tighter around my body.

"Farrah, what have you done?!" Padar runs toward me and jumps head-on into the swirl of energy. Bright flashes of blue and silver whirl around us. Thunder echoes from his roar as his tanned skin glows blue. I gasp in shock.

In an instant, Padar changes. His torso grows bigger, his teeth sharper, like a vision from a nightmare. "What was your wish?" He is frantic as he rips the ring from my hands, but I can't move, can't compute what I'm seeing. "Farrah, snap out of it. What did you—"

"What is happening to you? What is going on? Why are you blue?!" I scream, my body now free to move. The figure, who I *think* is my dad, is fighting against the swirl of energy erupting from the ring. Waves of thunder roll off him as light from the ring swirls faster and faster, but Padar doesn't even look *scared*.

Unfortunately, I'm scared for the both of us because I can barely recognize Padar. He turns to me, the whites of his eyes glowing purple. "Run now. Get out of here before he gets you too," his voice booms, loud and deep, like it's coming from every direction. It shakes the cliff and sends me flying backward. I get an awful feeling in my stomach as I cover my head with my arms.

"Padar, just let go of the ring. It's doing something strange to you," I yell, because that has to be it, right? "Drop it and we can get out of here!"

Impossibly, two things happen at once.

A boy with milky white eyes and hair appears in front of Padar. The boy gasps in surprise, like he's just woken up from a nap.

And a cyclone wraps around them both. Padar's clothes thrash against his body as he shouts something at the boy. The boy's eyes lock on mine for a second. His mouth puckers as if he's eaten something sour.

I try to get a better look, but I blink and he's gone. Finally, a light bursts from Padar's chest as he crumples to the ground.

No.

I run over to him, falling on my hands and knees. His shirt is torn, exposing his blue skin, and there are so many silver scars that resemble lightning bolts trailing from his arms to his chest. For a second I'm too afraid to touch my dad—too afraid to allow whatever changed him to change me. But then I see my phone sprawled on the ground, with our photo staring back at me, and I snap out of it.

"Padar, wake up. Padar. Open your eyes." His eyes stay closed. I have to fix this. Somehow. My training from Girl Scouts kicks in, and I call 911. I hold on to him, tears leaking from my eyes. "I take it back. I take it all back. Just please wake up."

He doesn't. Instead, the scars on his body burn bright—so

bright—but I don't let go of him, because I'm scared of what it means if I do. As the glow starts to dim, so does Padar, until the unthinkable happens.

He vanishes, like dust through my fingers.

The wind slows, and starlight catches on the ring next to my phone. The ring shimmers one last time, and when the light fades, I notice there are now seven gems embedded in the gold.

Only one gem glows.

Only one whisper remains.

One fate for another, it says in my head. *Your wish has been granted.*

CHAPTER TWO

THE GIRL WHO CRIED JINN

Red and blue lights dance against the state park sign. Adults in dark navy uniforms are running around and whispering to one another.

I curl up tighter in my soggy blanket and stare up at the starry sky from the rear of the ambulance. The back doors are propped open. I pinch my cheeks because I'm getting that prickly feeling behind my eyes, and the only thing worse than having your dad disappear (literally) on your birthday is crying like a baby about it in public.

Tires crunch on the dirt parking lot, and a gray car door slams shut.

"Farrah, where are you? Farrah?" Madar—wrapped in her winter coat—is near tears. She shakes one of the EMTs. "Where is my daughter?"

I want to tell her, *I'm here,* but everything feels so heavy.

There's an annoying buzzing in my right ear that won't go away.

Finally, she spots me and wraps me in her arms.

"What happened?" Her big brown eyes look me over as she runs her hands along my face, my damp hair. "Where's your father? How—"

"He disappeared, Madar." My teeth chatter from the cold as I hug her tight. The prickly feeling only gets worse, but I swallow it back. "He gave me a ring and then there was a storm and then he was gone. Like, *gone*, Madar—"

"Is that so?" Madar goes stiff as she glances around, like she's expecting something to pop out from the shadowy forest. There's a look on her face that makes me nervous. "Don't worry, I'm sure he's fine. Come, let's get you home. You must be freezing." Her arm guides me to the car, but something feels wrong.

The leaves crinkle in warning in the breeze. The buzzing gets louder.

"But, Madar, we can't just leave him." I look back at the trail and imagine the cliff, the storm, the mysterious boy with white eyes. My wish. The way Padar looked. The voice. The lights of the police cars and ambulance stain the trees and signs. "It's my fault he's gone. Something bad happened to him because of me—"

Madar cuts me off. "Don't you ever blame yourself for your father's reckless behavior. After all, people don't *vanish*." She lifts me into the passenger seat and tucks my hair behind my ears. "People leave," she mutters while gently shutting the door.

"It is my fault. I made a wish and then Padar turned blue, like—like a *jinn!*" I say frantically when Madar turns on the car and drives away. That's got to be it. Everyone knows jinn are responsible for wishing objects. I try to swallow the feeling that Madar is wrong. "Look, I can prove it. Do you see how it's *glowing,* Madar? Madar. Madar, can you just stop driving and *look?*" I hold up the ring and explain what I saw, hoping it'll change her mind and she'll understand there's something really wrong.

My mom keeps her eyes fixed on the road, refusing to look, refusing to listen, like this is just one more trouble I've added to her already-full plate that's ready to break. Worst of all, Madar seems *scared.*

"Listen to me when I tell you, Farrah jan, our life is not a fantasy; there is no magical rainbow or story or thing that will take us away from our problems. You were exhausted, freezing, seeing things. What happened has nothing to do with jinn or you. I know it hurts to have him run off like this, but you don't need to defend his bad behavior with a story," she says quietly. "Now, please, settle down and trust me when I say the best thing for all of us is to go home and never speak of this again. Do you understand?"

"But—"

"I mean it." Madar's voice wobbles as she drives. "Not a single word. For all of our sakes."

OF COURSE ALL I WANT TO DO IS TALK ABOUT IT.

But in the few days since Padar vanished, the adults have been very secretive, having hushed conversations behind closed doors they think I can't hear through. Though I can only make out bits and pieces of their whispered talks, I can feel the rumbles of gears turning, like something is about to change, I just don't know what yet. All I know is my family is talking a lot about what happened on my birthday—just not with me.

"I'm sure there's a logical explanation," Arzu says while using the ledge of my rowhome as a balance beam. I'm sitting under some twinkling string lights with a tablet, doodling in a drawing app. The emergency access door to our rooftop is propped open. Arzu and I have been using the roof as our idea spot for years. It's one of the things we have in common: we do our best thinking in high-altitude situations. No matter how hard Arzu tries, I don't think a series of backflips is going to get me to smile. Deep down, I know that what happened to Padar had everything to do with my wish. Which means it's all my fault.

"Take me through it again." Her curly hair whips in the wind as the moon and stars glitter all around her. Center City winks in the background. "Maybe you're missing something."

"There's nothing to miss," I say while making angry brushstrokes. Blue slashes across the page. "He was telling me a story about the darkness and light and making the right choices. . . . The last thing he said to me was to run before he gets me too. Next thing I know there's this . . . jinn boy who shows up and Padar is gone." The words are sticky and slow because I don't want a repeat of Madar's reaction, but I'm pretty sure the boy was a jinn. Or maybe a ghost—but definitely *not* human. I lie on my back and gaze up at the inky sky. Wide white eyes stare back at me. Was the boy the *he* Padar was warning me about? I shiver. "All that was left was this."

The present inside the box.

A ring.

I take it from my pocket and examine it for the fifty-third time. My tablet slips off my lap and slides next to my shoes. The golden ring looks worn, like it's been wished upon a thousand times before. Around the ring are seven gems— but only the dark sapphire-blue one is glowing right now. I remember my dad's blue skin and shudder all over again. The other gems are bright and vivid too. Ruby red, emerald green, amethyst purple, carnelian yellow, pearl gray, and quartz white. But those gems weren't there before my wish. I have so many questions. What is this ring? Where did it come from? Why did my dad give it to me?

Did it make my dad disappear? Or was it the boy who came out of the ring? Did he put a curse on my dad that transformed him? Is there a way to get Padar back, or will he be gone forever? And the biggest question—why didn't any of it faze my dad? It's like he *knew* it was all real.

My thoughts are jumbled with guilt and questions and zero answers. I stare at the half-finished drawing of my dad—giant, blue, transformed. Nothing makes sense.

"Hmm. Hm. Hm. Hm." Arzu jumps down from the ledge and snatches the ring from my hand. "What if you spooked your dad with your wish?" She brings it up to one of the fairy lights strung along little poles and squints an eye. "Maybe this was his way of saying goodbye. A gift to remember him by."

"He wouldn't give me a box and then leave me all alone in the woods." I try not to frown, but it really stings when your mom *and* best friend don't believe you. "Glad to know you think I'm making it all up too."

"Hey, I never said that." Arzu rushes over, her hazel eyes wide. She plops her hands on my shoulders. "I really *do* think your dad was up to something fishy. It just might not . . . involve jinn. And not to be mean or anything . . ." Her eyes settle on my tablet. She looks at it curiously. "But your dad does have a habit of not sticking around, you know?"

"It's an *annual agreement—*"

"I'm just saying," Arzu interrupts. "It's not like you know your dad that well. Maybe this is just how he is. And I wouldn't blame you if you thought up some story to explain him leaving again. I get that it's easier to think he got wrapped up with the magic of jinn because . . ."

It's better than thinking he doesn't want to see me anymore.

"I'm not making it up. Now you sound just like my mom."

I turn around and cross my arms over my chest so Arzu can't see how much her words sting. "Once I convince my mom and grandparents that I'm telling the truth, we'll get to the bottom of this. They'll help me find him. They just need a little more time to come to their senses."

"Right, you're right," Arzu agrees uneasily. "I'm sure you'll find out what—"

Arzu's phone buzzes in her pocket.

"Oh shoot." The little screen lights up her scrunched face. "I've been summoned home. Discussion to be continued, okay?" She grabs her backpack and slings an arm around my shoulder. "Come on, don't look so blue. It'll all figure itself out. I bet money on it."

"You don't have any money," I grumble while packing up my stuff.

"Well, if I *did*, I'd bet it." Arzu leads us back to the emergency door. "You'll see. Your dad will show up with an explanation, and things will go back to normal. I'm sure of it."

The wind picks up just as Arzu goes down the stairwell. It curls around me, blowing my hair over my face. A buzzy sound, like a voice, rings in my ear.

He's coming for you.

"Hello?" I whirl on my heel. "Is . . . anyone out there?"

The wind continues to swirl around me, tugging at my shirt, my hair, my shoes, saying the same thing until it roars in my head like a waterfall.

I look out, past the roof, to the twinkling city and freeze.

By City Hall's clock tower, there's the boy with white hair hanging from one of the clock's arms, staring at me.

"You coming or what?" Arzu yells from the stairwell.

I startle and blink.

He's gone.

"Hey, wait!" I jump and wave, in case the boy reappears again. I cup my hands around my mouth and yell, "Who are you and what have you done with my dad?" It can't be a coincidence to see him twice now. "I'm not afraid of you! Show yourself!" That boy has to know *something*.

"What was that? I haven't done anything to your dad," Arzu shouts back from the bottom of the stairwell. "Farrah, don't make me come back up there. You know I hate stairs!"

I keep staring at City Hall for five, ten, fifteen more seconds until my eyes start to burn. *Show yourself. I know you're there.*

The boy doesn't come back.

When I can't hold my eyes open for a second longer, I blink away my disappointment.

"That's it, I'm coming back up!"

"Coming!" I slam the emergency door shut and run down the stairs. *Maybe they're right. Maybe it was all in my head.*

So then why does the buzzing wind follow me all the way down the stairs?

Why can't I shake the feeling that whatever took my dad is coming for me next?

DINNER IS PRETTY QUIET AND TENSE WITH OUR LITTLE FAMILY of four sitting in our narrow dining room. Since I've never met my dad's family, it's always been just the four of us: Madar, Bibi jan, Baba Haji, and me. Normally, I like spending time with my mom and grandparents. We do lots of activities together. (Most of them revolve around *not forgetting where we come from*, aka reenacting lots of games my grandpa played as a kid; this involves *so many* card games.) The past few days have been anything but normal. Ever since my birthday, it feels like there's been a dark shadow looming over my mom as she spends more and more time in her bedroom on the phone.

"Take a second helping." Madar fusses over my grandpa, plopping a concoction of basmati rice, cardamom seeds, rose water, and veal on his plate. Bits of rice sprinkle in my drink. "The meat is extra fresh."

"How can meat be extra fresh when it's already dead?" I conduct precise surgery as I squint my eyes and pluck the offending pieces of rice out of my now-ruined soda. "Dead things can only get more dead, not more fresh."

Baba Haji's silverware screeches like nails on a chalkboard as he and my grandma exchange disapproving glances.

"Farrah jan, that's not appropriate dinner conversation," Bibi says in Farsi. Her hands flutter along her spotted headscarf. "One should never take death's name so easily. Brings bad luck."

"It's a little too late for that," I mumble, and sink deeper into my chair. "Bad luck is all I know lately." The only thing worse than forks scraping on china is silence and three sets of eyes glued worryingly on me. I focus singularly on stabbing my pumpkin dumplings, over and over again.

"You see, there she goes again," Baba Haji mutters very quietly and fast in Farsi at my mom. "Behaving unpredictably, like her father."

"Dada jan, please."

"What's so bad about being like my dad?" I grumble, and continue stabbing my dumplings until they're a pile of mush.

"Nothing, janem." Bibi jan fakes a tight smile, but I know she's lying. Apparently, acting even a little bit like my dad these days makes the shadows heavier around Madar's face. I can't help feeling guilty for the little spark of joy at having something in common with him. Especially since my mom refuses to talk about my dad. It's tradition to not talk about him. After my birthday when Padar drops me off at home, Madar pretends the visit never happened.

"We just worry your father puts silly things in your head," Baba Haji says while taking a sip of his water. "Stories like talking rings that are best not to be entertained or used as an excuse for his reckless behavior."

I sink further in my seat, embarrassed when I realize my mom and grandparents have been talking about me behind my back. "But it's not a story, it's *real,* and I can prove it if you would listen to me."

"Not this again," Baba Haji groans.

"If you would look at it—"

"I don't need to see anything from that father of yours," Baba Haji cuts in. His cheeks and ears go red when he loses his temper, and I stare at my fingers in my lap, trying to blink away the prickly feeling behind my eyes. A moment of silence goes by. Then I hear my grandpa sigh. "I didn't mean to be so harsh," he explains, a little softer. "If it will help, let's see it, then."

Finally. My heart darts in between the little strings that are pulling tight, ready to hand over the ring. Once he touches the ring, he'll understand. He'll feel the unexplainable energy, see the way the blue gem glows, hear the voice that whispers and buzzes in my head. Then he'll help me and we'll find Padar together. I'm sure of it.

I give him the ring. Bibi jan leans in, squinting as Baba Haji brings the ring close. He runs his fingers over the grooves with a strange expression on his face.

Again, the whispers rumble and whirl around my head, wrapping my thoughts with the same question: *What is your heart's truest wish?* I can feel the whisper circling through my ears and weaving toward Baba Haji and Bibi jan.

Madar, strangely, keeps looking away. Her face is a thundercloud of an emotion I can't read.

"Do you hear it?" I ask tentatively.

"I don't hear a thing." Baba Haji tosses the ring at me and leans back grumpily in his chair. "Did you?"

Bibi jan solemnly shakes her head, but she doesn't look me in the eye when she says, "No, my dear. Nothing at all."

"But . . . the blue gem. See here? Can't you see its glow?" It's like my heart's been flushed down the drain. I look at the ring. Why can't they feel what I feel? See what I see?

"It's just a regular ring, janem, and nothing more," Bibi jan says softly. "I think it's time we put this theory to rest, yes?"

A blanket of tension lies on top of us when I don't respond. Instead, I angrily start shoveling dumplings into my mouth to keep the prickly feeling away. If the adults won't help me figure out what happened to Padar, then who will? How am I supposed to find him and fix what I've done?

Bibi jan sighs when I continue chomping on dumplings and ignoring her.

"You see what I mean?" Baba Haji asks Madar. "We need to decide what we're going to do. I don't think being here is good for us anymore." He smooths his wispy white hair back. His thick black brows draw together. There's a piece of shredded carrot wedged somehow in the space between them. I don't tell him. "We need to decide about the house and Farrah's future—"

"I would rather we not discuss it at the table." Madar cuts in quickly.

My thoughts come to a screeching halt. The dumplings turn sour in my mouth. "Discuss what?"

"Don't talk with food in your mouth, jan."

I spit it out and home in on Baba Haji. "What about the house?"

"Farrah!"

"I didn't even chew it. Look, it still looks like a dumpling." If you squint, like, really hard, but that's not the point—the point is something big has been happening behind Madar's closed bedroom door, and I need to know *now*. "What about the house?"

"And I think that's it for dinner." Bibi makes a tired sound as she starts to clear away the plates.

"Farrah, I—" Madar sighs wearily, like there's so much weight on her shoulders, she can barely move. "I think it's time we try to move on from all this. Get a fresh start, away from the chaos your father has caused."

Baba Haji's watery gray eyes stare kindly at Madar as he clasps his wrinkled hands on top of hers. "We can always stay at your sister's home in New York and figure it out from there. We won't tell anyone; we'll just go and he'll be none the wiser."

Padar. They're talking about my dad. And moving. And—

"It's for the best," Bibi agrees, and adds her hands on top of their support huddle.

"The best for who? We can't move!" I push away from

the table so hard, my chair topples backward and hits the wall. "Philly is where we belong. I'm not doing it. *No way.*" I've lived my *entire* life in this house. Every dent in the hallways, the pencil markings Madar would take to measure my height, the patches of unfinished painting projects—I've memorized every moment in this house. Twelve years of memories. Moving has to be illegal, especially when I'm halfway through sixth grade. I should have never told my family about the ring. I should have kept it to myself, figured it out on my own.

"Your khala Fazilat has a lovely home right next to the water in Patchogue we can easily—"

"Khala Fazilat's house smells like stinky sewage and I. Won't. Go. They're mean and judgy and I don't like them!" Ever since I was born, my mom's side of the family has kept their distance from us, and now we're going to live with one of them? No way. "Madar, please. I take it back, you were right, I made it all up. It was all a story, so we don't have to move, right?" Madar is the sensible one. She doesn't act on rash emotion—she's been our family's rock forever. She takes a long time to answer, but when she finally looks at me, her eyes watery and pinched shut, I take one step back and then another.

"It's not just about the story, janem. Maybe a change of scenery would be nice." She rubs her eyes with the backs of her hands. "For the rest of the winter break. Just to see."

"But I need to be here." I hate the way I sound, like a

whiny kid. "My whole world is here." Plus, I need to be around to find Padar. I need to come up with a plan. I can't do that when we're in New York. I wasted so much time waiting on my family to help me, but obviously their idea of helping is making everything *worse*.

"I know you're too young to understand this now, but your world will change many times in your life, sometimes in an instant," Madar says. "It's scary, but we'll get through it together." She spreads her arms wide, ready to hug me. Problem is, a hug isn't going to fix the idea of moving or leaving my dad.

"I can't believe this!" I bolt out of the dining room. "First I lose my dad, and then I lose my home! It's like you're actively trying to make my life worse. I wish I were the one who disappeared!" I stomp up each step to emphasize each word.

"Farrah, you can't mean that." Madar reaches to grab me, but Bibi holds her back.

"Let her go cool down," she says quietly. "She'll come around to the idea."

I slam my door shut, hoping they get the message loud and clear.

I'm not moving.

CHAPTER THREE

THE (SHORT AND TRAGIC) LOVE STORY OF MY PARENTS

There's a soft knock on my door. "Go away." I draw the blankets up to my neck. When I see the door open, I turn around and wiggle my way to the side of my bed that's next to the wall.

"Can I come in?" Bibi's sweet voice floats through the darkness. She turns on the LED lights all around my room and picks a preset light show (the blue one, my favorite). The lights bounce and play against the shadows, making it look like we're underwater.

"You're already in," I mumble, still keeping my back to her. "And ocean lights aren't gonna get me to—"

"It seems I've made too much ice cream and thought you might like to help me finish it. Such a shame to let it go to waste, you know. Your grandfather doesn't like sweets, and it's just too much for your mom." She sighs loudly. "But if you're not hungry, well then—"

"Wait." Ice cream changes everything. I sit up abruptly. There's a twinkling knowing in Bibi jan's eyes when she hands me a bowl.

"Well, go on and scoot. I have to sit somewhere in this mess." She chuckles and settles in next to me in my twin bed. There are papers, books, clothes, and climbing supplies scattered around my floor and all over my desk. Art supplies spill out of drawers, and I'm almost running out of space on my walls from all the drawings, calligraphy, and photos I've taped up. With the right lighting, I like to think I'm drifting away in an ocean of memories—something a new home could *never* offer.

"It's not a mess, it's organized chaos." I shovel spoonful after spoonful of Bibi's homemade ice cream into my mouth. It's not because I love the taste—it's vanilla, rose water, and pistachio all mixed together; it's kinda weird—but because if for some reason we do move, I don't want to miss out on a nighttime tradition with my grandma (even if she's trying to ruin my life).

"Slow down there." Bibi laughs. "You'll get a brain freeze if you keep that up."

"Too late." I drop my spoon in my empty bowl. "Are you going to finish yours?" I eye her half-full bowl, and she swats me away with a gentle push.

"Let an old woman enjoy her sweets in peace." She sinks back into my pillows and pulls me into a hug, which really isn't fair, because my grandma is the softest pillow ever. She doesn't say anything, but I watch how she looks at my stacks of books—mostly fantasy and climbing guides. Her gaze lands on one stack that I like to call my jinn research pile (it's mainly notebooks filled with the stories told to me over the years), and she sighs.

"I know you're angry at your mother," she begins. "And I can't blame you for being upset with her. If I were in your shoes, I'd feel the same way. In fact, I did feel the same way you do when my mom did something similar to me."

"Really?" I think for a second. "You had a mom who bossed you around too?"

"I wasn't always the wise old woman you see before you. I was a little girl once." Bibi jan nods and lays her chin on top of my head. "Oh yes, I was a little bit younger than you when we had to move from Mazar-i-Sharif to Kabul. It was quite hard on me. I had to learn to make new friends, learn a whole new way of life."

I didn't know this about my grandma. It's hard to picture her as a kid (it's hard to think she ever *was* a kid—aren't old people just born old?) since she doesn't have any photos from that time, so I end up just picturing myself.

"What did you do about it?" I ask.

"Well, I certainly didn't stomp up the stairs and slam my door, like a certain little girl I know," she teases me. My face gets red. "I rebelled, in my own way. I got lost in stories, in books I tucked away full of creatures and magic. I imagined I was part of a powerful, magical prophecy, and that we had to move to keep hidden from the jinn who wanted to interfere."

I gasp. "Really?"

"Really. You know, we're more alike than you think." She pushes my hair away from my forehead.

"But you think that's all they are," I mumble, and poke my fingers together, remembering her reaction to the ring. "Stories."

"I like to think there's a nugget of truth in every tale, my dear. And I would never deny the existence of jinn."

"Then why does no one believe me?"

"I believe in how you feel, but . . ." She holds me closer. "There's so much of this world we don't understand, we can never say for certain what is real and what isn't. What's more important is what feels real to *you*. When you get to my age, sometimes you forget the part of yourself that once was young and starry-eyed." She sighs and continues her speech. "When I was your age, what felt real to me when we moved was my anger. I was so mad because I didn't know *why* it was happening. It didn't feel very fair then, and I don't think it's very fair now to be doing the same thing to you without explaining why."

"I don't want to hear why. I just want it to go away." I push away from her and sit crisscross on my bed. My bangs flop around my forehead, and I search in my sheets for my tablet to finish my drawing. She's doing that adult thing where they pretend to understand but don't. When Bibi doesn't continue speaking, my curiosity gets the better of me. I look up. "Okay, you got me. Maybe I want to know a little bit."

"Ask and you shall receive." She smiles while putting our ice cream bowls on my night table. "Your mother, grandfather, and I moved here—yes, this very house—when your mother got accepted to a college here in the city. She wanted to go so badly, I remember her asking day and night if she could go. I never wanted to stand in the way of her dreams, so we made a decision and came together.

"At first, everything was perfect. We got adjusted, started making a routine, but then, in that first year, your mother started coming home later and later, and there always seemed to be a secret smile glued to her lips, like her head was somewhere up in the clouds." Bibi pauses here. "Like she was in love."

I stop my drawing when I realize what my grandma is saying. "We're not supposed to talk about that," I whisper. My eyes go wide, and a million questions pop up—questions I've never been allowed to ask.

"I know, my darling, but I think you're old enough to hear just this part." She pushes my bangs out of my eyes. "One day, in the spring, I saw your mother being dropped off by a handsome stranger, and it was breathtaking how happy they looked. I thought, *Finally, love has come for my youngest child.* Of course, I pretended I hadn't seen, and waited for the day your mother felt comfortable enough to tell us about him."

"And?" I feel like I've unlocked a new bonus level, and I want to know it all. I don't care if it's gross or weird. "What did he say to you when you met him?"

"Well, that's the thing. When the day arrived, we prepared to meet him. I had never seen your mother so nervous—she would have lost her head if it weren't attached to her. She had made a fuss about everything—what to wear, what to cook, what we could and couldn't say. I held her hand on the couch, and the three of us waited and waited and waited." Bibi jan's brows furrow as she remembers. "But he never came, and it was like he just . . . disappeared. Vanished right before her very eyes, if you will. No calls. No messages. Nothing. It devastated your mother to the point where she stayed in bed for months. She lost herself in those dark days and got out of bed only when she realized she was going to have you. Strangely, soon after you were born, your father just . . . showed up. No explanation. Over the years, we've come to accept that this is simply his way, to disappear and reappear without notice. But that isn't a way to raise a daughter, so he came up with a rule that worked for everyone." Bibi jan's eyes tear up at the memory. Her voice catches as she gazes lovingly at me. "I admit, I had a hard time accepting our situation in the beginning, but I saw how the idea of you brought her back to the light, and we are so blessed to have you, janem. But I have reason to believe this incident with your father reminds her of that time, and maybe it's just one time too many for your mother to bear."

"Wait. That's it?" That's so different from what I've been told my whole life, that my parents weren't together because they couldn't be. Because it wasn't accepted. Because the way they went about their relationship was wrong. I think Bibi reads the confusion on my face.

"We thought it would be easier to give in to a cultural assumption, instead of a sad truth that didn't really have a tidy answer, that sometimes, for whatever reason, things don't work out the way we had hoped. Now you know the real reason why. Your father's heart was elsewhere, and your mother chose to move on in the best way she could."

"So Padar *chose* to leave us?" I glance down at my drawing. The blue lights splash against Padar's half-finished face. My dad never mentioned it was his idea to see me once a year on my birthday. If he made the rule, then why once? Why not more?

Maybe he knew I'd ask why.

Maybe he didn't want to answer.

"Oh, my darling, my intention wasn't to make you sad," says Bibi jan. "I know I can't make it any better for you, but what I can do is ask you to follow this. Just like I did. Just like your mother did when she had you." She gestures at my heart and holds me close. "Your heart will never steer you wrong, not once. Even if the choice is hard, it will always work out in the end. Okay?"

"If you say so." I feel for the ring in my pocket and squeeze it tight.

"I knew you'd understand." Bibi jan slowly gets up and takes the dishes out of my room.

I don't understand, though. Maybe Madar is still hurt over what Padar did, so that's why she doesn't want to believe me. Maybe Madar thinks Padar chose to leave, which is why I can only see him once a year, but maybe he made the rule because . . .

I take the ring out of my pocket and stare at it.

Maybe he was mixed up in something dangerous.

Something magical.

If I can just find him, then Padar can explain, once and for all, *why* he never showed up that day, why he made the rule. Maybe Madar's hurt can be fixed. After all, if he knew about this magical ring, he was probably tangled up with magic then too. That has to be it.

The adults aren't going to wake up, so I need to find Padar on my own. I should have known waiting for them to believe me was a bad idea. I mean, they didn't do anything way back before I was born when he disappeared the first time, so why would they do anything now? In my mom's eyes, this is just another disappearance, but what she doesn't know is that this time, it's on me.

I'm the one who opened the box and made a wish, so I have to be the one to get him back. I unleashed whatever was hiding in that box with the ring. What if the boy ruined my wish and made Padar disappear? What's going to stop him from turning me into dust too?

I gulp.

What if he turns *all of us* into dust?

I can't let that happen. I've got to find the boy first, before he finds us.

This could be bigger than moving, bigger than not getting Padar back.

I make sure I'm extra quiet while I pack an emergency bag (filled with climbing supplies, my tablet, some fuzzy sweaters, a scarf, and snacks, because you never know when you might need a sugar boost). I tie the ring on a thread around my neck. My harness clatters from its hook on my desk, spilling more organized chaos all over the floor. It sounds like an avalanche of noise.

Whoops. I guess quiet was never my style.

Little shadows flicker from the light by my window, adding to the underwater feel.

I shove my window open and shiver against the breeze. Before climbing out the window, I close my eyes and remember the story Bibi jan told me of Madar and Padar and slip it into a neat box in my head for safekeeping, right next to the image of Padar and me from the cliff.

I'm coming to find you, Padar. I'm coming to find the truth. I wrap my hand around the ring again.

"Farrah." Madar is walking up the stairs. "Want to watch the next season of that show you like with the aliens? I've got popcorn going."

It's now or never.

"I'm just gonna go to bed," I call out. "Maybe tomorrow!"

Without hesitating, I take a deep breath and jump into the night, hoping Madar won't freak out too much when she finds out I'm gone. Just in case, I leave my favorite blue chalk bag on my desk to let her know that she doesn't have to worry.

I'm going to fix everything.

For her. For all of us.

CHAPTER FOUR

WHEN WORLDS COLLIDE

I swing out the window and latch on to my fire escape. I've taken this shortcut to the roof so many times, it's practically muscle memory by now. My heart is *whoosh*ing in my chest as I dyno to the next building's fire escape. I climb up it until I'm on my neighbor's roof. The low-hanging moon lights the gray sky.

Way off in the distance, City Hall twinkles and waves.

The plan is simple. If I can just make it there, I'm bound to run into that boy. If my dad's warning is true, he's going to find me anyway, and I'd rather face him head-on than by surprise. Once I get to him, I'll demand he bring my dad back (and hope he doesn't have any tricks up his sleeve).

I breathe hard through my nose and run. There's a tingle in my fingers that bolts down to my toes as I prepare to roof-hop. The rows of brownstones have a huge gap between street intersections. Sometimes, when I can't sleep, I climb up here in the middle of the night to practice roof jumping. (Arzu tried to join once. Let's just say, it didn't end well.) I know it's dangerous, but when the wind blows against my back and I get ready to run and leap, I imagine I can do impossible things, like run so fast that not even the wind could catch me.

"Yaaa!" I swing my arms and leap. My sneakers crunch onto the ledge as I scramble and continue to run, jump, land. Repeat. My breath swirls like slinky coils in the air as I go. *Be faster, better, stronger,* I think as I jump. *Be the best.* Soon enough, the roofs zip by, and the City Hall clock tower is getting bigger.

When I run like this, I like to pretend I'm in a race against the moon. Everything is a competition to me—and because of that, I always win. I can't remember a time I wasn't first in class or sports. Losing just isn't an option, and being the best also gives my mom one less thing to worry about. It's easier for everyone this way.

I look to the side just to get a peek of the moon when something strange happens. There are shadows forming along the sides of the roof to my left and right. Which wouldn't be weird . . . if they seemed like normal shadows. I slow down to get a good look at them. One starts to twitch, like an ink blob. I stare even harder, curious as they twitch more and more until they start to resemble shadows of people.

Then they do the most unshadowlike thing ever: they open their eyes and blink.

"This isn't real. This isn't real." I rub my eyes and jog nervously away from them. "This isn't—aah, stop looking at me! Shadows aren't supposed to have razor-sharp teeth!"

One shadow, with its bright red eyes and gleaming teeth, lunges. The static screeches in my head. *Give back what doesn't belong to you, little one.*

"Now you're in my head? I didn't give you permission!" I shout. I try to make the next jump, but I trip over my scarf that's come loose from the side pocket of my pack. I stumble and twist to catch the ledge. The scarf just tangles more around my ankle, causing me to miss it.

Uh-oh.

You know that feeling when your stomach drops to your butt when you're in trouble?

That feeling that screams, *This is very bad.*

Well, this is way worse. Because I messed up the jump, and I *never* mess up a jump.

My body crunches against the brick as I fall. "Ughhh!" I clamber for something to hold on to, but I'm falling too fast. I brace myself to hit the concrete. My scarf rips and gets stuck on someone's second-story outdoor window garden. It catches me, and suddenly I'm hanging upside down by my ankle.

That was a close call.

"Well, that was incredibly foolish, if I do say so myself." The clock tower boy materializes in front of me. He has a mess of white hair hanging in his face. "Your form was all wrong."

"Get away from me!" I swipe at him. My scarf twists, and all the blood rushes to my head. "I was distracted by those blobs chasing m-me." It's so cold, my teeth are chattering. My bag keeps riding up to my neck, and no matter how hard I try to wriggle free, I can't reach up to untie the scarf from my ankle.

Above me, the shadowy figures multiply.

"What are those creepy things?" I squirm and twirl, but it's no use. I'm stuck.

"They're shadow jinn, of course. It's what they do. They're *shadows*," the boy says. "But they're not really *here* here, if you get what I mean. They're more like puppets. Which makes them a bit pesky to deal with, since, you know, you can't really kill them. Being puppets and all."

"They're *what*?" The static screeches in my head the closer he gets to me. My ring burns under my shirt. The boy's eyes widen in surprise.

"You mean to tell me you don't know what you've done, then? With that ring?"

"What I've done? You're the reason I'm in this mess!" The glowing eyes of the shadow jinn are looming closer, and I really don't like the way they're staring at me and the ring. The boy moves to my side, like he's about to touch me. "Don't take another step! You turned my dad to dust, and I won't let you do the same to me!" I swat him away.

"Why would I turn anyone to dust?" he asks.

"Because that's what evil jinn do."

"I did no such thing."

"Yes, you—" I swipe at him again when he tries to get close to my ankle. "Stop trying to confuse me!" My thoughts are getting sludgy, and the longer I hang upside down, the harder it is to think.

"What I'm trying to do is help you. You're the one who is doing the confusing here." The boy sighs. "Now, if you'd just let me untie you—"

"I'll untie myself. Just stay where I can see you."

"And if you can't?" he asks, narrowing his pale eyes—they're actually a very light gray. His black shirt and pants billow in the chilling wind, making him look a lot like a ghost with his washed-out skin and face. "Just because you can't kill a shadow jinn doesn't mean they can't kill you. And it looks like you've got about thirty seconds before they do exactly that."

"I am not going to fall for your tricks. When I get out of here, I'm going to—" I'm scrambling for my ankle, but my head feels like a ripe tomato. The shadow jinn are racing down the brick walls. I panic. "Okay, fine! Help me!"

"Help me, what?" He smirks while sticking one hand in his pocket.

"This is no time for manners!" Though I really don't want to say it, I realize I'm not gonna get out of this without his help. "Fine, you win. Help me, *please*."

He disappears and materializes right next to me. He bows comically before brushing his hair out of his moonlit face. His hands are covered in ink. "At your service. The name's Idris. Don't forget it." He unties the scarf and I fall to the ground. "But if you don't mind, I suggest we run. Now and very quickly."

"You don't need to ask me twice." I'm bolting just as three shadow jinn jump down and smash into the flower box. They screech as they tumble into trash cans and bikes.

"Quickly, this way." Idris zips left and right, flickering in and out of sight like a ghost, into an alleyway that's pitch-black.

"No way. I can't see down there."

"That's the *point*." Idris pops back out and drags me into the alley. "Shadow jinn need light to materialize. No light. No shadow." He puts one hand on the brick wall while leaning over me, keeping an eye out as the herd of shadow jinn run straight past us. Their blocky arms and legs wobble unsteadily as they search.

"I guess that makes sense," I grumble in the dark, but now that the threat is out of the way, I push Idris and point at him. "What doesn't make sense is why you and these other jinn are stalking me."

"I don't think saving you from imminent death counts as stalking. Also, *you're welcome*." Idris rubs the center of his chest. "You really pack a punch for someone so small."

"I am of average height for my age, but that's beside the point." The point being if Idris really did have something to do with my dad's disappearance, then it wouldn't make much sense for him to help me out just now. But if Idris isn't the *he* my dad was talking about . . . I crouch into a ball and rub my face in my hands. Then I'm back to square one. "Let's say I believe you. Then why were those things chasing me?"

"If I had to guess, it probably has something to do with that cursed ring you're carrying around."

"Cursed?" I tug the ring out. The single gem shines like a beacon in the dark alley.

"And the fact that, you know, you are what you are." Idris's eyes flicker eerily against the glow of the ring.

". . . A girl?"

"A *jinn* girl," Idris corrects me.

"I'm a—" I almost snort-laugh (which would have been *very* embarrassing). "I think you must have hit your head somewhere because I would know if I was an all-powerful mystical being."

"I'm flattered you think I'm all-powerful," Idris says, amused. "I hate to break it to you like this, but if it quacks like a duck and smells like a duck and looks like a duck, then it's probably a duck."

"I'm not a duck either."

"It's a metaphor." Idris tugs at his hair. "Or an analogy? This isn't the point." He sighs in frustration. "Let's try this a different way." He looks out from the alley before making sure the coast is clear and pulls on my arm until we're under a streetlight. "You fell from a building at a height that should have broken bones, but you're fine. Why is that?"

"I'm lucky . . . obviously."

"Look at your arm and tell me this is just luck."

"I—" I look at my hands, flip them over. They're just normal-looking *human* hands. Sure, they've got cuts and scratches. Calluses and bruises. There's a big scrape on my forearm that's gonna sting for a bit. Only, something weird happens. The scrape goes from angry red to pink to gone right before my eyes. "How . . . ?" All the cuts start to heal, one by one, until they're all gone.

I've had cuts heal pretty fast before, but never like *this*. I keep on staring at my hands. Could it be? Me? A jinn?

But *how?*

"Fine, okay. I didn't think you'd create calculations in your head about this. You're only half jinn." Idris claps enthusiastically as he encourages us to keep walking down the street. "Your mom reeks of human one thousand percent."

"You smelled . . . my mom?"

"No, of course not. That is disturbing." Idris pinches the bridge of his nose like an old man. "I simply can tell, okay. It's a jinn thing, I can't explain it. Here, smell me, maybe you'll get it."

"I am not going to smell you." I'm beginning to wonder if looking for this smell-obsessed boy was a good idea when I realize what he just said. If Madar is all human, that means so are Baba Haji and Bibi, which means the only way this theory would be possible is if . . . "Are you saying . . . my dad is a jinn?"

"Finally! She gets it. And for a moment, I was worried this argument would never— Why'd you stop walking?" Idris turns around and looks curiously at me.

I adjust my backpack and keep looking at my hands because no way, right? Because that would mean it wasn't my wish that changed Padar. I quickly search in my bag for my tablet and look at my drawing. With big, shaky breaths, I turn the screen and show it to Idris. "So you're saying this is what he normally looks like."

"Oh wow, athletic *and* artistic? Impressive." Idris leans in closer. "Yes and no. I mean, he probably has a few forms— all jinn do—but this is closest to his true form, if that's what you're asking."

My brain feels like it's short-circuiting. *This is his true form.* I think back to the way Padar's voice changed when he transformed, the way he wasn't scared at all when he took the ring from me, when he spoke with Idris. And it was Padar who brought the ring in the first place. . . .

All the stories he told me of phoenixes and faeries and dragons and jinn . . .

He didn't just get mixed up in magic. He *was* magic.

"I'm sorry to have to bother you during what seems like an important moment, but, uh, we've got bigger problems right now." Idris looks down at our shadows. They start to twist and move on their own.

"Not again." I hop around, but my shadow hops right with me. "I do not have the brain space for this too!"

"They're not going to leave us alone until you give that ring to them." Idris jumps out of the way as his shadow turns 3D. It stands right in front of him with a wicked smile on its face.

"Not in a million years!" I might not know all the details about why this ring is so important, but what I do know is I can't let these strange blobs take it. I bolt as fast as I can, but it looks like my shadow is gonna be tough to outrace. It blocks my way down the street. *Okay, think, Farrah. You've gotten out of stickier situations.* But we're in the middle of the street and there's nothing close enough for me to climb and the shadows are multiplying.

"They've got us covered." I spin in a circle. Idris and I are back-to-back. "They're closing in fast." I hold the ring tight in my fist, wishing for a pause button. Where's a shadow jinn–fighting tutorial when you need one? I glance at Idris and nearly smack him. "Why are you smiling? This isn't the time to laugh."

"I'm sorry. I'm a nervous laugher." Idris wipes his hands on his shirt before reaching into his pocket. He pulls out a jeweled pen and gives it a click. "This one's on me, but next time, you've got to deal with the shadow jinn on your own. Okay?"

The shadow jinn are so close, I can make out the details of my own face on one of them. It flashes me a peace sign. Now, that is creepy. No one should witness a shadow version of themselves this up close and personal. It reminds me of the monsters I used to be afraid of as a kid. You know, the things that live under your bed (and yes, of course I still check).

"Unless you've got a sword in that pen, I don't see how this is going to end well." The shadow jinn growl right before they lunge. This is it. I shut my eyes and brace myself for the worst.

"Didn't your parents teach you what happens when you're at rock bottom?" Idris laughs while throwing his pen into the air. "If you can't go left or right, sometimes the only way out is up." A wispy cloud materializes from the pen and wraps around us. "If you're going to survive our world, you've got a lot to learn, Farrah Noorzad."

And just like that, we float all the way up into the starry sky, leaving the shadow jinn reflections of ourselves behind.

CHAPTER FIVE

I'M A *WHAT?*

I open my eyes to an inky black sky, filled with gray clouds zipping all around us. The moon winks right above me. I rub my eyes to make sure I'm not dreaming.

When I look again, I still see Idris and me, sitting on a humming cloud as it zips along the sky in a straight line. Little ribbons of white fluff wrap around Idris's body, holding him in place. I look at my own legs. Every time I try to move, the ribbons move with me, sorta like the world's comfiest full-body seat belt.

"Whoa." I think my brain chip has officially fried. "This has got to be a dream." I pinch my leg, just in case. It hurts.

"Not a dream, unfortunately," Idris mutters before throwing his arms out wide. "Welcome to the airways, the *only* way to travel if you want to get anywhere fast." The wind blows Idris's hair out of his face.

"This is . . . amazing."

"Yeah, it's pretty spectacular if you've never used it before." He's completely relaxed, like this is as normal as a car ride on the highway. Until he stares at the ground. A small frown wrinkles his face. The little lights from buildings resemble toy towns. "Everything looks so different down there."

"Like Legos." I lean over a little bit to get a good look. It really is quiet up here. "I've only seen the city like this from an airplane window." But this beats that by a million.

"I wouldn't get too close to the edge. You could fall," Idris warns. "Wouldn't want to have to rescue you twice, now."

"I can take care of myself," I snap back, and sit in the center of the cloud.

"You don't have to take it personally."

Problem is, I do. There's this feeling inside that's tough to explain. It was already hard enough living with only half my history. I can recite by heart all of Madar's family tree without breaking a sweat. But ask me about my dad? It's always been a wide hole of nothing.

And what I thought I knew . . . was wrong.

Like Arzu would say, *It's hard to ignore the facts when they're staring right at you.* Or in this case, floating away on a cloud from a small army of shadow jinn with a smell-obsessed jinn boy who knows way too much about me.

"What's got you worried now?" Idris taps my forehead.

"I-it's true, then?" My cheeks get hot-splotchy when I look at Idris. "That my dad is a jinn."

Idris nods solemnly.

"Which means so am I."

"Half," Idris corrects me. "Do you . . . need a minute?"

"No, I'm okay." I look out at the stars splashing around us. I'm really not okay, but I don't need Idris to know that. I don't need him to know I've got a million questions bubbling up, like if my dad is really a judge who lives in Abu Dhabi or if that's a lie too. Or why did he hide that he is a jinn in the first place? And what about any half-siblings? Do they exist? Are they like me? Or are they full jinn, like Padar?

The questions start to get crowded in my head, so I open up a little box in the corner of my brain, dump them all in, and seal it shut. No more thoughts, no more problems.

"Can this cloud do anything else besides float in circles?"

"That's up to you." Idris settles back and draws in the air with his pen. Our cloud makes its sixth big circle over Philadelphia. "Where do *you* want to go?"

"I'm not so sure anymore." I tug on the ring. The blue gem glows as if it's listening. "I guess I really did change my fate when I made my wish."

"I'm glad you did. Otherwise I'd still be stuck in there." Idris rubs his head nervously. "It wasn't the most . . . spacious place to be, that's for sure."

"What do you mean?"

"It's how the ring works," he explains. "To use it, you've got to exchange another person's fate for it, like a . . . trade or something."

"So then why were you stuck in there?"

"Because I didn't *know* that at the time." Idris's cheeks get pink. "So I got trapped as punishment. Obviously."

Red alert. "Hold on a second." I really look at the ring now. "You think I've trapped my dad in here?"

"It's possible." Idris takes a deep breath before sticking out a hand. "Let me see that." I slip off the ring and give it to him. He brings it close to his eye, flips it around, smells it, and then finally says, "Strange. It looks like your wish hasn't exactly gone through yet. See the gems? They're not all lit." He hands it back to me. "Whatever you wished for, it's waiting for something else before it goes through."

"What does that mean?"

"It means that maybe there's a way to get your dad back. I don't know for sure, but I do owe you a debt for, you know, getting me out of there." Idris tries to play it like it's no big deal. "And if you're certain you want to release him from that ring, then I might know who could help."

"I'm guessing this help isn't close by?" I ask.

"It's not. And I won't lie to you, it's not going to be an easy trip. You'd have to leave this world behind for a little while." Idris shakes his head. "You could always turn back. I would if I were you."

"A different world?" I murmur.

Idris nods.

I take a deep breath and look at Philly. From up here it feels tiny, as if I could squash it with my foot. The lights twinkle in goodbye, like they already know what I'm going to choose. I wave back. Deep down I know if I go home now, I'm always going to wonder.

"I want answers." For me. For Madar. For my family. I stare bravely at Idris. My hair ripples behind me. "I want to fix this mess and . . ." *Find out who I really am.*

"Adventure it is, then." Idris looks considerably cheerier at this. He stands up and points east. "Prepare yourself, it's going to be a long ride." Our cloud shoots forward, and we race against the moon and the glittering stars.

I stand up too and let the wisps of the cloud wrap around me. My hands glide against the wind. It reminds me of my tenth birthday. Padar and I had planned on driving out to New Jersey to do some high-altitude trail hiking. He used to tell me it was his favorite place to be, sitting somewhere close to the sky. Through the *whoosh* of the wind, I can almost hear him say, *Where the world is quiet, way up high, that is where you will find me.*

I didn't get it then. But now I imagine Padar standing next to me, just like he did when we were on the cliff. I imagine his arms wrapped around me as he whispers, *Your adventure has only just begun, janem.*

"Where are we going exactly?" I ask against the rush of wind.

"To the place where the seen world ends and the unseen world begins. To the Qaf Mountains, of course," Idris replies. "The gathering place of the seven jinn kings. If you're looking for answers, they're the ones to ask."

"Seven jinn kings?" I try to think back on Padar's stories, but I'm drawing a blank. "Why would they help us?"

"*You*," Idris corrects me. "And they'll help you because your dad is one of them." He gives me the most serious look, like he hasn't dropped the biggest bombshell on me. "Obviously."

CHAPTER SIX

THE CITY OF JEWELS

"My dad is a judge in Abu Dhabi," I say automatically, but the words feel so wrong now. Somehow, finding out my dad is a jinn king takes the cake—the puzzle that was my dad has exploded into a million pieces that I'll never be able to put back together.

"He most definitely is not." Idris settles in on his side and sleepily yawns. "I'd tell you more, but maybe after some rest? All this life-saving has been exhausting."

"Idris, if you fall asleep on me, I will—"

He's out in three seconds. His snores add to the symphony of the wind.

"You can't be serious right now." I jab his side with my foot, but he doesn't even wince. He really is knocked out. I make sure to record a video of him as payback for dropping that information on me. Who does that and then decides to take a nap?

Hours pass, and it doesn't matter what I do (jump on the cloud like a trampoline or sing horribly), Idris sleeps through it.

I end up lying on my back, counting the stars that *whoosh* by like painted lines on a highway. Every once in a while, I see other clouds zipping by too, all with passengers. I wave, mesmerized by the sight, but everyone seems to mind their own business. I try doodling on my tablet, but nothing I do can get this thought out of my head:

My dad . . . a jinn king.

Now, that's a story I can't wait to tell Madar and Bibi. Once I visit the other jinn kings and get my dad back, I'll finally have proof that I wasn't making it all up. That it's real, all of it.

If they don't already know, the whispers buzz.

I sit up, suddenly alert. It's that voice again. "Who are you and why do you keep talking to me?" With Idris asleep, I can't ask him. And since there's no shadow jinn up here, it couldn't have been them. "Is it you?" I stare at the ring. The blue gem glows a little brighter but makes no sound. "My mom would never lie to me about this. Never. You heard it yourself, they all think it's made-up. A *story.*"

The ring is quiet, but weirdly I can feel its silence, like it's *smiling.*

"Stop messing with me. It's not funny." I hug my bag and sink a little deeper into the cloud, holding the idea of Madar's and Bibi's awed faces when I return with the truth. Once I tell them, it'll change everything for the better.

Actually, why even wait. With that thought, I take out my phone and type out a message to Arzu.

you're so lucky you don't have any money because you def lost our bet!

I send her a selfie with a snoozing Idris and the airways behind me.

believe me now?

My eyes get heavy waiting for the messages to send, and slowly I drift off to sleep too.

"Hey. Hello. Rise and shine, princess. Time. To. Wake. Up."

Something sharp pokes me in the side, and my hand goes flying. "I'm not ready for school," I blurt out when my hand smacks my alarm clock.

"What was that for?" Idris is holding his cheek, looking betrayed.

"Oh, it wasn't my alarm." I sleepily rub my eyes, shivering. "It's a little chilly up here. Does this cloud have a heating feature?"

"You're not going to apologize?"

"For what?" I zip open my bag and search for another sweater to put on.

"For this!" Idris points at his face.

"Oh." I blink after finding the fuzziest sweater in my bag. I jam my head in before answering, happy to be warm. "You shouldn't have poked me."

"I also shouldn't have saved your life," he grumbles while squinting into the distance. "Not like I had a choice," he mumbles even quieter. The sun has turned the sky pink, and rising through an ocean of seafoam-green clouds is a floating mountain range made of the brightest, greenest emeralds I have ever seen. My jaw drops.

"What is *that*?"

"Home." Idris's face relaxes as he sits up in relief. "Welcome to the Qaf Mountains." Our cloud slows down, and I notice that the airways are a little more crowded here. Curiously, instead of floating through the main gates with the rest of the clouds, Idris veers lower, guiding us under a mountain.

"Um. I think you're going the wrong way?" I look back, and just as we dip out of sight, I see the shadow of something huge fly over us. Something that looks a lot like—

"Is that a simurgh?" I scream, jumping up to get a good look. "A real-life Persian phoen—"

"SHHHHHHHH. It's just a dragon. Relax. The simurgh doesn't come out at this time of day." Idris covers my mouth with his hands before looking around suspiciously. "Can you not draw attention to yourself for a minute?"

"Why?" I ask, but Idris ignores me as he cautiously steers us all the way under the mountain. The bottom is a dark, unpolished emerald. Very tough and solid, but it smells sweet, like holy water. "Why can't we enter the normal way?"

"Because." Idris starts knocking on random spots on the stone. "It would be in our best interest to enter the City of Jewels . . . this way. Just in case." He knocks again, and this time something clicks. Idris breathes a sigh of relief when a tiny little tunnel appears directly above us.

A very dark, tiny tunnel.

"I am not going in there." While I may not be afraid of heights, I really don't like small, dark spaces.

"Suit yourself." Idris jumps up, grabs a little handle in the tunnel, and starts to climb. "But so you know, I'm going to put that cloud back in my pen when I get to the top."

"You wouldn't."

"Guess we'll find out!" His voice echoes farther away the higher he climbs.

I wring my fingers, take a deep breath, and stare at the dark tunnel. *Okay, Farrah. It's just a ladder. Just a—*

My foot slips into the cloud as it starts to shrink. It's getting smaller and smaller. . . . "You are extremely rude, you know!" I huff, put on my backpack, and jump up to grab the last rung of the ladder right as the cloud fully disappears.

"I could have fallen to my death!" I climb the ladder faster than the speed of light and end up bumping my head against Idris's shoes.

"No, you wouldn't have," he says when he hits the top. He wiggles whatever is blocking the way, and a little shard of sunlight trickles through. Noises rise above us. "You just needed a little motivation to get going is all." He pushes himself out of the tunnel and reaches a hand in to help me up.

"And if I didn't?"

"Then I'd get the cloud to bring you back." He rolls his eyes. "Obviously."

I blink in surprise because I can't believe I've been outsmarted by a boy.

"This is the moment where you say thank you." Idris waits a second before sighing. He covers the entrance of the tunnel with a slab of grass and pats it down. It looks like we're in an outdoor garden. There are glass benches scattered along a glass walkway that leads to a large street. "So you don't say sorry, please, *or* thank you? You've really got to work on your manners. Especially if you're going to ask a favor from those jinn kings."

Oh right. We're here to see the kings. My stomach is in knots when I remember all the details from last night. Idris walks over and plops down on one of the glass benches with a troubled look on his face. "Do you . . . have any suggestions on how to do that?"

"Yes. First we sit on this bench and soak in the smell of

these berry bushes." To be even weirder, Idris plucks a handful of berries from the bushes next to the bench and rubs them under his armpits. "Then there's something you have to know before we go out there." He points at the busy street ahead of us. Past the shade of trees, tall buildings loom. "I'm not liking all these surprises." I sit on the other side of the bench. "And I am *not* rubbing a plant under my armpits."

"How do you think I feel having to explain everything to you?" Idris asks, shaking his head. His hair flops over his face. "It's no fun for me either, you know. I don't even know how long I've been gone, so maybe what I'm about to tell you isn't true anymore, but judging by your lack of knowledge on the jinn world . . ." His eyes get really sad at this. It makes me nervous.

"Well, spit it out, then."

"So your dad isn't just a jinn king; he's *the* Judge of the Supreme Court of Jinn and rules over the realm of Jupiter— but even so, there are . . . rules in the jinn world that cannot be broken," he starts. "Rules that the jinn kings are *supposed* to uphold." Idris gives me a hard stare.

Rules. At least something makes sense here. That sure sounds like Padar. I wait for Idris to continue, but he keeps looking at me like I'm supposed to get what he's saying. "Rules like . . . ?"

"Like the fact that in the jinn world, we aren't allowed to mix with the mortal world, aka *humans*." He stops again, waiting for me to get it. "As in, it's forbidden. As in, half-jinn are *against the rules. . . .*"

"Oh." I blink, and something sinks deep down inside me. "So I'm not allowed to be here . . . at all?"

"You're not allowed *to exist*," Idris clarifies. "At least, that was the ruling . . . What's the year right now?"

I tell him.

"Oh . . . then, about a hundred years ago," Idris says quietly.

"So you're saying my dad, preacher of rules and lessons and *this is just how it is*, is actually the biggest rule *breaker*." My stomach feels really upset now. My eyes start to sting. "If I'm not allowed to be here, why'd you bring me, then? Shouldn't you have a problem with me too?"

"Because a deal's a deal, and I owe you one." Idris seems to snap out of his somber mood and offers a handful of berries. "Plus, I never said *I* had a problem with half-jinn. So, if you want to get to the kings before a crowd starts to form at their court, then you've got to erase that human-world smell off you and get a move on."

"Oh great." I go pale at the thought of having to face six other jinn kings.

"It's not as scary as it sounds," Idris promises. "Are you ready?"

No, but I imagine Madar's encouraging face saying, *You can do it,* and force myself to stand up. "Let's go."

We hurry out of the little park and into the bright, sunlit sidewalk. The glare hurts my eyes, and I bump into something very solid.

"Watch it," a massive jinn, with jagged wings tucked into the slits of his jacket, grumbles. "God, where is that human smell coming from? Smells like rotten cabbage." He wrinkles his nose and wipes his side a few times before heading into the park.

I sniff my armpit. "I don't smell like cabbage," I mumble, trying to keep up with Idris's pace.

"Told you to use the berries," Idris says. He slows down as more jinn crowd the sidewalk. "Behold the City of Jewels, the capital city of the Qaf Mountains." He steers us fully out of the park area, and I'm awestruck. We pass by towering, sparkling buildings made of stained glass and emerald. It looks like someone scooped up part of the land and built a city right in the heart of the emerald mountains. It is . . . the most beautiful place I've ever seen in my life.

"There really is no place like home," Idris mumbles while also staring at the glittering city. His eyes scan faces and places, searching for something. "Even though it's changed so much, it's still nice to be back."

I immediately start taking pictures. (I know we're on a mission, but I also need *proof* to share with Arzu that I was right and she was wrong.)

"What's that?" I point.

In the distance, there's a floating stadium covered in lapis lazuli, giving it a bright blue-and-gold glow. I cover my eyes with the back of my hand. Two diamond-shaped kites cut across the sky in the stadium, followed by cheers.

"Kite fighting." Idris frowns. "I was never any good at it, but it's popular here."

"Is there anything you like?"

"Not getting caught breaking the rules is pretty high on my list right now." At that he smiles. "And reaching destinations, speaking of which."

We stop in front of a huge building—it reminds me of City Hall, but much prettier, with way more mosaics and gems. "That building is really fancy." Like, even fancier than the Prophet's Mosque in Medina. I feel out of place with my leggings, fuzzy blue sweater, and hiking backpack.

"When you're a king, you have to be fancy." Idris points. "The court is just inside here. Come on, you'll have time for sightseeing later."

We pass through the domed entrance, with a set of balance scales engraved over the stone archway. The ring hums against my sweater, and the static gets annoying in my ears.

Time is running out before wishes become reality, the voice says.

"Did you hear that?"

"Hear what?" He looks back and throws out his arms to block the way. I shake my head and glare at the ring. "Well, we made it. Welcome to the Supreme Court of Jinn. Before we cross through the arch, a warning: you might experience a slight tingling sensation when you walk through. It's perfectly normal."

"Okay." I step through the arch.

It definitely does *not* feel normal.

Stepping into the court feels like I chugged a pot of Madar's coffee *and* an energy drink (which I have done once, on a dare; it didn't end well). Energy vibrates through my entire body, making it hard to not fidget and wiggle my arms.

"Please stop acting so weird," Idris mutters as our footsteps echo through the quiet space. "The point is to *blend in,* not stand out."

"I'll try, but no promises." I shove my hands into my sweater pockets (and still wiggle my fingers in secret to get the energy out). I look up. The high ceilings are covered in murals with colorful gemstones. A sea full of sapphires, rubies, opals, all pulsing and glowing. The jewels wind down around walls and pillars. Huge stained-glass windows cast hazy strips of sunlight on our faces. The deeper we go into the building, the more energized I get.

"Why do I feel like I can run a marathon without stopping?"

Idris shrugs. "It's enchanted. Anyone with ill intent won't be able to pass through. There was an incident in 1875, if I'm correct. Huge disaster. Took forever to repair the building."

Guards line the hall as we walk down. Their dark eyes follow us as we pass through the final arch. Arabic scripture glitters in onyx jewels above. It is so pretty.

"Thanks for the history lesson." I want to ask more about it, but I'm too busy turning the corner, staring at the walls, trying to read the calligraphy . . . that I don't notice I've walked into a huge room with seven massive thrones, all in a neat line. They shine from the enormous domed skylight. White and gold pillars make a wide circle around the thrones. The white marble floor gives the illusion of walking on air. It's so clean, it's hard to know which side is real and which side is reflection. I feel like I could walk into the floor and come out through the upside-down version of the throne room . . . where six massive jinn are sitting and chatting.

I suddenly feel very, very nervous.

"Idris, you didn't say that the jinn kings are huge and—"

"Big enough to rip our heads off?" Idris nervously laughs from behind the corner. "But in my defense, if I told you they were terrifying, you wouldn't have come, and, well, a deal is a deal. We're even now. Good luck!"

"Hey! You can't leave me alone with them!" I yell, a little too loud. It echoes and catches the attention of the kings. All their heads (one jinn king has *four* heads) turn to stare at me with their glowing eyes and sharp teeth.

And they don't look happy.

"What is *that rancid smell?*" one of them says, scrunching their dark face.

"Oh god, is that a human?" the king with four heads grumbles. All eight eyes narrow at me. I death-grip the ring and start to hyperventilate. "I— I'm . . ." *Too scared for words.*

"You have exactly five seconds to explain why you've so rudely interrupted our breakfast meeting and dared to bring that cursed ring of fate into our court," the giant jinn, sitting in the first throne, demands. His voice booms and shakes the room. Little rocks fall from the pillars. "And answer wisely, child. Your life depends on it."

CHAPTER SEVEN

THE SEVEN (ER, SIX) JINN KINGS

Here's a pro tip: it's probably best not to barge into a room full of powerful giant jinn kings before they've had breakfast.

"Please don't eat me," I think out loud as I take a step back.

"Don't flatter yourself," the jinn on the seventh throne snorts. "We have higher standards than that." He's really tall—at least ten feet—and his huge crown hangs around one long, pointed ear, teetering like it's gonna fall off and crush me if he makes a wrong move. His dark red skin shines against the glittering dark red of his throne. By his feet, I notice something engraved in gold at the bottom of the throne, where *King Al-Ahmar of Mars* glitters.

Oh boy, if he's anything like Ares, the Greek god associated with Mars . . . then I'm in trouble (though I suppose the Greek gods are really just all-powerful, larger-than-life jinn).

From where I stand, I can confirm that these jinn are all-powerful, larger-than-life, and *angry*.

"Ahmar, it's too early to be picking a fight." The jinn king sitting in the first throne—*King Barqan of Mercury*, reads his throne—rubs his face while adjusting his green robes to flow like a waterfall on the ground. Inclined against his blue throne is a spear crackling with lightning. His face and body are the color of midnight, with two elegant horns sprouting from each temple. His skin sparkles and glistens as he leans over to the throne next to him and mutters something in the ear of a jinn who is wearing clothes that shine like the sun. The light around his head makes his hair resemble a flaming golden halo. I have to shield my eyes to look at him. I squint and read *King Al-Mudhib of the Sun* on his throne.

"It's highly irregular that Shamhurish is absent for this long." The shining Al-Mudhib takes a sip of tea from his gold teacup before narrowing his eyes at me. "I suspect our little visitor might have something to do with it."

They all turn to look at the empty throne in the center of the line. It's much plainer than the other thrones. *King Shamhurish of Jupiter* is engraved there, along with lots of symbols I can't read.

"It—it was an accident," I blurt out as all the jinn kings loom over me in their thrones. I rip the ring off its thread and let it dangle in front of me. "My dad gave this to me, and I might have wished on it and accidentally trapped him inside."

"He *what?*" King Mudhib chokes on his tea. "Why would he retrieve a ring he sank into the ocean in the first place?"

"Did you say your father?" A ghostly-looking jinn draped in silver—*King Al-Abyad of the Moon,* I read—puts his long fingers together as he looks at me curiously with golden eyes. He breathes deep, smelling the air. His eyebrows rise. "A half-human, but I do detect Shamhurish's scent. Curious indeed."

I immediately regret not taking the berries.

"Shamhurish, you never cease to surprise." King Ahmar rubs his hands together at the idea of a fight. "I will happily take the charge against him. It's been so *boring* around here."

"Ahmar, the last time you took justice into your hands, you nearly split the earth in two." A giant, winged jinn king—his throne is engraved with the name *King Maymun of Saturn*—hits Ahmar on the head. "And a whiff of our dear friend doesn't prove anything. How can we be sure the girl isn't lying?" A scary smile stretches across Maymun's thin face. He looks like the stuff of nightmares. "If you let me into her dreams, I'll be able to find out for sure."

"What are dreams going to prove?" King Ahmar blows a raspberry. "My way is much better."

Hidden behind the commotion, I notice a boy around my age peering behind King Barqan's watery-looking throne. His bright green eyes narrow when he sees me. His black hair is pulled tight into a topknot with little pieces falling out on his forehead and around his pointy ears. When I blink, the spear and the boy are gone.

"It's too early for all this noise." King Barqan pinches his nose and motions for me to come closer. "You, what is your name, child?"

"Farrah Noorzad." I make direct eye contact with him. Madar always told me looking someone in their eyes makes you seem a lot more confident than you actually are. But that doesn't stop my knees from knocking against each other when King Barqan leans forward.

"And what, foolish half-human child, did you wish for that involves the esteemed Shamhurish?" he asks.

I think back to the day on the cliff with Padar. I remember the pinching in my heart to not let our time together end. "I wished to not be hidden." My face feels like it's on fire, like I'm reading my private diary notes out in front of a room of strangers. "I wished to have a place in my dad's world."

The room groans as King Barqan gazes intently at me.

"She's lying." The four-headed jinn king—*King Zawba'ah of Venus,* his throne reads—flicks his wrist, and three of his heads shift into a small whirlwind of smoke and disappear. He stares pointedly at King Barqan. "Unless you're already concocting a talisman to settle the matter."

"I haven't decided yet," King Barqan mumbles. It feels like his eyes are rummaging inside my head and poking around my heart. There's something off about King Barqan's ancient eyes. They don't fit his youthful face. I don't like it, so I look at the floor . . . only to find the reflection of his eyes staring right back at me. Double creep factor. "Because if what the half-human says is the truth . . . Tell me, child, how many gems are glowing on that cursed ring?"

"Uh, one . . ." I bring it closer for him to look, but King Barqan quickly moves his body away.

"I don't want to *touch* it."

"Oh, sorry." The blue gem is still bright since Padar disappeared. But wait. A second gem, a red one, flickers on. "Um. I think now it's two."

"What do you mean, it's two now?" King Barqan narrows his eyes nervously. "Can you not count?"

Suddenly, the courtroom rumbles, like it's fighting against being split in two—and it's losing. A large pillar cracks, and I jump out of the way right before the falling debris squashes me.

"What is going on?" roars King Ahmar. His large body erupts with light. "What is happening to me?" Thin white lines are running along his arms and legs and face, the same as what happened with Padar, until he too vanishes like dust.

"This . . . is quite bad," gawks King Maymun.

"I . . . didn't mean for that to happen, I swear!" I stare at the ring in my hand as the last of the dust disappears into the red gem. It glows angrily at me. "But you can't deny that's pretty good proof. . . ." I scratch the back of my head and laugh nervously. "Sooo . . . you think you can undo it and get them both out now?"

"Undo it? *Undo it?*" booms King Barqan. He stands up, lightning crackling and snapping around him as his already-large body gets even bigger. "Farrah Noorzad, while I cannot confirm the truth of your origin, I can see you have made a grave mistake. If it is confirmed that you are indeed the . . . child of Shamhurish, then not only have you disrupted our breakfast court and brought a cursed object into our fold, but you have also made a wish that threatens the careful order of our jinn world." He mutters to himself, "This is exactly why we have *rules*," before pointing a finger at me. "Have you any idea what all this means?"

"No." I hate how small these kings make me feel. How am I supposed to *prove* my dad is my dad when he's not here? I take a few steps back. The bubbles are fizzing and bouncing in my stomach, and I'm not sure if I want to burp or throw up, but neither is good. "I don't have a clue about any of this! That's why I came here, so you could help me save my dad."

"Please stop calling him that." King Barqan wrinkles his nose.

"But he is!"

"Enough!" he growls. "There's a reason why that ring was never meant to be found again, and yet, like what was foretold, fate has brought us this travesty."

"Told you we should have been stricter with the no-humans rule," whispers King Maymun to King Abyad. "But nooo, tracking dreams is too unethical. Everyone needs their privacy."

"Like I was saying," King Barqan says while glaring at

King Maymun, "half-human abomination, your wish to change the threads of your fate means undoing the magic that the seven of us enacted one hundred years ago to banish any jinn with mortal blood from our realm. Simply put, you traded us for yourself. And should all seven of us be locked in that cursed ring . . ."

"We'll be trapped for eternity. Our world will be doomed. All our futures will be *ruined*." King Abyad fills in the dots just as his stomach grumbles. "And all before I get my omelet."

"So what you're saying is . . . you can't snap your fingers and make it all go away?" I look nervously around the room. The only thing worse than losing is disappointing people. And right now, I feel like the world's biggest disappointment.

"While I would like to snap my fingers and be done with *you*, unfortunately the wish can only be undone by making a deal with the original jinn who created the ring, which may be our only hope." King Barqan groans as he sits back in his throne. "I can't believe I've lived long enough to say this, but, Farrah Noorzad, regardless of your heritage, the only way to save all of us is for *you* to travel to the original jinn's realm. Only there can you undo your wish."

"You can't be serious, Barqan." King Maymun stands, his wings flapping once. "Did you not see what happened to Ahmar?"

"I think we all saw what happened to Ahmar."

"Then you understand that I cannot allow *my* fate to be in the hands of some incompetent mortal."

"Well, *we* cannot enter that forsaken jinn's realm, so it has to be her," King Barqan reasons. "She would need a chaperone, I suppose. But *who* would dare go there willingly?"

"Absolutely not! You want to alert *more* jinn to this situation?" King Maymun shrieks.

"Then *what do you propose we do?*" King Barqan squeezes his eyebrows in frustration.

"I don't know, anything else!"

I take a step back from the bickering jinn kings and try to think it through.

Is the situation bad? Yes. Could it be worse? Nope. Definitely couldn't be worse. But there is a teeny chance that I can get my dad (and I guess King Ahmar) out of this ring. All I need to do is imagine it's like an elaborate scavenger hunt. Track down this original jinn. Make a deal. Undo the wish. Problem solved. Three steps. It's just three steps. My social studies projects require more steps than that (and I've got the highest grade in that class, so this should be fine). The only information that's missing is *where*.

"We are going to be here all morning if you two continue squabbling like children," King Mudhib adds to the conversation. "Perhaps I can parse through my index of prophecies? Zawba'ah could aid me. Surely, there must be a link. . . . This simply cannot be a coincidence. On that, I'm sure you can all agree."

Surprisingly, the remaining jinn kings nod their heads at this, even King Maymun.

"That . . . might be helpful," King Barqan considers.

"Glad to be the voice of reason." King Mudhib takes another sip from his cup. "I only hope it's not what was fore—"

"Um. Sorry to interrupt, but where exactly is the original jinn's court?" Hopefully it's not too far. I don't want to be gone too long. Madar is most definitely going to kick my butt if I don't get back home soon, and I don't want to make her worry more.

"In a place where none of us can venture." King Barqan sighs. "The Realm Beneath the Unseen. The realm of Azar, the oldest known fire jinn."

"Oh, no no no. You see? The thing is already getting curious." King Maymun's face turns frightening as dark energy gathers around his wings. "I say we follow Mudhib's plan, search the prophecies, and then execute the abomination, as stated in the rules."

"Execution isn't always the first answer, Maymun." King Barqan turns on the winged jinn. "But there is something called *tact and timing*. . . . There are questions that need to be asked, truths to be exposed, fates to be considered, before making such a decision. We can't risk our careful order by acting rash."

"I mean, killing her *could* get her soul to the Realm Beneath . . . no?" King Mudhib wonders aloud. "It would be much easier to leave the physical body behind. But if the prophetic investigation involves the prophecy of calamity, then it would be impossible to. . . ."

So I was wrong. Things have definitely gotten worse. Way worse. Maybe the *he* my dad warned me about was many *hes*. Either way, I need to get out of here.

I doubt they'd let me leave this room alive, so with the jinn kings bickering about my fate, I take one small step, then another, sidestepping the dark little wisps floating away from King Maymun. When I get far enough away without them noticing, I run out of the court, and I don't look back.

CHAPTER EIGHT

PROBLEM-SOLVING 101: NEMESIS EDITION

❖

There is no way I'm going to be able to do this.

How am I supposed to evade five jinn kings that want me dead *and* get into the Realm of Beneath and Unseen . . . whatever that means.

I can't even remember what the place is called. I'm supposed to go there by myself? Alone? To face a jinn who creates cursed rings and who knows what else?

No way. This mission is impossible. Where is the restart button? I'd like a redo, please, at this whole wish-upon-a-cursed-ring-of-fate thing.

"This day could not get any worse," I mumble while bumping into more jinn as I exit the Supreme Court of Jinn. "Sorry, didn't see you there."

"Didn't see me? I am eight feet tall," the jinn screeches as a hot liquid spills down his shirt. "I just bought this *yesterday.*

Do you know how hard it is to find the right tailor in this city on short notice?"

I keep on moving and try to ignore the lingering stares and whispers as I figure out what to do next. At least I'm not being followed by the kings . . . yet. I retie the ring around my neck and fish out the ripped blue scarf from my bag. I wrap it around my head to block out the stares while hurrying out of the square around the Supreme Court. Waves of jinn file in and out, getting ready to start their day. Adults wear colorful and formal clothes (probably to go to work); I spot kids around my age, racing past each other in fancy school uniforms. Something small sparkles on each kid's chest, like a gem. If I weren't on the run for my life, I would ask them if they're students like me, if they have sixth grade here too. I want to know what jinn life is like in the clouds. If Padar's world is as magical as it looks. There are so many questions bubbling up, but I keep them inside. I sigh, feeling lonelier than ever while watching two girls—one with curly hair, one wearing a hijab—linking arms and laughing together. It makes me miss my best friend.

This is *not* what I expected when I said I wanted a place in my dad's world.

When I'm sure the coast is clear, I slow down and try to trace my steps back to the park, hoping Idris might be lurking there, but I get lost. It shouldn't be so hard to find, but I'm not used to the way light bounces off the fancy emerald mountains that hug the city. Without clouds to block the sun, the sunlight hits the jeweled buildings and glass streets, hurting my eyes.

After twenty minutes of searching and bumping into many frazzled jinn, I find a glass bench and curl myself up into a tight ball. My eyes get hot because it isn't fair. At home my best friend and mom think all I do is make up stories. And then I get here, to a dream-come-true jinn world . . . only to find out the jinn kings think I make up stories as well. I'm tired of not being believed. And I'm tired of being a harami here too. All because my dad broke a rule.

Everything about this day is a nightmare, which sucks because this place is the prettiest nightmare I've ever seen. When I wipe my eyes and look really quickly, it feels like I'm back in a regular city, but when I *really* look, it's hard to ignore the way the air feels alive, or the way I can see right through the clear roads and watch the Earth gently spin below, beneath my shoes. Sometimes wispy clouds pass through the streets, making everything appear a little bit dreamier, a touch softer. Every once in a while, a big, winged shadow passes from above, and I can't help but drool at how majestically the flying beasts soar.

I couldn't imagine a more beautiful place, and that makes knowing I'm not wanted here a lot harder.

I wish Arzu were here to give me her signature pep talk. I stare really hard at her icon on my phone, thinking if I wish hard enough, the messages I sent last night will go through, but they don't. There's no signal up here, and that makes me homesick. Even though I know they won't get the messages, I send a quick text to my mom and Arzu anyway.

> you won't believe where I am
>
> this place is like a real live faerie tale

I attach the dreamiest video, hit send, and imagine what they'd say back. If I listen hard enough, I can almost hear Arzu's jaw dropping. I can almost feel Madar's hug while she scolds me for running off. I sniffle a little.

It's probably better I can't message them now, especially since it'd just add more stress to Madar's plate. I can't forget the dark shadows across my mom's face. Imagine how she'd react if she knew what those jinn kings said about me. Yeah, it's for the best to figure this out on my own. Plus . . . I'm not sure how that conversation would go, like, *Hi, Mom, I'm okay but guess what I'm still a harami out here too only it's way worse and now I've got to go to some scary jinn realm to save my dad before he's trapped forever please don't be mad.*

No, that'd make Madar even more stressed out and worried. Still, I wonder what they're doing right now. I know if Arzu were here, she'd be pointing excitedly at the glittering café across the street. *It's the perfect backdrop for my next dance routine,* she'd squeal while bending sideways to find the best angle.

The café, Divine Delights, really is pretty. The domed

storefront is all frosted glass, with light blue trim that makes it resemble the fluffiest marshmallow you've ever seen. Jinn walk in and out of the revolving door, arms filled with sparkling pastries and steaming glass to-go cups. My stomach grumbles when the aroma of heavy cream and buttered tea wafts toward me. Oh right, I guess it's been a while since I had something to eat. I wonder if jinn take human money. . . .

I'm about to finish taking my last photo when I notice a boy sitting by himself at one of the tables. I gasp. I'd recognize that white hair anywhere. "There you are, you sneaky traitor!" I barrel through the glass revolving doors and march right up to where Idris is sitting. "Thought you could get away from me, but now—"

"Not you again," Idris groans through his arms. He is sprawled dramatically across the table. His head is tucked into his forearms. There is a steaming cup of tea next to him. "I told you, a deal is a deal. You got me out of the ring, and I got you to the Supreme Court. Now leave me alone before you get us both in trouble."

"You mean you left me to fend for myself *and* lied to me about how terrifying those jinn are!"

"Keep your voice *down*," he hisses while pulling me into a chair next to him. He keeps his face turned away from me. "What part of *not allowed to exist* don't you understand?"

"Well, I didn't realize *not allowed* meant *sentenced to die*. I thought it meant, like, not allowed!" Like how kids aren't allowed into R-rated movies.

"Look, I can't explain everything to you," he snaps. "I did what I had to, and that's it."

"Fine." I adjust my scarf to hide my face from the other customers in the café. "But when I fail at getting to the Beneath Unseen Realm to undo my wish and destroy the jinn world as you know it, I hope you remember this talk and feel bad that you didn't help me."

"Hold on." At this Idris looks at me. His eyes are red and puffy. A little bit of tea sloshes out of his cup, but somehow the pot next to him floats up and gently refills it. "You have to go *where?*"

"Have you been *crying?*" I watch in shock. "And is that teapot sentient like Mrs. Potts in *Beauty and the Beast?*"

"Beauty and who—you're confusing me." Idris pushes his cup in front of me, and the little swirls of steam tickle my nose. "Explain. What happened back there."

I tell him what the jinn kings told me (and leave out the part where I'm technically on the run from them).

"You have to go to the Realm Beneath the Unseen?" Idris stares at me like I've grown two heads (which actually seems like the least shocking thing I've seen here).

"From your expression I assume this is very bad."

"It is much worse than bad," Idris whispers. "It's not a pleasant place. It's a jinn realm that was removed from our world to keep us safe. It used to be called the Underworld, but some people felt the name was misleading. Under which world, human or jinn? Because that would be two different worlds. And so it's been the Realm Beneath the Unseen ever since."

My heart stops when it finally clicks. *"The Underworld?"* Visions of fire and suffering flash before my eyes. Somehow everything just got so much worse.

Idris clicks his tongue. "The Realm Beneath the Unseen," he corrects me. "Not to be confused with other common Underworlds."

I sigh. "Can't be that different if it's so terrible to go to."

"I wouldn't know, since I've never been to either." Idris clears his throat uncomfortably. "But if what you're saying is true and your wish goes through, then there won't be any more jinn kings." His expression turns serious. "Meaning the residents of the Qaf Mountains and everyone living in the City of Jewels would face a leadership crisis—" He clears his throat again. "I need to drink something with dark chocolate in it to process this. You should probably drink that if you don't want to keep smelling like cabbage here." He gestures at the cup he'd pushed toward me. "Excuse me." He walks off to the counter, where an attendant is taking orders. He grabs a little notebook from his pocket and starts scribbling in it.

"Do I really smell like cabbage?" I don't want to look around and ask, so I take a little sip of Idris's drink and nearly pass out from how good it is. Either I'm really hungry or this is the best tea in the world. It feels weird to say this, but it tastes like *home,* like Bibi's stories and Baba Haji's laughter and Madar's hugs—it tastes like missing things. I down the entire drink and watch in awe as it refills itself. "You really are like Mrs. Potts, aren't you?"

The pot doesn't speak, so I continue to sip and think about home and belonging.

The problem is, the more tea I drink, the sadder I get, until the missing feeling pinches too much and all I want to do is sprawl dramatically over this table. It makes me think about Padar. If he had told me who I really was, I wouldn't be here trying to save him.

Unless you're part of the problem, the whispers needle.

I jolt in my seat. There's that voice again. "What did you say, you cursed thing?" I bring the ring close to my face and squint an eye. The blue and red jewels glow like they've been eavesdropping this whole time. I pretend I'm talking to Padar. "If I'm the problem, then why did you bother giving me a wish in the first place if I can't belong here either?"

The ring says nothing, so I keep talking.

"Give me one good reason why I should undo my wish," I say to the blue gem. "Why should I help save you when you're the reason we're in this mess?" I don't understand why Padar and the other jinn kings agreed a hundred years ago to banish all jinn with mortal blood. What's so bad about that? And why didn't Padar tell me any stories about the jinn kings? Were all the stories . . . lies? Maybe what I think I know about jinn isn't what jinn are at all. I grew up thinking they were these monstrous, scary beings, and okay, while the jinn kings did behave quite monstrously, so far the rest of this place isn't so scary at all.

"And say I do help you," I continue talking to the ring. "I don't know where to start looking. It's not like your friends are going to tell me, and there aren't any big billboards with flashing *Book your next trip in the Underworld* plastered with driving instructions—"

A plate clacks on the table. On it is a shimmering tart the color of a galaxy. My stomach grumbles.

"It'll take more than an apology tart to fix—" I look up into a pair of angry green eyes. It's the boy who was behind King Barqan's throne. "You are not Idris."

Instead of introducing himself politely, like *no-I-am-not-Idris-my-name-is-so-and-so*, the angry boy points a lightning spear in front of my nose. It crackles with energy.

"Eat the tart," he demands.

"Um. Can you point that thing somewhere else? People are staring."

"Not until you take a bite and answer why you trapped my baba in that ring."

"Your . . ." I blink. "Baba?" I try to remember the name of the second jinn king that disappeared into the ring. "The jinn king of Mars?" Suddenly, the boy's aggression is starting to make more sense.

"Ahmar is not my father." His eyebrows furrow together (looking suspiciously like a unibrow).

"Then who is?" It's the way his eyes crinkle in the corners that makes my head spin. If it's not King Ahmar, then it's got to be . . . "I trapped my dad in the ring. Not yours."

The word *brother* rings in my head. I've got a brother.

"Well, that's impossible. I don't have any siblings." He scoffs. "And even if I did, my father would not have a half-human child. My dad would *never* break such a sacred ruling like that, so you could never be my sister." He pushes the tart forward with the spear again. "Why don't you tell me who you really are so we can get this over with, half-human!"

"I have a name, you know." I scowl at him. "So why don't you cool it with the half-hu—"

"Is there a problem here?" Idris returns with two empty cups. Two jugs filled with brightly colored liquid float behind him. He sits down in his seat. The cups clink together in greeting as they settle in next to the teapot already on the table. "I believe there's a sign that says 'no weapons allowed,' so if you don't mind, we are not interested in what you're selling. Please leave." Idris turns to me. "Would you like jade citrus mint or raspberry chocolate lemonade?"

This makes the boy even angrier.

"Raspberry chocolate lemonade, please," I say, because I'm angry too. I take a sip (it's just normal lemonade) and try to ignore how much it stings to hear *You could never be my sister*. To be honest, it's not like I dreamed about having a brother or a sister. (I do great by myself.) Being an only child rocks. I don't have to worry about sharing my tablet or my video games or having someone steal my clothes, but sometimes . . . it can get a little lonesome. On particularly lonely nights, I'd sit on the roof of my house and stare up at the stars and wonder what it'd be like to actually *meet* a sibling. If maybe I'd like having someone to share my games with, if they'd like sports and art just as much as I do.

I never thought it'd go like *this*. The way this boy is glaring at me makes me feel like I'm a science experiment living past its expiration date. More than mad, I feel a little glum, like another tally has been added to the *reasons why jinn don't like Farrah*.

"What's it going to take to get you to go?" Idris rolls up his sleeves. "You're disturbing me."

"Eat. The. Tart," the boy grits through his teeth.

"Fine, but only because I'm hungry and it looks nice." And maybe if we stop arguing, he'll get to talk to me and realize I'm not the enemy here. I pick it up and take one bite. It feels like someone threw warm honey all over my body as it makes its sludgy way into my brain. My mind turns into cloud soup. "Why do I feel so—"

"It's a truth tart." The boy also takes one bite, and I can see the tension fade from his shoulders. I bet he feels like cloud soup right now too. "It's infused with a very specific jinn essence so you can't lie. Now." He puts away the spear and draws up another chair.

"Finally, I can drink my raspberry chocolate in peace," Idris mutters into his cup.

"What is your real business here?" asks the boy.

"I told you already, to get my dad out of this ring." Little lights start to sparkle in the air and wrap around me like a warm hug. "So you better get used to it. . . . What's your name anyway?"

"Yaseen," he barks out immediately. The lights run to Yaseen and crowd around his arms, squeezing tight. A small strand of hair falls loose from his topknot and pokes his eye. "Are you really my sister?" He tucks the hair behind a pointed ear.

"Unfortunately," I mutter. The lights go back to me. So that's how this works. This truth tart is a two-way street. "Did you really think you were going to stab me with that spear?"

"Yes—" The lights squeeze Yaseen very tight, until his face turns red and he stutters, "N-no. Ugh! I'm not the one under investigation here."

Idris and I share a look, and Idris whispers a question in my ear.

"What happens to the jinn kings once the wish goes through?"

"I don't know." The warm feeling is back, but it's lighter now. My head is less soupy. "But we won't need to know, because you're going to do what I say and hand over that ring." Yaseen sticks out his hand. "Me and the real jinn will be taking over to clean up your mess."

Now, that stings. I know we only just met, but even I wouldn't be that mean.

"There's no way I'd giv—"

Yaseen is *fast*. So fast I can't finish my sentence when he rushes to steal my necklace. Unfortunately for Yaseen, he is also clumsy. His arm knocks over the cups and pots. Liquid sloshes everywhere.

"Hey, these are the only pants I have!" Idris shrieks as he jumps up.

Yaseen doesn't hesitate. He tumbles onto the table, his fingers inches away from my ring. It's too bad for him that I'm fast too. I jump up and grab one of the hanging decorations and swing. I swing over Yaseen and somersault into the middle of the café . . . straight into the rolling display of pastries.

They crash to the floor. Glass sprinkles all over my hair.

"What is going on?" a jinn patron screeches as his table gets knocked out from under him.

"This could all be avoided if you just do what I say and give me the ring!" Yaseen is charging, and I don't have enough time to get up, so I do the next best thing—I pelt him with as many baked goods as I can. They burst and boom in a flurry of color, feeling, and taste.

"This is not how a brother is supposed to act!" I throw a handful of chocolate truffles Yaseen's way. They explode onto his skin, and he begins to float very slightly in midair.

"Now you've done it." He grins. Somehow I've given him a superpower, and he's flying toward me with a lightning bolt. Great, just great. The bright bolt whizzes. I cross my arms in defense just as it hits me. I expect it to hurt a lot.

It feels like a pinch.

"Whoa." I look at my arms as the lightning crosses over my body. My skin gleams like armor against the energy. Yaseen's shocked expression mirrors mine.

"What the—" Yaseen stutters.

I flip my hands palms-up and watch the lightning as it trails up my arms. My skin appears to be fine, but each snap creates a little cut that heals faster than a blink—faster than when the shadow jinn were chasing me. The lightning stops. My eyes go wide.

"How are you doing that?" Yaseen is still in shock.

"I'm not sure." I glance at Yaseen. "Is it a jinn thing? Is everyone like this?"

"There's no way that didn't hurt." Yaseen raises his spear again. A bright glowing orb of light crackles, ready to attack.

Judging by his reaction, my fast-healing skin is *not* normal by jinn standards either. Somehow that thought makes me smile.

"Levitating malt balls or not, I cannot let you wreck the best café in town." Idris pounces on Yaseen, and they go crashing into three tables of diners. Two adult jinn grab them by the shoulders. "This is for spilling my favorite drink all over my pants!" Idris smears a handful of rainbow cream on Yaseen's face. There is a roar of commotion as Yaseen and Idris struggle to get out of the adult jinn's grips.

In the back of the café, the doors swing open and slam against the wall. A livid man covered in flour and wearing a chef's hat points at us and screams, "Get out now!" With a flick of his wrist, a gust of wind pushes Idris, Yaseen, and me out of the swinging glass doors and onto the very bright street. I land on my back and feel a crunch in my pocket.

"Oh no. Please, please, *please* don't be broken." I am covered in who knows what from those pastries, with a half brother who has anger problems, hundreds of miles away from home. And the only connection I have to my real life is through my phone, and it's . . .

Shattered.

I see red. "You broke my phone." I get up and turn on Yaseen. My whole life was on my phone. My texts with Arzu. My group chat with Madar and my grandparents. My last photo with Padar. And now I'm really cut off from my family. "Do you know how expensive it is to get this fixed? My mom is going to be so mad!"

"Even if I knew what a phone was, I wouldn't care." Yaseen's hair is all over his face. He's covered in little scratches. He bares his teeth—his sharp, pointy teeth. "Look, I'm not afraid to take that ring and you by force if I have to. I'll even make it easier on you. Give me the ring so I can save Baba, and I'll let you go back to where you came from." He shakes his head and assumes a fighting stance. "It's your choice, half-human. Don't make this harder than it needs to be."

"You still want to fight . . . after seeing your little toy stick do absolutely nothing to me?" I want to tell him *I'm* the only one who can save our dad, since the wish was mine, but the angry bubbles won't stop multiplying inside. . . . I mimic Yaseen's stance. If a battle of *who's the toughest* is what it takes to prove to Yaseen that I can do this, then I'll do it. "You're on!" Knowing Yaseen's lightning spear can't hurt me makes me a little more confident. There's something . . . really cool about the idea of being untouchable. Indestructible. Strong.

"While your . . . enthusiasm is inspiring, maybe try to take it down a few notches." Idris clears his throat and stands between us with his arms outstretched. "Because if word gets out that King Shamhurish's two kids are having an all-out war and one of them is a . . . *you-know-what* . . . no one is going to be fixing anything with the scandal that's going to spark."

This gets Yaseen to calm down.

"So what are you saying, that we . . . work together?" I ask.

"Ideally, I would rather stay out of whatever this drama is." Idris points his finger between me and Yaseen. "But it's clear that babysitter boy was sent to fetch you, and considering *I* now need a change of clothes, it works best if we all cool down and think things through. Firstly, with an apology for ruining my only pair of pants."

Yaseen grumbles, "I personally wouldn't use the words *babysitter boy.* . . ."

"The jinn kings made you look for me. . . ." I can't believe I didn't realize it sooner. That means the kings could be on their way here right now. What if Yaseen was just a trick to slow me down?

"Fine, you got me." Yaseen scowls while crossing his arms. "The kings couldn't leave their courtly duties. It's already bad enough that two kings are missing, so they sent me to make sure you don't do anything risky with that ring. But I don't want to spend any more time with you, so if you just give me—"

"I can't!"

"*Why not?*"

"Because if you want to free our dad, then you need me," I explain. "Or did your jinn bosses forget to mention that part? I made the wish, so I have to make the bargain."

Yaseen groans when it clicks. "Don't tell me we need to—"

"Work together?" Idris cuts in. "Yes. And unless you want the growing scene of nosy jinn to increase, I suggest we all accept that we can help each other and *get out of here.*"

Sure enough, there is a small crowd of curious jinn within the café who are not so discreetly staring at us. Yaseen notices too and gives in. "Since I've got no other choice, you and the half-human should follow me . . ."

"I have a name."

". . . this way." Yaseen walks briskly down the street.

"Hold on. Before I go anywhere, I need to ask you one thing." I rush closer to Yaseen so we're almost nose to nose. Because I don't want to freak Idris out, I ask quietly, hoping there's still a little bit of the truth tart swirling around in Yaseen's stomach, "Are the jinn kings really going to execute me if I go with you?"

"If the kings really wanted to do that . . ." Yaseen purses his lips. Little bits of frosting fall to the floor. "Then they wouldn't have sent me. All right?" His eyes narrow, daring me to not believe him. "And even if *I* don't like the idea of working together, you're going to need me too, to get to Azar's realm."

"What are you two whispering about?" Idris is busy wiping cake off his pants.

"Nothing important." Yaseen sighs and begins to walk away. "Like I said, this way." He points with the spear.

I sigh and choose to follow since it seems I don't have any other choice. If I run, Yaseen will chase me.

"At least you don't smell like cabbage anymore," Idris whispers while we follow Yaseen's lead. "That's a miracle in itself."

I roll my eyes and begrudgingly follow along.

If this is a sign of how the journey will go, then the jinn world is already doomed.

CHAPTER NINE

SOMEONE WORTH PROTECTING

"**W**hat is this place?" I ask when Yaseen does a quick double take down both sides of the street before pushing us up a set of glass stairs and into a dark (and very serious-looking) building.

"It's my school," Yaseen whispers as he tiptoes into the main hall. He leaves behind a sprinkle trail. The ceilings are so high, it looks like I'm staring up at a twinkling night sky. "Al-Qalam Academy for the Exceptional. We just need to get to the boys' quarters, and then we can—"

"Yaseen, there you are." A girl's voice calls from the right side of the enormous hall. It's strange—this school seems much larger on the inside than on the outside, like it's enchanted to take up less space. The girl walks with a group of other jinn kids who look a little older than me. I have to squint to really see them because there isn't much light. "We missed you in class this morning."

"Hey, Sufia. Yeah, I had . . . independent study at the Supreme Court. It was last minute, you know how King Barqan is," he lies. Because it's so dark, the group doesn't notice when Yaseen rudely elbows me and Idris into a curtain. My back presses against the cool glass of a very tall window.

"So no news about your dad, then?" Sufia asks.

"Um. No, not yet . . ." Yaseen laughs awkwardly. "But I'm sure he'll turn up soon. You know how he is, loses track of time. Probably out in another realm, doing kingly things."

"Is that what King Barqan told you . . . ?" Sufia pauses. "Before or after you decided to roll around in a pool of sprinkles?"

"Uhhhhhhhhhhhhhhh—"

"Ouch, watch it." Idris's elbow bumps into my shoulder, and for the second time, I am squashed in the dark with Idris. I'm about to push the curtain away when Idris shakes his head.

"He's got a point," he whispers with wide eyes. "Considering we're inside the academy for *royal* students."

"Royal?" I gawk and try to (very discreetly) peek around the corner of the curtain. The students are wearing the same school uniforms I saw this morning, only now I can see the tiny glittering pins stuck to their jackets. I recognize the two girls I saw earlier standing behind Sufia. "They don't look royal to me." I always imagined royalty to be draped in jewels or other expensive royal items, like crowns and capes.

"Well, only students who are descended from jinn

royalty—like certain jinn kings we know and other lesser jinn royals—can attend. So it'd be great if they didn't see you, or me with you, otherwise we'd be in a lot of trouble."

"Oh." But I have so many questions. "What's school like for jinn? Is it like regular school? In sixth grade, we have social studies, math, language arts, music class, science—"

"Is this really the time to explain human school to me?" Idris stands moodily by the window. "Human studies isn't something we learn unless that's our focused track."

"What was your focused track, then?"

"I'm thirteen and a half." Idris only gets moodier. "Focused track doesn't begin until you're fourteen, and not everyone gets one. There's an exam you must pass the year before."

"So then—"

"I would prefer if we don't talk about school anymore, all right?"

"Oh right. I forgot. It's been a while for you." He's been asleep for a hundred years, so maybe it's a sore subject for him. I go quiet and peek at Idris from the corner of my eye, feeling a little sorry for him too.

"I'll see you at talisman studies!" Yaseen waves nervously when Sufia and the rest of the group head back into another dark and twinkling hall. He rips back the curtain and says, "That was close. Come on, we've got fifteen minutes before they come looking for me again." He quickly walks across the main hall and through an arched corridor. It bubbles and warps when we walk through it, like it's stretching out into another large hall. Off-center, there's a series of stairs that wind up into the starry ceiling.

"This way!" Yaseen runs up the stairs, skipping two at a time.

"Who was that girl?" I ask. "She seemed worried about you."

"None of your business." It's hard to tell if Yaseen's face is red from talking to her or the stairs we're running up, but I have a feeling it's not the stairs.

"Why'd you lie to her?"

"Because it's *none of your business*," he grits through his teeth.

"Well, she seemed nice. You have nice friends." We go up, up, up the floors. Portraits and large tapestries holding Al-Qalam's insignia—a pen poised in between an open book—line the walls. The walls get more solid the closer we are to them, but when I look down below, the lower floors turn into an inky night sky again. You could really lose track of time in here. I try to imagine what it'd be like to go to this school. To be *exceptional*. There are grand arched entrances on each floor that buzz with their own energy. That's when I notice older students—teenagers, I think—poring over stacks and stacks of books in a library. I want to peek in and ask about the serious-looking students—what track are they on?—but Yaseen is moving too fast.

"Can we slow down for a second?" Idris wheezes when we reach the tenth floor.

"My room is on this floor. Almost there." Yaseen doesn't even look back, just swings open the door and goes through. The door slams in Idris's face. Idris and I share an annoyed look.

"Think he's always this intense?" asks Idris.

"It's 'none of my business.'" I use air quotes, then push open the door.

The first thing that gets me is the stench—it *definitely* smells like boys live here. I guess jinn aren't immune to cheesy feet smell. "Does anyone know what deodorant is?" I hold my nose as we pass by rows and rows of doors. Little orbs of glowing light float above our heads. "Or a shower?"

Idris breathes in deep. "Smells just fine to me."

"Stop smelling things and get in here," hisses Yaseen. He corrals us into his room and quickly locks the door. "And don't touch anything."

I don't know what I thought a jinn boy's bedroom would look like, but I wasn't expecting it to be so *clean*. It makes my organized chaos look like regular chaos. The room is small and square-shaped with a desk, a bed, a chest for clothes, and a bathroom. (So jinn *do* use the bathroom, another research point to write down.) I notice there aren't any mirrors. There's a big window that lets in light. I can see the back of the large Supreme Court building from it.

"Do you really live here? At school? And not at your house?" I ask while looking at the neat stacks of books on

Yaseen's shelves. There aren't any pictures or posters. I would at least have a picture of my mom in my room if I had to stay here for a whole school year. Why doesn't Yaseen? Maybe jinn don't care as much for their parents? Yaseen doesn't seem to care about anything, other than being inconvenienced.

"Yes?" Yaseen looks confused when he opens a chest next to his bed and rummages around. "Don't you? Now, where is it . . ."

"Doesn't your mom miss you when you're not home?" I know Madar would.

"Don't talk about my mother." Yaseen's face goes stony right before he falls all the way into the chest and the lid snaps shut.

"Oh . . . kay." I can't tell what's weirder—Yaseen's reaction or the fact that he was swallowed whole by a piece of furniture. I glance at Idris. "Moms and dads are important in the jinn world too? It's not just a human thing?"

Idris shrugs. "Depends." He's staring out the window with that searching look again. "Yes and no."

"What do you mean?"

"I mean it depends on how important you are to *them*," he clarifies, and says nothing more.

"Oh."

A second passes in awkward silence before the chest lid swings wide open again.

Yaseen tumbles out—sparkling clean and in his academy

uniform—with his arms full of books and a spare change of clothes. We bump into each other, and the books go flying all over the floor.

"Could you not make a mess of everything, half-human!" Yaseen is more agitated now. He hands a spare set of pants to Idris. "For your troubles," he mumbles.

"Could you stop calling me that?" I huff.

Yaseen sighs. "Could you just make my life easier and not speak?"

"Could you make my life easier and learn some manners?!"

We're caught in a glaring match. I can't believe I'm related to someone so mean. My head is going *red alert* when I notice the dropped books neatly rearrange themselves on the ground. Their pages turn until they stop on a monstrous drawing of a jeweled door covered in flames. The text is written in a script I can't read.

Curiously, this gets Idris out of his window-gazing stupor. He picks up the book, draws a little shape with his finger in the corner of the page, and reads it aloud. *"'While there is no known static gateway to the exiled Realm Beneath the Unseen, there are standard signs and requirements to discover an active gateway. Gateways are only found in mortal-inhabited areas. The land is generally volatile and unstable. Items forged from the fire of the Realm Beneath are helpful in locating potential gateways. . . .'"* His voices trails off as he skims. *"'Protection charms, whilst not necessary, are highly encouraged for safe return for jinn. For many mortals, returning to the mortal realm of the seen is impossible without said protection charms.'"* Idris drops the book like it cursed him. "And you *still* want to do this?"

"I have to. If it were your dad, wouldn't you?" Yaseen sits cross-legged on the floor while looking over the books. So I guess he *does* care about his parents—well, his dad at least. Yaseen must be pretty important to our dad if he cares this much. "Plus, I'm not the one who needs a protection charm," he mumbles to himself.

"I mean, I guess . . ." Idris's hands are in knots. His eyes go a little murky.

"Okay, so it can't be that hard to get a protection charm, right?" I pace around the room, trying to get the nervous tingling out of my fingers and toes. "There's probably a store I can buy one from."

"You don't *buy* a protection charm." Yaseen snorts. To prove his point, he walks over to his bed and plucks something from his pillow—it's a tiny crystallized flower that looks a little like a spider. "It's something someone *else* makes for you, not something you create for yourself." Idris and I crowd around Yaseen to get a better look. The tiny spider flower glowing in his palm radiates warmth and love in little pulses. Yaseen's voice gets tight when he says, "You have to give up a little piece of yourself—something that can never be replaced—to make it. That's why protection charms are near-impossible to get." I reach to touch the little flower, but Yaseen snatches it away. He pins it to his uniform jacket.

"Oh." That makes things complicated. "Well, there's got to be someone who would do that for me. . . ." My voice trails off when I realize that the only person who would is currently trapped inside my necklace. I look worriedly at Idris. "Do you have a protection charm?"

Idris returns to the window, lost in his thoughts. Maybe he didn't hear me.

"Who gave you yours?" I ask Yaseen.

Yaseen clams up and picks at his eyebrow. "None of your b—"

A little bell goes off outside Yaseen's room, followed by a faint call to prayer. I've never seen someone look so relieved to go pray. "Well, that's my cue." Yaseen scurries around his room, plucking books off his shelf and stuffing them into an extremely small pouch. "I've got to take care of a few things to keep up appearances. Stay here until I get back. *Don't touch anything.* I'll know if you do." He gives me a pointed look. "We'll leave the city and look for the portal tonight, when everyone goes to sleep." He turns on his heel and shuts the door. It glows red for a second.

"Wait, I can help—" I yank at the door. It's locked. "Hey!"

"It's for your protection!" he says through the door.

"My protection or yours?! Unlock this door now!" The more I try to pull it open, the hotter the doorknob gets. I let it go and fan my hand. "How am I supposed to try to get a protection charm when he's locked us in?" I grumble and kick the door. My shadow moves a half second slower than my foot. Great, we're stuck in here until Yaseen gets back . . . that is, if he comes back. "Now what do we do?"

"Should have seen that one coming, Noorzad." Idris is still at the window, seemingly unfazed by our current situation. He's writing something in his notebook. *"Look for the portal tonight,* he says. Even I almost believed him." Idris's eyes go a little cloudy as he turns the page, like someone put a film of white over his irises. I gulp. That's a little weird. Must be another jinn thing.

I notice the book Idris was reading earlier and crouch down to scan through the pages. There are so many drawings of gateways, charms, and what the realm looks like, but I notice one thing missing. "Can I ask you a question, Idris?"

"Hmm," he says, distracted. He's scribbling very quickly. Little bits of ink smear on his fingers.

"There aren't any pictures of Azar in here, and it's got me wondering . . ."

Idris shudders. "Must you say his name?"

". . . why is he so dangerous?" I glance up as Idris sighs and closes his notebook. "Besides making this ring, what's so bad about him?"

"I don't know all the details, but he's rumored to be the oldest living jinn in our world," Idris explains while picking at an ink stain on his thumb. "Older than the seven jinn kings, and infinitely more powerful. We're taught that many centuries ago, he wanted to expand his fire kingdom into the Qaf Mountains and eventually rule both the seen and unseen worlds, starting with the City of Jewels. So the seven jinn kings banded together to banish him and put his realm beneath ours to keep everyone safe. That's why it's called the Realm *Beneath* the Unseen."

"But?"

"Are we really safe?" Idris turns his sad eyes on me. "I mean, from . . . ," he whispers. "The tricks of a jinn king?"

Safe and *jinn king* aren't words I would normally put together, but after my first impression of the seven jinn kings, who are incredibly terrifying, I can't imagine how much worse Azar must be. I remove the ring necklace from around my neck and examine the five remaining gems. It's hard to imagine how something so small could steal so much.

"Why create a ring that only makes your life worse when you use it?" I wonder out loud.

"If I knew the answer to that, I would have stayed home and woken up to my normal life," says Idris. "But instead I go from being imprisoned in a ring to imprisoned in this room trying to figure out a way to survive going to the Realm Beneath, where I could very likely become imprisoned *again*."

"You don't have to tag along. You can just go home."

"Yes, I do—"

"No, you don't—"

"I can't find a home I can't remember," Idris quietly admits. He sniffles once while looking out the window again. "Everything is so different now. The roads are mixed up in my head. I can't . . ."

"Oh." Something clicks about seeing Idris curled up on the café table earlier. "When you left me at the court, you went to look for your house." *And couldn't remember where to find it.* Which means . . . he's all alone. No parents. No grandparents. It hits me for the first time. Idris is lost in his own hometown.

Idris doesn't say anything.

"Maybe someone at the court might know—"

"I doubt the kings would care about me. I'm not like you." Idris rubs his face and tugs on his earlobe. He takes a second to steady his breathing. When he looks at me again, you wouldn't be able to tell anything was bothering him. "So, since your crisis is a little bit bigger than mine and I've got a spare set of pants, I figure there's nothing left to do except help you. That is, if you want my help?"

"Well, you did save my life once before," I ponder.

"I can be very heroic when needed—"

"But you also deserted me back at the court."

"In my defense . . ." Idris scratches behind his ear before smiling sheepishly. "There is no defense. I am sorry about that, but I'm positive I can make up for it. Actually . . ." I watch Idris as he carefully pockets both his notebook and the book I was looking at. He scans the room. "I can make up for it right now." A little light blooms in Idris's face when he reaches the chest. "Rookie mistake." He kicks it open and gestures at me. "Let's get out of here and find you a protection charm."

Without warning, Idris jumps into the darkness of the chest and disappears.

When I don't jump in after him, his exasperated face peeks out of the chest. "Come on, Noorzad, it doesn't bite."

Something doesn't feel right about this. Wouldn't he want to search for his missing family?

"Why are you helping me now when you don't have to?" I shift my weight from foot to foot. "Especially since being around me is just going to put you in more danger."

"Because I am an accomplice, and I'm sure your brother is already telling the jinn kings I helped you, but mostly . . ." Idris sucks in his cheeks and taps the side of the chest. ". . . I don't want to be alone."

"Oh." That sounds like a pretty good reason to me. "Well, I'd be a huge jerk to say no." If I were in Idris's shoes and woke up a hundred years later to a whole new world with no mom or grandparents, I would really need a friend too. And it wouldn't be so bad to have one jinn friend with me on this journey.

"Thanks, Noorzad. You won't regret it." Idris smiles. "I can't believe a single wish turned both our lives upside down."

Oh right, I don't know why I didn't ask earlier. Since Idris was trapped in the ring, he must have made a wish too. "What did you wish for?" I ask, suddenly curious.

"Does it matter? It's not like it went through."

"It matters a little—"

"Noorzad, we don't have all day," Idris interrupts. "And I personally don't want another meeting with the jinn kings, unless you do?"

"Nope, definitely don't want a repeat of this morning." I watch Idris disappear into the chest and, after a second, jump right in after him, wondering what made Idris want to wish upon a cursed ring of fate in the first place.

CHAPTER TEN

WHERE EVERYONE PRETENDS

We pop out of the chest and into a very large library. Tall windows replace one of the walls. The drawn curtains make everything dark, similar to a night sky. The rows and rows of books glitter like stars, just waiting to be picked up and read.

"How did the chest get us here?" I climb out in a daze.

"Looks like it was enchanted to this spot," answers Idris. "Explains where he got all those books."

"Enchanted . . ." When I look down at my shoes, I notice I am wearing an academy uniform (and I'm somehow magically very clean). There are three thin silver stripes that run up the side of the pants that remind me of shooting stars on the airways. On the matching jacket, the same stripes are around the cuffs and line the lapels. I spy the school emblem right above my heart. Emerald-green buttons glitter on the jacket and match the soft silver dress shirt underneath.

"I need one of these in my house." I touch my hair with awe. All the sticky toffee is out. "This would save me so much time. Goodbye, showers!" I swish my legs in the dark navy pants, liking the sound they make when I walk. "This is the best outfit I've ever worn in my entire life."

"Your brother has a very strange obsession with cleanliness and studying, it seems." Idris frowns as he tries to adjust the slightly too-small uniform. While he digs back in the chest for his clothes, I keep hearing the words *your brother* out loud. I'm still getting used to it. "Here, in case you need this." He hands my pack over. "What's the matter? You look like your favorite faerie just died."

"I've never had anyone say—I mean, I've never had a brother—I mean, I guess I *have* a brother, but . . ." I pick at the school emblem on my jacket. "It's hard to explain. I feel happy and sad about it at the same time."

"I get it." Idris doesn't ask any more questions. Instead he says, "But seriously, you should put that bag in your pocket."

"I don't think it'll fit. I'll just wear it on my back."

"Do you want to go back to smelling like cabbage? We need to blend in if we want to get out of this school, and we can't do that with that ugly thing waving around like a human-shaped red flag."

"My bag is nowhere near human-shaped."

"Don't say I didn't warn you." Idris pinches the bridge of his nose. "Since we're here, I'm a little rusty on the mechanics of creating a protection charm. While I grab the books we need, you can look through this book and find the clues on potential Realm Beneath gates." He puts the book we were looking at in Yaseen's room in my hands and starts reading the floating signs in the library. They warp and flicker between languages. "I'll meet you back here in fifteen minutes, okay?"

"Great." I wave and watch Idris disappear into the maze of shelves before looking down at the book in my hands. I take a deep breath and open the pages. It's not in English. I groan. I know I'm a fast learner, but even I won't be able to learn to read the Arabic script fast enough to understand this book. I look around, wondering if there's someone I could ask for help. If my phone wasn't busted, I could have easily used a translation app.

Help a half-human, the voice in my head says. This time it sounds deeper, less a whisper and more like someone speaking from over my shoulder. *I doubt it. These jinn would banish you the second they discovered who you really are.*

"You again?" I whirl on my heel, my heart fluttering a mile a minute. I look at my necklace and notice the gems are glowing brighter than usual. I don't know how or why, but it doesn't seem keen on wanting to leave me alone. I chew on my lip and nervously whisper back, "I guess I won't let them discover who I really am."

Clever girl. The voice feels like it's smiling. *Show them what you can really do. You need not be afraid when it's they who should be afraid of you.*

"Afraid of me?" I peer down the starry rows of books, but no one's there. It's just me and my twitching shadow, reaching for my neck. "What do you mean, what I can really do?" Hold on. I squint at the shadow on the ground and make a peace sign. My shadow makes a peace sign back. No twitching. I sigh and shake my head.

Pull yourself together, I think. All the stress and magic pastries are finally getting to me. I'm sneaking around a magical library with a talking ring. I can almost feel Arzu's *Are you serious?* face. Real or not, the voice is right. No one is going to help me here, and even if I could trick them into helping me, I don't need that. I can do this by myself, and when I do, it'll be enough to show the jinn kings there's nothing wrong with being a little different.

That's why being the best is important. People make exceptions for the exceptional all the time. Maybe half-jinn were a problem in the past, but maybe they weren't as good as me. Maybe I'll be the first one to impress them, change their minds, be the exception. After all, Padar gave me the ring for a reason, right? Right. Even if it was cursed, a part of him *wanted* me to change my fate, so that's got to count for something. Once I do all this, then I'll be able to tell Madar the truth so she'll understand *why* Padar disappeared. Then maybe we won't have to move at all. Maybe everything will be okay.

With my new positive thoughts, I huddle into a quiet corner and flip through the pages. Even though I can't understand the looping Arabic script, I can sorta piece together what's going on with the pictures, but it doesn't give me any new information. The truth is, the answers are gonna be in the details. When I reach the page with the protection charm symbol, I gently wrap my fingers around my glowing ring and hold it closer to my chest. For a minute I pretend I too have a tiny glowing pin on my academy uniform.

I pretend that I am someone's worth-protecting.

I pretend I belong.

With a big sigh, I gently close the book and wait for Idris to return. He's going to have to read for clues. But curiosity gets the better of me, and I decide it can't hurt to take a small peek around the library while I wait. All I need to do is fit in, and no one will know the difference. I quietly slip my bag off my shoulders and do what Idris asked. I put it in my uniform pocket. Magically, it fits. "I really need five pairs of these pants," I mutter quietly to myself. Then I carefully peek out of the nook I'm in and wander down the starlit rows of books. This library looks a little different from the one we passed by earlier, with the older students. I wonder if each grade has their own study space.

I reach the edge of the library, where there's a large clearing and a set of huge stained-glass doors. A few kids around my age pass by me without a glance and open one of the doors, letting in a slice of sunshine that cuts against the starry universe of the library.

I wish we weren't in such a rush. I want to know how it

all works. Clutching the book to my chest, I wonder what it'd be like to study on the sunny deck that stretches and yawns out over the jeweled city, to say hello to the sparkling green mountains every morning on my way to class, to learn more about what someone like me could do in a place like this, where simurghs and faeries and dragons and jinn are real, where no one calls our stories silly.

"Are you lost?" Sufia's voice startles me. Her big brown eyes blink in confusion as she waves.

"Oh!" I stumble back and nervously laugh. "No, not lost, just thinking."

"I do that sometimes too," she says brightly. "Especially now with midterms coming up next month." Her pin sparkles on her silver uniform sweater. Three navy stripes run down the sleeves. "I only ask if you're lost because you're in the third-year study and I've never seen you in here before. Are you new? A first-year?"

"Um, yes." My brain scrambles for an excuse. "I must have taken a wrong turn. That's why I can't find anything in here. It's so dark, everything looks the same." I smile sheepishly before inching back. Idris is going to be so mad when he realizes I've gotten myself spotted.

"You get used to it." Sufia shakes her head. "It's just like this in between the winter solstice and spring equinox. You'll see, it gets quite pretty when the new year rolls around. It's my favorite time of year at the academy. The walls turn the dreamiest color and sparkle in the best way."

I nod.

"Sorry, I've rambled for too long. I'm sure you don't care for boring things. I'll see you around." She holds out a delicate hand to shake. "I'm Sufia, by the way."

"Farrah."

"What a pretty name." Sufia dazzles with her wide smile, and my cheeks get red. I can see why Yaseen likes her. She's kind. "If you get lost again, look me up." She winks and waves. Her soft brown hair swishes gently against her sweater as she catches up to her friends on the balcony.

I should probably get back before Idris has a heart attack. I take one last look around and grip the book tighter. Maybe it wouldn't be so bad to move, if I could move here.

Even if it were only for a little bit.

Just to see the halls of the academy bloom and change for the new year.

Just to see if Al-Qalam Academy for the Exceptional is the place where I could be someone who belongs.

BY THE TIME I HURRY BACK TO THE MEETING SPOT AND huddle down against a bookshelf, I realize I am not alone.

"Did you secure the girl?" an urgent voice asks on the other side of the bookshelf.

"Yes, King Barqan," comes a reply in a voice I instantly recognize—Yaseen's. "Just like you asked."

I should have seen this trap coming. Idris was right.

King Barqan sighs in relief. "Good, that's reassuring. We can't have a half-human freely wandering our city with so much hanging in the balance. The others will be happy to hear it. We haven't been able to calculate exact figures on how much time we have, but based off rough estimates, we have a week, maybe a little less, before the wish completes."

A chill creeps into my fingers and toes. Only a week? I go completely still and try to catch what they're saying.

"Um. What should I do with the girl and her friend, then?"

"Friend?" King Barqan sounds surprised.

"I found her with another boy."

"A friend . . . This doesn't bode well if the half-human already has accomplices. Perhaps it was a blessing she ran off. Maymun almost convinced me to eliminate her at our meeting." King Barqan sounds like he's pacing. "But now I'm thinking she could be useful to gather information. We don't know how deep this may run, if they're in cahoots with Azar. He always finds a way to meddle in our affairs after we locked him away in that cursed place. Which means we need to act quickly. Take this. One for her and one for the friend." There's some shuffling, and curiosity gets the better of me. I remove a book from the shelf. It opens up a little space where I can peek through and see King Barqan hand something small to Yaseen.

"What is it?" Yaseen looks confused.

"It has Maymun's talisman inscribed. . . ."

There are light footsteps a little farther in the sparkling library, which makes King Barqan bring a finger to his lips. Just my bad luck, I see it's Idris making the noise. He is walking quickly down the rows of shelves, waving at me and mouthing very quietly, *I've got it, let's go.*

"Not now," I hiss while crossing my arms in an X. I wish I could send him a message with my mind. *I'm on a stealth mission; stay where you are.* "Stop moving!" I whisper as quietly as I can. Idris only moves quicker. I'm too distracted; I don't catch the rest of King Barqan's message.

". . . in a drink and we'll do the rest. Is that understood?" King Barqan glares at Yaseen, who shrinks back a little.

"Are you sure there isn't—"

"Yaseen, there is no room for questions. There is no more discussion on this matter." King Barqan goes cold as a light purple aura glows off him. Yaseen's eyes turn glassy and dazed for a second. It's so scary a sight, I have to turn away. "Understood?"

"Yes, sir."

"Good," says King Barqan. "Do this, and we will see that you don't have to repeat the year. We can't have you failing second year *again* now, can we?"

"I won't disappoint."

I look back in time to see King Barqan swish away, his green clothes trailing magnificently behind him. Yaseen just stares at the item in his hand with a puzzled look on his face. Very slowly, I put the book back, right when Idris reaches me.

"What is the holdup!" he whispers angrily. "What part of 'it's time to go' don't you understand?"

A shadow moves and footsteps pass by us. Idris goes still and crouches beside me. We see Yaseen walk right past us. *Don't do it,* I think when he stops again and looks at the small objects in his hand. I know we got off to a rough start, but somewhere, deep down, he's got to see me as his sister. Maybe there's still a chance we could work together as a team to save our dad. After a moment of hesitation, he slips them into his pocket and makes a beeline for his chest.

My cheeks start to pinch and my legs turn into jelly when I watch him disappear around the corner. Suddenly, all the warm feelings about belonging shatter.

"We've got about two minutes to get out of here before Yaseen realizes we're gone." Idris gets up and tugs on my arm. "What is with you? I thought you'd be halfway out of the city by now."

"I was just hoping—" I shake my head. Just because Sufia was nice to me doesn't mean she'd act the same if she knew what I am. I hug myself. It was silly to imagine seeing the new year here. It was silly to fill my head with a daydream. Madar was right. Our life is not a faerie tale. "You were right. We don't have a second to lose."

"*Finally,* true appreciation." Idris smiles as we zip out of the library, through the starry archways, and down the midnight stairs. "Took you long enough to get with the program."

"Yeah," I say, without looking back at the academy. I swallow the tickle of disappointment in my mouth and keep running. "From now on, no more distractions."

CHAPTER ELEVEN

AN UNEXPECTED DETOUR

We almost make a clean getaway.

"Hey, there you are," shouts Yaseen when he spots us halfway down the block. His hands tug at his hair as he steps into the bright sunlight of the academy's entrance. "Hey, stop! This wasn't what we agreed to!"

"Whatever you do, don't look back." I grab Idris's wrist and drag him with me. (Idris is *not* a very fast runner, unfortunately.) I use my anger and disappointment to propel us through the crowded streets.

"There's got"—Idris huffs—"to be"—and puffs—"a better way." I lose my grip on his wrist when his ankle rolls. He tumbles onto the glass ground, scraping his palms. "Oof!"

Leave him. The whispers swirl in my head. *He'll only slow you down.*

For a second I think about it. I could go faster without Idris, but then that'd make me a bad friend and probably just as bad as Yaseen for accepting King Barqan's deal. There's only one correct way to handle this. I stand in front of Idris just as Yaseen is gaining speed. He reaches inside his jacket pocket, and I know in about five seconds he's gonna start swinging that annoying lightning spear around again.

"I think I sprained it." Idris winces as he wobbles on his feet.

I do the only thing that feels right. "I'll hold him off, but you figure out a way to get us out of here," I shout as I run full speed toward Yaseen. A small crowd of passersby stop to watch in curiosity.

"Academy kids and their dramatics," one adult mutters as they walk past.

I spot metal poles above me. I jump up and swing round and round. When a lightning ball zips its way near me, I let go and fly directly toward it.

"Didn't your mom ever tell you being a bully isn't nice!"

"Don't talk about my mom!"

Without thinking, I draw back my fist and punch the ball with all my force. It sizzles and crackles and surprisingly shoots back toward Yaseen. I . . . don't know what I was expecting, but it definitely wasn't *that*. My hand doesn't even hurt.

"How are you doing this!" Yaseen yelps, and dodges the attack by jumping into a bush.

Idris blinks as he clicks his pen and waits for his cloud

to take shape. "D-did you just *punch* a ball of lightning with your bare fist?"

I drop down onto the ground (quite epically, if I do say so myself) and jog back over to Idris. "Do you think the café gave me powers?" My mind is whirring with possibility. If that's true, then we've got to stop by the shop to stock up on every tart and truffle.

"I doubt it," Idris mutters. "I can't be completely sure, but I think entering the unseen world is activating your dormant jinn abilities."

"If being here for a few hours activated super healing and super strength . . ." I stare at my hands and laugh. "Who knows what a few days or a month could do. I wish I had come here sooner. This is the best thing to ever happen to me!"

"Don't push it," Idris warns. "Jinn abilities are seldom what they seem at first glance."

"Blah, blah." I'm still on an adrenaline rush as little wisps of Idris's cloud start to circle around our legs, lifting us up in a warm hug.

"Idris, let's blow this Popsicle stand!" I whoop as the cloud belt locks me in.

"What?"

"Just go while he's still distracted!"

"Hang on tight." Idris steers us straight up and past another lightning bolt. "It's gonna get a little bumpy." We move so fast, even my shadow is having a hard time holding on.

It's not fast enough—something *thunks* onto the edge of the cloud. I turn around. Yaseen is crawling his way up onto our cloud. The wind pushes my hair in my face, and I get up too, ready to push him off.

"What is with you?" he yells, and quickly rolls away from my shove. "I thought we agreed we were going to work together!"

"That was before you lied to us."

"When did I lie to you?" He lunges for me and we collide, rolling and pushing one another as he tries to reach for the ring. "You're making my life harder for no reason!"

"No, you are! You said locking us up was for our protection!"

"It was!"

"No, it wasn't, and you know it." I try to move away, but Idris makes a sharp turn, pushing us past the tallest buildings until we're soaring in a spiral near the peak of the emerald mountains. This unlucky choice of steering pushes me closer to Yaseen. His fingers clamp around my ring and yank—breaking the string. Idris turns the cloud again, and Yaseen loses his balance.

Two horrible things happen at once.

Horrible moment #1: Yaseen drops the ring.

Horrible moment #2: Yaseen's face gets very, very green, and he starts to vomit from motion sickness.

"The ring!" I shout as I watch it tumble down into the clouds, heading straight for Earth.

"My stomach!" groans Yaseen.

"My shoes!" shrieks Idris, but then he recovers himself. "Okay, actually, they're *your* shoes."

"Forget the shoes! Dive down and chase the ring, Idris!" I shout, but Idris has slowed down our cloud and is fussing about the shoes. "Come on! Now is not the time to worry about hygiene!"

Yaseen is about to jump out of the cloud to follow the ring when, without warning, a third horrible moment happens:

My shadow unravels and lets go of the cloud. I watch in horror as my shadow opens its red eyes and winks at me (with *my* face) before zipping down to scoop up the ring.

"Oh no," I whisper.

"What is a shadow jinn doing all the way up here?" shouts Yaseen.

Soon enough, Idris's and Yaseen's shadows peel off and shift into wobbly birds.

"Why are there more of them?" he continues shouting.

"That." Idris throws off his shoes. "Is." The ring glitters in my shadow jinn's mouth. "Very." Then it loops the loop and disappears into a wave of clouds. "Bad."

Right before we lose sight of the shadows, my shadow jinn looks back. She winks and whispers, "Is this really worth protecting?"

"Please don't tell me that just happened." Yaseen is holding his stomach as reality sinks in.

We lost the ring.

THE TIMING COULD NOT BE WORSE.

Getting to the Realm Beneath with a protection charm was near-impossible by itself, but now we've lost the ring that's holding my dad and Ahmar, and it's all Yaseen's fault.

"This is all your fault," I say to Yaseen for the hundredth time. The wind slaps my hair into my face as Idris tries to search for the shadow jinn. "We needed that ring to bargain with Azar!"

"My fault?" He wiggles his way to the edge of the cloud— just far enough away from me and Idris. "Do you have memory loss or something? Like maybe mentioning that you had a shadow jinn stuck to you this entire time? They're Azar's little henchmen. They're his eyes and ears in our world. Now that thing knows our entire plan. Whatever they hear, they report back to him!"

"You had one stuck to you too." My cheeks are burning. "And you didn't notice either, so . . ."

"Because Azar's creations normally can't get into the Qaf Mountains."

"Can you two be quiet for five seconds?" Idris grumbles. "Blaming each other isn't going to get us out of this situation. And can you stop saying his *name*."

"I haven't even started blaming you yet," Yaseen continues. "But now that you mention it, don't think that I didn't notice that slowdown."

"No one asked you to come along, you know." Idris ignores Yaseen and looks very seriously at me. "We need to think about what to do next. Maybe we can still do this without the ring."

"How can you release someone from a trap if you don't have the trap?" Yaseen hisses. "We need that ring back."

"I'm just trying to find solutions. Your snarky remarks aren't helping anyone," Idris retorts. "Noorzad, did you find any more information about the gateways?"

"Oh." I look down at my knees. "About that. I couldn't actually *read* the specifics—"

"What do you mean, you couldn't read it?" Idris asks.

"I can barely read Arabic, and I can't understand it," I say quietly. "I thought I could if I tried hard enough. Some words are the same in Farsi, but not very many."

"It's okay." Idris sighs and holds out his hand. "Just give me the book, and we'll figure it out now."

"Okay." I try not to focus on Yaseen's critical stare as I pull my bag out of my pocket and look through it. Only, the book isn't there. I freeze. "I—I think I might have left it in the library . . . by accident."

Idris stays quiet.

Yaseen keeps staring at Idris.

I feel my face flush with embarrassment. I never mess up like this. "I—I think I accidentally put it back on the shelf after . . ." *Eavesdropping on Yaseen and King Barqan.*

"Luckily, I always check out two copies from the library

for this exact reason." Yaseen surprises us by sitting up tall. His pin glows on his chest. He digs in his pouch and holds up an identical book. "Aren't we lucky?" Idris frowns as Yaseen flips through the pages and reads. "It doesn't say we *need* anything specifically from the Realm Beneath to access a gateway. It's just *helpful* in locating where a gateway is, but we still need the ring to free my dad."

"So without the ring, our dad is doomed," I say.

"Not necessarily," Idris interjects.

"Explain," says Yaseen.

"If the shadow jinn have been listening to us this whole time, then I doubt they'll leave us alone for long. I think what they're hoping for is to waste our time. That's what *you-know-who* wants, isn't it?" Idris sits in a thinking position. "They want us to waste time looking for the ring because it'll distract us from getting to the gateway . . ."

". . . so we'll have less time to prepare surviving the Realm Beneath." I piece the rest together and nervously look over my shoulder. "Because they haven't really gone away, have they?"

"Exactly." Idris beams.

"I'm not so sure about this . . . ," Yaseen mutters.

"No one asked for your opinion." Idris turns to me and says, "I can see which sibling is the bright one." Then he slaps his jeweled pen into my hand.

Yaseen scowls but says nothing.

"Um, thank you, but why are you giving this to me?"

"Because we are staying the course, Noorzad. Which means if you want a chance to survive the Realm Beneath, we've got to get you that protection charm first." He stands behind me and guides my arm up and down—the cloud moves up and down. "See, pretty easy, right?" Idris gives me an encouraging smile that makes something flutter in my stomach. "Just picture where it is you want to be in your head, and the cloud will take you."

"That's cool and all, but there's one huge problem with this plan, Idris." The airways shimmer in front of us as I steer past other clouds. "I don't have anyone in the jinn world who . . ." *Thinks I'm worth protecting.*

Yaseen makes a face when he hears that but mumbles, "It doesn't need to be a jinn."

"Did you say something?" I ask.

Yaseen clears his throat and begrudgingly says, "It doesn't need to be a jinn. Humans"—he shudders—"count too. Un-fortunately."

"They do?" I whisper, looking back and forth between Yaseen and Idris.

"Obviously." Idris's grin fills his whole face. "Know where to go now?"

I nod.

"And you thought the half-human was the bright one . . . ," Yaseen mutters under his breath, then clears his throat. "Before I regret my genius suggestion, mind letting us know where it is we're headed so I can prepare myself?"

"That's an easy one. I'm a little surprised you didn't guess it already." I point the pen forward and picture exactly where I want to be. "We're headed home."

CHAPTER TWELVE

WHEN SHAPE-SHIFTING IS AS PAINFUL AS IT LOOKS

It takes longer than I thought to float back to Philadelphia. Enchanted clouds, apparently, do not move as fast as airplanes. Idris tried to copilot with me but ended up falling asleep about two hours ago. I've never met a person who sleeps so much. Yaseen kept his nose in his book the entire time, reading furiously.

I try not to peek back at my brother, who is still holding on to a huge secret. Since he has nowhere to run, maybe if I ask him, he'll come clean about his deal with King Barqan.

"What? Do I have something on my face?" asks Yaseen when he catches me staring.

With Idris asleep, I quietly say, "I might not be the sister you wanted, but our dad is depending on us to work together."

"Okaaay." Yaseen gives me a blank stare. "Isn't that what we're doing?"

"Is it?" I glance at his pocket, where he slipped whatever King Barqan gave him.

"If you're talking about—" Yaseen's words go sludgy, like his mouth is full of chocolate. He clears his throat and tries again. "I didn't lie to you whe—" His face goes red when his words get stuck in his throat again. He sighs. "There's nothing to worry about except saving Baba, okay?"

"You promise?"

Yaseen stares at me for a few seconds before nodding. "Now if you don't mind, I've got a lot of reading left to do." He turns around and goes back to his book.

"Okay." It's not okay. My stomach hurts when Yaseen turns away. I thought I could say, *I know your secret, you liar!* But after losing the ring and trying to get a protection charm, I feel really small, like I'm disappointing everyone. I've always been the best, and now I'm not.

It's better to recharge and focus on what's important right now. Getting the charm. Maybe then my stomach won't hurt and I'll be strong enough to call Yaseen out. And tell Idris. I should definitely let Idris in on what I know, so he doesn't think I'm tricking him too.

I just hope nothing bad happens until then.

We arrive right before sunset. Philadelphia's city lights wave goodbye to the sun just as the moon peeks through the clouds. We circle and loop as our cloud slowly descends. My stomach is in confusing knots. I don't know what's worse—knowing my brother is lying to me or having to explain the truth to Madar and my grandparents.

At first I was excited to tell them, but what if learning I'm half jinn changes how they feel about me? I know that one reason for finding Padar was to get the truth about why he left Madar a long time ago, so we can stay in Philly, but this secret affects more than moving. It can change the way my family sees *me*. I can picture Baba Haji's disappointed face now. *I knew something was wrong, just like with her father.*

What if the truth changes everything for the worse?

What if it makes me lose Madar too?

I peek at Yaseen, who is watching the passing buildings very intently. He picks at the corner of his eyebrow. I know I shouldn't, but I can't help but wonder if all this would be easier if I were 100 percent jinn or 100 percent human.

I wonder if Yaseen thinks the same.

Even though I'm upset with Yaseen, there's a tiny part of me that wants to know more about him. Family is family, after all (even if he denies it). "Have you ever visited a human city?"

"No. Why would I?" asks Yaseen. "I'm the son of a jinn king. My life has nothing to do with humans." He keeps tugging his eyebrow, like there's something that doesn't quite add up in his head about his father. *So then why would a jinn king secretly spend time in the human world?*

"What about your mom?" I ask.

"What about her?"

"You always mention your dad, but what about your mom? Is she a jinn queen too? What does she do?" I imagine Yaseen's mom, an extremely glamorous jinn queen, with bright emerald eyes to match Yaseen's, since he really doesn't resemble Padar that much. She must be extremely patient to deal with his attitude.

Yaseen is silent for a second, like he's remembering something sad. "My mom is—"

The cloud hits some turbulence—a flock of pigeons—that jolts Idris awake.

"No, milk chocolate is a travesty, don't make me drink it." His gray eyes blink rapidly when he sees the skyline of Philadelphia come closer. "Ah, nothing like waking from one nightmare to another."

"I happen to like milk chocolate," Yaseen mutters while wiping his eyes.

"You have no taste buds."

"No, *you* don't have any taste buds."

"Noorzad, please, settle this discussion." Idris gestures toward me.

"Um, milk chocolate is okay." I ignore Idris's shriek of betrayal and focus on the small smile that pops up on Yaseen's face. His eyes still look faraway, and I wonder again what else there is to the story of Yaseen's mom.

We land softly on the bridge that connects Center City

with University City as 30th Street Station gleams in the twilight. Trains drift lazily in and out of the city. Idris and Yaseen continue to debate why milk chocolate should (*"shouldn't,"* corrects Idris) exist.

"Why would anyone like dark chocolate? It's so bitter," Yaseen mutters as he looks at the golden-blue Schuylkill River. There are a few brave rowers rowing through the last drops of sunlight. He loses his train of thought. "Whoa. That's . . . pretty peaceful-looking."

"The rowers? Yeah, I've always wanted to try, but my mom says I'm not old enough yet." I point off to the distance. "You can't really see it from here, but there's Boathouse Row. I like to watch the boats go by too. When the sun is just right, it looks like they're sweeping across the sky."

"Yeah, but they're *not* actually flying. It's just an illusion." Yaseen crosses his arms as his shoe taps against the concrete bridge. A little line forms between his eyebrows, but he keeps on staring at the boats. "Why can't I feel anything on this bridge?"

"What do you mean?"

"It feels so . . . boring." Yaseen keeps tapping his shoe on the bridge. "Where's the essence? The flow of energy?"

"I think it's because humans are non-magical, so they don't use essence like we do to keep their world running," Idris explains. "I don't think they really need it."

"I can already tell I don't like it here," mutters Yaseen.

Now that Idris mentions it, I do feel normal back on solid

ground. I take a deep breath. Here, the air isn't buzzing with energy like in the Supreme Court and the café and the academy. It feels like good old regular home . . .

. . . good old regular *boring* home.

This makes me frown. I'm supposed to be more excited to be back home. The plan is to stay in Philadelphia. So why are starry libraries and emerald mountains popping up in the back of my head?

Suddenly, I feel very nervous about talking to my mom.

"If you're going to puke, please try aiming for someone else's shoes." Idris waves a hand in front of my face when I don't move. "What's the matter?"

"Nothing." I hold my hand to where my heart is racing. "Just a little sleepy from all that driving." I shift my bag straps to both my shoulders and start walking. "It's this way. Oh, and keep an eye out for shadows that don't have people attached to them." Which is easier said than done since the shadows from the sunset only seem to get longer and longer. At least none of them look suspicious.

We walk block after block. Yaseen keeps checking his shadow every two seconds.

"I'm pretty sure that's just your regular shadow."

"Can't be too careful."

"Can you stop," I whisper, holding the straps tighter. "People are staring at you." It isn't until the third block that I really notice people squinting their eyes at us. Yaseen keeps his arms rigidly by his sides, careful not to touch anyone.

"They won't bite you," I say as we pass Market Street.

"Of course they won't," he replies. "They can't bite what they can't see."

"What?"

"Allow me to demonstrate." Yaseen stops by a food truck and ties his hair into a topknot. The man inside the truck looks at Idris and me.

"Aren't you cold, little girl?" he asks.

"No, I'm—" *Not cold.* Wait a second. It's the end of December. I should be freezing without a jacket on. I look at the uniform and then look at Idris (who has never worn a jacket, now that I think about it).

Idris just shrugs.

"You know, you look familiar." The man is squinting at me just like the other people. "I feel like I've seen your face before." It makes me sweat.

"Well, I've never seen you before, and my mom tells me I shouldn't talk to strangers." I nervously eye Yaseen, who picks up a rock and stands right in front of the ordering window. He lifts the rock and starts spinning it around. It's very silly, but it gets the food truck man's attention.

"I just get the feeling I've seen your face. . . ." He gets distracted by the rock. "What is—" Yaseen then chucks the rock at Idris, who scowls.

"I will not be an accomplice in this." He throws the rock back at Yaseen, who then tosses it inside the truck.

The man proceeds to scream, "Astaghfirullah, it's jinn.

Jinn! Get out of here now! We are closed!" He shuts the sliding glass window.

"Oh." I should have realized Yaseen and Idris would be invisible to humans. It's the most basic fact we learn about jinn—they only appear to humans when they want to. How could I forget? I look at my hands and wonder if that's something I could do too. Super healing, super strength, *and* invisibility? I mean, talk about an unbeatable combo. Arzu is going to freak out when I tell her.

"If you're done tormenting the human, can we get back on track?"

"Oh, now you're in a rush, huh," retorts Yaseen.

Idris grumbles and stalks ahead. His notebook is in his hands again. He drums his fingers against the top page, like he's waiting to write something down. Quietly, he mumbles, "Now that we're out of the jinn world, maybe I'll be able to see something useful."

"See what?" I ask.

Idris spins around, surprised. "Oh, nothing. I meant—" His face goes white. "Noorzad, please tell me you have a long-lost twin in town."

"No, why?"

"Because then, who is *that*?"

We all look over where Idris is pointing. Slinking on the edge of the Chestnut Street sign, a horde of shadow jinn form on the corner as they zip and dart into the local mall. Half of them run inside, knocking open the doors and bumping into startled people, while the other half flatten and warp around the side of the building. They head up to the abandoned observation deck on the fifty-seventh floor.

But that's not what turns my legs into cement.

It's the duplicate girl standing at the mall entrance waving at me. Her red eyes wink just as the ring glints in her hand. *Find your worth-protecting yet?* Then she disappears into the building. A chill fizzes all over my body. That's the realest she's looked so far. Which makes me wonder—*why* is she taking on my reflection?

"Come on, let's go," Yaseen urges. "If they're here, it means we're heading in the right direction. I say we get them while we can."

"I don't know. . . . What if they're just distracting us again?" Idris questions. "We should stay the course and try for the ring *after* we get the protection charm."

"*Why?*" Yaseen presses. "It's literally right here. I say we should take the chance now while we have it."

"Because Noorzad needs the protection charm."

"No, she doesn't *need* the charm. She's not all mortal," Yaseen says. "What she needs is the ring."

"Says the full-jinn who only cares about himself."

Yaseen blinks. "What jinn says 'full-jinn' to another jinn?"

"Noorzad, please, a little help?"

I'm about to tell them to stop arguing so I can think when

a swirl of paper rustles by my feet. It has a picture on it. My picture. It says: MISSING CHILD.

"Oh, this is bad." I guess Madar didn't get the hint with my chalk bag.

"How did we not notice them?" Idris looks over my shoulder. "They're everywhere." My face is plastered all over the mall entrance. "An unfortunate picture choice, though. This photo is . . . a tragedy."

"This isn't the time for jokes." My ears burn as I dart behind the food truck. "Yaseen is right. It'll be easier if we have the ring."

"Ha!" Yaseen gloats. Idris rolls his eyes.

"But I can't go in there," I hiss. "Mall security will spot me in a second if I do."

"What is a mall security?" asks Yaseen.

"Guards."

"Why didn't you say that in the first place? There's only one way to fool guards, in my experience. . . ." Yaseen's eyes trail across the street to a Philly gift shop. "You need a disguise."

"No, that's not—wait, yes. That's exactly what I need."

"Come on. We don't have time to waste." Yaseen doubles back and heads right for the shop. "The sooner we get the disguise, the sooner we can get the ring, and then we'll be back on track to find a gateway."

"There's just one problem." I stop Yaseen from opening the shop door. "You can't take things from stores here. You need *money*." I point at a blinking security camera outside the store. "Otherwise they'll think *I'm* the one stealing." The last thing I need is to get in more trouble.

"Fascinating." Idris blinks up at the camera. "Where do they put the eyes?"

"I know what money is." Yaseen sighs, big and heavy, plucking my hand off his shoulder. "I didn't think I'd have to resort to desperate measures here, but it looks like it can't be avoided. . . ." Yaseen seems like he's bracing himself, but for what?

"Do you think they'd notice if I borrowed this metal soul recorder to study . . . ?" Idris is hopping up, trying to grab at that camera.

"It's not a soul recorder, it's a—"

A horrible cracking noise, like tree branches being snapped in half, takes my attention away from Idris, who shrieks and loses his balance when he spots Yaseen.

"You could have *warned* us," he moans while covering his eyes.

"What is going on?"

Yaseen's arms and legs snap and break into horrible shapes. I immediately cover my eyes (okay, I peek a little) just as his torso twists and contorts. His shadow gets larger until he's six feet tall.

My jaw hits the floor when he turns back to look at me, his bright green eyes glowing like two headlights in the dark.

"Ready?" His voice is deep, like an adult's. His body is edged in a dark purple aura. "Let's do this." He opens the shop door and cheerily calls out to the clerk, "Good day, human attendant!"

Holy mother of—

Yaseen can shape-shift.

CHAPTER THIRTEEN

JINN SURE DO LIKE RIDDLES, HUH

Note to self: shape-shifting does NOT look fun.

Yaseen dabs some sweat from his forehead as he walks around the shop very suspiciously. "Very nice stuff. Nice things you have here, human attendant." I notice he's very careful not to let anything touch him.

"Excuse my . . . uncle. He's got anxiety about . . . germs." I scramble for an excuse as I death-grip my backpack straps. Idris smiles and waves, like this is the most normal thing in the world. The clerk doesn't notice him.

Instead, he leans over and asks, "Is there anything I can help you fine folks with?" He keeps one eye on Yaseen as he checks out his reflection in the mirror.

"We're all good. My uncle is just a weird person." I laugh nervously and bolt for the racks in the back of the store. I grab the most inconspicuous items—a large black hoodie, big cheetah-spotted sunglasses, and a pink hat that says *LOVE*—

and gesture furiously at Idris, who is staring at magnets. With Yaseen distracted, this is the perfect time to fill Idris in.

"Idris, get over here," I hiss.

He walks right over. "I don't know if the hat suits you, it feels—"

"Forget the hat," I whisper, keeping an eye on Yaseen on the other side of the store. "Something happened back at the academy."

Idris listens patiently while I explain the conversation between King Barqan and Yaseen.

"I knew the jinn kings had something up their sleeves," says Idris.

"I was going to wait until after the protection charm to tell him we know."

"Or . . ." Without missing a beat, Idris puts an arm around my shoulder and walks us farther back into the shop. "We keep the secret to ourselves. Let him think we're clueless."

"Why?"

"Think about it. If he knows we know, we lose our advantage," Idris explains. "This way, we can keep a lookout if he tries anything sneaky. Let him think he has the upper hand."

"I guess . . ." Something about it makes my stomach turn, though.

"Hello? Where are you guys?" Yaseen hisses from the fitting rooms. "Can we leave yet? The smell of rotten cabbage is killing me."

"Trust me, Noorzad." Idris's pale eyes stare intently into mine. For a second I feel like he can see right into my head. "Have I steered you wrong yet?"

"No." I look away. "But—"

"I'm glad you agree." Idris takes the clothes from my arms, walks promptly toward Yaseen, and dumps them into Yaseen's hands.

"Get these human things away from me," Yaseen yelps in his normal voice, and tries to hot-potato them back to Idris.

"This is your plan, Yaseen. We've got the clothes. Now what's the rest of the strategy on getting out of here?" I stand in the middle of the two boys, preventing Yaseen from throwing the clothes back at Idris. "There is more to the plan, right?"

"Of course there is." Yaseen grimaces. "Just watch and be amazed."

He straightens and walks briskly toward the counter. Then he throws the clothes on the counter and makes direct eye contact with the clerk. A shiver runs down the clerk's spine when Yaseen's body continues to crack and bend to be even bigger. He's shape-shifting again, and it makes me queasy to look at.

Yaseen starts to glow with a cold purple aura. I double blink because I think I've seen this glow before. *"Listen as I compel. A gift for the girl and all will be well."* What comes out of Yaseen sounds a lot like the voice that rustles in my head. I want to ask Idris what he's doing (and why he's speaking in such horrible rhyme), but I can't. Something in my head is telling me to wait and watch.

"Yes, of course," says the clerk in a monotone voice. His brown eyes are glazed over with a dreamy smile. "Take whatever else you like. On the house." He packs the items into a paper bag and hands it robotically to Yaseen. "Enjoy your time in the City of Brotherly Love."

Yaseen grabs the bag (with two fingertips) and steps out of the door. A chill runs down my back when the door opens and all the sunlight diverts around Yaseen, like it's too afraid to break through the dark purple aura when he's like this. He turns, his green eyes glowing. *"Let's go,"* says Yaseen with a smirk.

My legs move on their own, sticky and stiff, out the door. Idris too.

"This isn't funny. Stop showing off and release me now," Idris protests when Yaseen breaks the spell. The dark aura disappears, and once again I am forced to watch him shapeshift back into his normal self. "You know it's against the rules to do that. *Jinn must not compel one another.* It's written in the court's constitution!"

Compelling. So that's what it's called. I remember where I've seen that glow before. King Barqan in the library. At least . . . I think that's what I saw. Is Yaseen being . . . compelled too?

"You know what else is written in the court's constitution?" Yaseen twists his back and stretches out his wrists.

He looks very, very pale and sweaty. Then he does something strange. He whispers low in Idris's ear, "You think I can't tell there's something weird about you too?" He hands me the bag of clothes. "Here."

Idris goes very still.

I blink in surprise. "What's he talking about, Idris?" My stomach flops when I put on my disguise.

"I have no idea." Idris throws an arm around my shoulders. "I think the human fumes have gone to his head. You ready to get that ring back?"

"Yeah, but . . ."

"No better moment than the present!" Idris marches off toward the mall, leaving Yaseen and me to stand awkwardly together. Yaseen narrows his eyes at Idris as the dark purple aura finally goes away. He glances quickly at me and raises an eyebrow. "How long have you and Idris been friends?"

King Barqan's scary image flashes in my head. "Longer than I've known you." It isn't a lie, but I'm not going to fall for his information-gathering for the jinn kings (compelled or not).

If it bothers Yaseen, I can't tell. He just keeps staring at Idris with a troubled expression. After a second he shakes his head, muttering, "It's just a little weird. One second he says, 'Forget the ring,' the next he's racing toward it." Yaseen goes to catch up to Idris.

Now that I think about it, it *is* a little weird . . . but I'm sure it's all a part of Idris's plan to stay one step ahead of Yaseen. That's gotta be it. As I run to catch up to them, I think about the cold purple aura that glowed around King Barqan and Yaseen. A jinn king wouldn't break the rules like that, right? They wouldn't force someone to do something against their will, would they?

Unless they really thought I was a threat . . .

I grip my hands into fists. Whatever the jinn kings had planned, they'll see when I save them all that there's nothing to be afraid of. If King Barqan really did compel Yaseen to lie to me, then *they're* the ones to be afraid of.

I'm not dangerous. At least, not any more dangerous than a regular jinn.

Are you sure? the voice asks.

"One hundred percent!" I shout with my whole heart.

We'll see about that, the voice slithers. *We'll see.*

WE PUSH PAST THE "CLOSED TO THE PUBLIC" SIGN AND THE security guard manning the elevator (with Yaseen's creepy shape-shifting help). Apparently, the rules can be bent when it comes to compelling pure humans. (There aren't any rules, as an FYI; humans are fair game.)

"How do you keep track of all these rules?" I whisper, keeping a lookout for suspicious shadows.

"First-year Bylaws for Beginners class, of course," Idris replies. "Don't humans do the same?"

"I think so, but we're just now learning about the US Constitution."

"Isn't that a little old to be learning about the rules of your leaders?" Yaseen asks.

"Maybe, but I've never really liked the rules anyway. And leaders get things wrong all the time; that's why there are amendments, you know," I explain. "Our Constitution has twenty-seven of them. How many does yours have?"

"Twenty-seven? We don't have any. I guess humans are a bit more shortsighted than jinn," Yaseen remarks as we walk past a giant green statue. "What a strange . . . green stone."

It's Benjamin Franklin's shoes and legs. "Why would anyone put this in the center of a small room?"

"It's Ben Franklin, don't you know?" We step into the elevator. I hit the button for floor fifty-seven. Idris's and Yaseen's knees buckle when the elevator rumbles and shakes before it heads up ("a metal death trap," Idris mutters).

"Who?"

"Electricity?" I point at the elevator wall. All the windows are covered with pictures of Philadelphia. There's one picture of a kite. "He flew a kite in a lightning storm?"

Yaseen shudders. "Why would anyone do that to a kite?"

"Well, how did jinn discover electricity in the Qaf Mountains?"

"What's electricity?"

My eyes widen. "It's what powers all the lights, phones,

video games, buildings, elevators. . . . It's what comes out of that spear you keep throwing around!"

Suddenly, Yaseen understands. "Oh, you use that for power? That seems silly. It's so unpredictable. Jinn essence is much more stable than lightning. But I guess if you don't have magic, you've got to get a little inventive." We watch the numbers go up in silence. Idris is too preoccupied with motion sickness to say anything. Yaseen hesitates. "What are . . . video games?"

"You don't know what *video games* are?" I whisper in shock. "They're only the best invention ever. It's like a box that can transport you to different worlds, where you can fight bad guys and be whoever you want to be."

"That sounds . . . nice," he says quietly. There's a curious smile on his face, like he's trying to imagine it. "Kinda like what we're doing now."

"Yeah." I smile back.

We're quiet again by the time the elevator reaches the fifty-seventh floor. Only, the doors don't open.

"What's going on?" I keep pressing the open-door button, but the elevator makes a weird gears-crunching noise. My stomach drops. "Are we . . . stuck?" It looks like the doors want to open half an inch, but then close again. The elevator starts to swoop down the floors. I press 57 again.

"This doesn't feel right," Idris mumbles.

"They're messing with us," Yaseen says. "To waste time."

"This isn't funny!" I bang against the elevator door. "Some

people have very real fears of getting stuck in elevators and other small spaces. People like me! Let us out!"

The lights in the elevator flicker on and off, like they're laughing at us.

"Shadow jinn can't think. You can't talk sense into them." Idris crosses his arms with his eyes closed, trying not to puke. "They don't have souls to do what they want. *You-know-who* is the one who controls them."

"They don't have souls?" I frown. "That seems a little sad." The elevator groans when we reach the top floor again with a small ding. The doors don't open.

"If the doors are stuck, why don't you, you know . . . ?" Yaseen gestures toward my arms. "If you can punch lightning, opening a door shouldn't be so hard."

Idris and I blink ten times in surprise.

"What?" asks Yaseen.

"Are you saying something *nice* to me?"

Yaseen scowls and crosses his arms. "Just open the door so we can get out of this death trap, okay!"

"I second this." Idris clutches his stomach.

"Okay." I take a deep breath and face the door. I shake out the jitters from my fingertips and toes and crimp my fingers in between the tiny gap in the elevator doors. If I have super strength, this will prove it.

Show them what you can do, the whisper bounces in my head.

"Yeah, yeah, yeah," I mumble, and pull with all my

strength. For a second the doors don't budge, but then something wiggles, just an inch. My arms are burning as I continue to pull the doors apart. The metal screeches and groans, but it's enough. The doors unstick and open the rest of the way on their own.

I did it! Another achievement unlocked! My heart is racing a mile a minute. I wonder what else I can do. Lift a car? No, maybe that's pushing it too much. I turn around and throw a thumbs-up at the boys.

Yaseen and Idris both have looks of horror painted on their faces.

"What's wrong?"

Yaseen just points.

I turn back around. It's pitch-black when the elevator doors fully open.

None of the light from the elevator buttons reaches past the open door. It's like it's blocked. Even worse, the darkness seems . . . alive. Like the floor is wiggling and squirming. Little dark red eyes linger at the very middle of the floor where Ben Franklin's giant dusty green head is placed.

"Again, can someone tell me *why* they thought putting that green thing in the center of a small space was a good idea?" whispers Yaseen.

"I've got a bad feeling about this." Idris ignores Yaseen. "Anyone vote for going back downstairs and forgetting this ever happened?"

"Don't be a baby," hisses Yaseen. "I didn't come all this way to back out now."

"So why don't you go first, then?" Idris pushes Yaseen's shoulder.

"I got the clothes *and* the book on the gateway. It's your turn to contribute."

Both boys are glued in place, their knees knocking.

I sigh. I guess that just leaves me, then. Only, I really don't like dark spaces.

"You got this, Farrah. Nothing can hurt you," I whisper to myself, and take the first step forward into the dark. *We must face the things that scare us* is a mantra in my head as I feel the darkness seep into my shoes. I gulp and imagine myself as a bright, bright light facing down the darkest and longest night of the year. When the elevator doors close ("Seriously?" Yaseen mutters), there is nothing to see. Idris and Yaseen huddle close behind me.

"Grab my hand so we don't get lost." I reach behind me and feel Idris's shaky hand hold on to mine. Idris then extends a hand out for Yaseen.

"Only because desperate times call for desperate measures," Yaseen clarifies while grabbing Idris's hand. Even though I'm scared, it makes me feel better that Yaseen and I have at least *one* thing in common.

"Hello?" I call out into the dark, keeping my eyes glued on the two red glowing dots. I take one step and the darkness ripples. I take another, and it continues to pool and get deeper, so now it's around my ankles. "Are you sure they can't think for themselves?"

"One hundred percent," Yaseen responds. "All we have to do is grab the ring and get out."

"They've got to want *something* to go through all this trouble," I mumble to myself. If they just wanted to waste our time, they wouldn't have come back. Right?

An idea comes to me. I fish my phone out of my pocket and press the home button. Little shards of light filter through the cracked screen. "We'll never find out what they want in the dark like this." And if the only way for them to fully take shape is by bringing a little light, then . . . "Maybe this will help." I walk closer, and the ripples get even bigger, like waves up to my calves, until I shine my phone directly at the red dots.

The red dots blink. A shadow face forms. *My face.* She smiles and says, "Well done." In my voice!

I don't like it at all.

"Is that . . . us?" Idris squints into the narrow light. "Can you make your light beam brighter?"

"It's called a phone. I've said this so many times before." I manage to somehow navigate the cracked screen and turn on the flashlight. The light beams and divides the swirling dark into two waves, coming up on my left and right side with Ben Franklin's head in the middle. Very Moses.

"I do not look like that. I've got way better hair," Yaseen mutters, and straightens so he's no longer crouched behind me. The shadow version of himself does the same. "Well, that's a little better."

"Why are you doing this? What does your master want?" I call out. "Are you just wasting time for the wish to go through?"

The shadow me continues to smile. It is very, very disturbing.

"Clever girl. A wish of your caliber requires time. There are many fates that must be rewoven, rewritten, redone. We are not meant to ask why our master commands; we simply obey," she says while toying with the ring on her finger. "But just because we are meant to obey doesn't mean we can't . . . take a little detour when the opportunity presents itself."

"A detour . . ." So they do want something. I start walking to the left as the shadow puppets move to the right. They keep on smiling, with their beady ruby eyes hungry on us.

"Silly being mixed with mortal blood," Idris's shadow jinn laughs. "Mortals have always been consumed by what they want. And how they always want! More and more. Makes one wish. Then wants another. And another."

"Guys, I am getting a really bad feeling." Yaseen looks up at the swarming black masses around and above us. "Like . . . lightning-spear bad." He makes a move to his back pocket.

"No, wait." Idris waves his hands to keep me talking to them. "Something feels odd about how they're acting."

"Everything is odd about how they're acting," hisses Yaseen.

"There's nothing wrong with changing your mind," I call out to the shadow jinn. We keep matching their movements. I continue walking to the left, following the circular hallway. I bump into a glass divider next to a vending machine. "Sometimes it can stop you from making a big mistake."

"Your kind makes the same mistakes over and over again," Yaseen's shadow puppet blurts out. His arm is poised in the same exact way as Yaseen's. Like it's just waiting for the right moment to unleash whatever is hiding inside. "What makes you worthy of your soul? What if it's time to give someone else a chance to wish too?"

"Hold on a second," mutters Idris, like the answer just dawned on him.

"That's it! I'm tired of talking about dumb wishes and who gets to make them!" Yaseen loses his temper and unleashes King Barqan's lightning spear. "You want to see a mistake, well, here's one! Your puppet mind tricks are over!"

"Yaseen, no!" Idris tries to stop him but it's too late.

The light is blinding as Yaseen unleashes a lightning storm right at the three puppets. The hung kite rattles against the blast.

"Took you long enough." Yaseen's puppet is a mirror image as he unleashes his own dark-purple-and-red lightning storm. The way I see Yaseen's jealous rage reflected in the puppet is scary, like he's fighting with himself. "Now the real fun can begin!"

Everything happens too fast. I lose sight of the puppets as the waves of darkness crash down on all of us. Idris's eyes go completely opaque for a millisecond, and he stares directly at me. Then he pushes me out of the shadow puppet's punch.

"What is happening to your eyes?" I screech while I tumble into the waves.

"TURN OFF THE LIGHTS!" Idris yells. "I know why they brought us here. It's a trap!"

"Over my dead body." Yaseen's spear is locked with the puppets as they strain against each other. It's enough to light up the entire observation deck.

"Your body will be if you don't stop!" Idris continues to shout and dodge.

I'm so preoccupied with watching Yaseen (he's a *really good* fighter), I don't see my own shadow sneaking up behind me.

"Gotcha." The puppet's legs sweep my feet, and I go tumbling to the ground.

"Aaah." I roll out of the way the second her fist punches down. "Why can't we talk this out? What's got you so mad?" My reflection keeps on moving, like she's got too much bubbling energy in her fingers and toes and can't get it out. *Like me . . .*

"Why don't you stay still!" she cries when I scramble onto my hands and knees. Once I'm up, I turn around to face her. Unafraid, I charge at her, and I give her a taste of her own medicine. I use all my strength to push her . . . only, my hands sink directly into her chest.

"Tsk. Tsk. Tsk." She smiles as the shadows wrap around my wrists and try to pull me in even more.

"Don't let them touch you!" Idris is batting away the shadows as quickly as he can. He jumps over a desk and throws brochures at his own puppet. "They brought us here because they want *us. They want to be us.*"

"That would have been nice to know earlier!" I scream and tug as hard as I can to release my hands. On the third tug, I break free and hold my hands to my chest. They're dark, almost the color of a shadow. . . .

Oh, that's not good.

"Running is futile," my shadow says while stretching her arms. Her hands are tan like mine. "I'll have your soul in no time."

I run anyway. Through the crashing light from the twin lightning spears, I look up. If super strength won't work, I've got to do the next best thing. Climb.

"Aha, skylights!" Right above me are rows of metal bars that lead up to the domed ceiling. I scramble up on Ben Franklin's head and avoid the shadows trying to claw at my ankles. Then I jump and catch one of the metal beams.

My shadow puppet is hot on my heels. She leaps and swings onto the metal beam next to me, and I have to do a double take because she moves just like me. Her sad, hungry eyes lock on to me.

We stare at each other for a second. It's like looking in the mirror.

"Why would you want to be me?" I ask through shaky breaths. "My life stinks!" If she's been following me this whole time, she should know there are a million other kids who would be better picks.

"Why don't you guess?" She mimics my shaky breathing right back. For a second I think she's going to stop, but I notice the way her toes wiggle in her shoes (the same way my toes wiggle in my shoes when I'm gearing up for a big jump).

I leap up and grab another beam the second she jumps. My heart is stuck in my mouth as I climb up, up, up. "Ouch!" My head hits the glass ceiling. There isn't any room to move up. I'm trapped. "Guys . . . I'm running out of space here."

"Yaseen, stop using your spear!" Idris shouts. "They're going to win!"

"No, they won't!" Yaseen shouts back.

"It's light that gives them form." Idris trips and falls backward. "Don't . . . let them touch you." The shadows overpower Idris, and he is swallowed up. "They'll . . . seep into . . . you. . . ."

"Idris!" I squint through the waves of darkness, but I can't see him anymore. *Think, Farrah. Think.* My hand grips one of the skylights a little too hard—it breaks off, causing part of the glass ceiling to crack. Little shards of glass rain on my head. The dark sky stares back at me through the small hole. "Ahh!" I lose my balance and pinwheel my arms to keep steady. My shadow smiles and lunges. There isn't much time before she catches up to me. I know what I've got to do. "YASEEN, TURN OFF THE LIGHT!" I chuck the broken skylight at my shadow puppet and leap toward Yaseen.

"I don't think so." The red eyes of my shadow puppet glint in determination as she follows. Down I tumble with a scream as we both land on top of Yaseen.

Our heads knock together. Little stars dazzle in front of my eyes.

"Oww, my head." The lightning spear is knocked out of Yaseen's hands. It flickers as the shadows swarm us. "I can't fight them off. There's too many." Yaseen runs for his spear, but he's not fast enough. The red smiles of the shadow jinn light up as they drown him in the dark.

"No, Yaseen! Fight them off!"

"And then there was one." My reflection stands in front of me. She grabs my arm and holds on tight. I can feel her fire, her determination to be *me*. I try to break free but can't. She is *strong*.

"You could choose anyone else." Little tears prickle in the corners of my eyes. "Why me?"

"Because you're the girl who made the wish. The one who defied the odds, lived undetected by the kings," she says with the saddest eyes I've ever seen. "If you could defy the odds of your fate, why wouldn't I want that for me? Why wouldn't I make a wish for me too?"

I watch as we swap—her face becomes more real while I become more shadow. Panic makes it hard to think, hard to run away. If I lose what makes me *me*—my soul—will I turn into a puppet too? Maybe this is how I get to the Realm Beneath after all. As a shadow of myself.

I stare back at the shadow jinn and I can feel how sad she is, how sad all the shadow puppets are, but there's something else, something strong in her eyes that makes me feel small. I don't know how to fight against myself.

What if it's better this way? What if this is like pressing reset on a video game? Maybe this shadow could have better luck than me.

"If you have to do this, please be nicer to my mom, okay? She deserves a better daughter." I struggle not to fall into the coldness of the shadows. My reflection blinks in surprise. "I ask you to please just . . . tell her I'm sorry." *For running away. For not coming straight home to tell her the truth about Padar and me. For adding more worries to her plate. For being weak when I should have been strong.* "Maybe you could be a better me, for my mom," I whisper. "If that's what you want."

Surprisingly, my reflection hesitates. Her face—my face—is puzzled. "No one's ever *asked* me to do anything."

"It's part of having a soul," I say sleepily. It's getting harder to keep my eyes open, to keep being me. "You can choose to do whatever you want, you know."

She keeps staring at me, more uncertain now. "A choice," she mutters.

Suddenly, the ground shakes and rumbles beneath us. My reflection loses her balance and falls over. A growling, angry voice booms into the observation deck. "I gave you form, and I can take it away. Devour those children and you will wish you were merely a shadow when you face my wrath."

Wait a second. I know this voice.

It's the one that's been in my head.

The whispers go haywire as the shadow jinn screech and swarm.

The lightning spear finally loses its light, and my shadow puppet's sad face is the last thing I see before the darkness takes over. "A choice is all I wanted," she whispers before her voice is swallowed up too.

All is still.

I feel the weight of the shadow jinn slink off me as I sit up. I look at my hands and watch color come back into my skin. I'm me again!

Yaseen is sleepily rubbing his head. "I have the worst headache."

"Am I still alive?" Idris's hair sticks up from the back of the room.

"There's no more light." I scramble and search around for the ring. "They can't take shape without light. Quick, everyone, find the ring."

"Wait, what's that?" Yaseen croaks.

At the very top of the room, I see the tiny hole I made in the glass ceiling. Slowly, the shadow jinn leak out little by little. They're escaping through it.

"What a waste. Enjoy the rest of your time as you are," the voice of Yaseen's shadow puppet taunts. "This time next week there won't even be a soul to steal."

A glimmer of red, blue, and gold winks through the hole before it's gone.

"No!" I bolt up. "You can't take the ring!" But it's too late. Soon the starry night and skyline wink through the tinted glass walls, free of all shadows. Like everything is back to normal.

When the last of the shadow jinn escapes, the whispers leave me with a message.

A reward for my puppets' disobedience. A clue for the destination you seek. Look for a land that is destined to burn for two hundred years, the voice instructs. *That is where you will find me.*

I look forward to finally meeting you, Farrah Noorzad.

I gasp in horror because it's just clicked.

The voice in my head. It was never the ring or the shadow jinn.

It's Azar.

CHAPTER FOURTEEN

WHEN YOU'RE TIRED OF LOSING

I look forward to finally meeting you, Farrah Noorzad.

I am suddenly very, very freaked out. How has the forbidden fire jinn king been in my head this whole time?

"I can't believe they got away again," Yaseen laments as he double-checks the ruined observation deck (just in case).

"Oh, I can"—dust tickles Idris's nose and he sneezes—"one hundred percent"—and sneezes—"believe it." He holds the last sneeze in and then sags in relief. He looks out through the weak filtering light as the moon splashes silver across the skyline.

"You guys didn't hear anything just now?" I ask nervously.

"Besides Yaseen's complaining?" Idris shakes his head. "Why? Did *you* hear something?"

"I think so." I quickly explain the voice (minus that last line) to the boys.

This just makes Yaseen act moodier.

"Hmm. Why would the shadow jinn give us a hint like that?" asks Idris.

"It was probably their master just getting control back on their strings." Yaseen dusts off his uniform and sighs when he notices how dirty he is. "But I wonder why they're talking through you." He crosses his arms tightly against his chest, looks out the glass window, and says very quietly to himself, "What's so special about *you*?"

"Are you seriously jealous about this?" We almost lost our souls, and he's mad that *I'm* the one who got the message? I point at my head. "I would love to not deal with these buzzing voices, so if you want them, take them. It'd be a lot easier."

Yaseen is quiet for a long time. When he does speak, his voice is tight and scratchy. "I'm not jealous. I just don't understand."

"Understand what?"

"Why Baba would go through all this trouble for a half-human." Yaseen looks away from the window and walks over to where the spear is. It transforms into half its size. "After all, if it weren't for *you* and that wish, we wouldn't even be in this situation. I've been working so hard at school this past year." He tucks the spear in his back pocket. "If anyone here deserved a wish from Baba, it was me." He finally looks up at me with accusing eyes. "There are a million better wishes I could have asked for instead of this foolish one."

Now, that stings. "My wish wasn't foolish." I try not to shout, but there are so many mixed feelings bubbling in my throat. I'm mad because the shadow jinn got away. I'm sad because I also wonder why me. And I'm hurt because Yaseen sees me as a forbidden half-human and not a person with feelings.

But I don't like feeling hurt or sad, so I let the anger take over.

"What does a son to a jinn king even *need* when you already have everything?"

"It's *none of your business*."

Red alert. There's that phrase again. Anger zips and courses through my fingers and toes. The bubbles are already pushing up and out of my mouth. "Well, if you would have listened to us, maybe you could have asked him yourself, but since you don't like to listen, the shadow jinn got away with our only connection to our dad." I poke him in his chest. "Maybe that's why I got a wish and you didn't." I poke him again, harder. I can't stop the angry feeling. "Maybe he liked me more than you, even though I'm a *half-human*." Energy is zipping through my body. I open both my palms and give him one hard shove. "Maybe you weren't good enough for a wish!"

Yaseen's eyes widen in surprise as he goes flying backward into the air. He lands on the ground with a *thump*.

That's right, the voice encourages me. *Show them what you can do. Show them what it's like to be strong.*

Yaseen's tiny protection charm goes bouncing off his uniform, and he scrambles to catch it. With shaky fingers, he puts it in his pouch. "Even if I wasn't good enough for a wish, I'll still be more than you'll ever be. Wish or no wish, at least I know where I belong."

We are caught in a glaring match.

"Guys, this is starting to get a little too mean. . . . I know we're disappointed about the ring, but let's cool down." Idris looks worriedly between us. "Let's just take a deep breath and—"

But why should you? the voice asks. *After all, he's the one with the secret.*

"You mean at the bottom of your class?" I guess from his secret conversation with King Barqan. I don't care if he was compelled or not. I look down at the ground and say, "You try to act like you're better than me, but at least I've never had to worry about repeating a school year."

Yaseen freezes. All his anger melts away. "You knew—" Again, his voice goes sludgy, like he can't get the words out.

"You're right, I knew about your conversation with King Barqan!" I shout, letting the energy snap and crackle like armor around my skin. "And I feel like a fool for not doing this sooner!"

An aura glows and shatters around Yaseen's mouth. "Wait, I can explain now."

It's too late for more lies, the voice says. *No more listening to bad advice.*

It should make me happy to know that Yaseen *was* compelled, but I've got too much energy fizzing in my fingers and toes. Too much of everything. I don't think about Idris or the way Yaseen seems to fold in on himself. I feel like a supernova ready to explode.

I run to the elevator and jam the buttons to close the door. Right when the doors are about to close, they get stuck. I use the fizzing energy to shut them all the way. Yaseen and Idris are running to catch up. It's the longest second of my life shutting those doors. When they finally close, I'm left with my foggy reflection in the metal doors, but I've had enough of looking at myself. I put the hood of my sweater over my head and pull the strings tight.

When I get to the ground floor, I dart past surprised mall security as they lock up the mall.

"Hey, kid!" the guard yells. "There's no running here!"

Run far, run wide, little one, Azar's voice urges. *But the truth will always catch you. Can't you see why they're afraid of you now?*

"Stop talking to me! I don't want you in my head anymore! I just want everyone to leave me alone!" I run, even when the cold air knocks all the oxygen out of my chest. Because this is something I can do. I can run and jump and climb and climb and climb until I'm so high up in the sky, nothing can reach me. Not Yaseen's secrets with jinn kings, or Azar's whispers.

The only problem is, the fight with the shadow jinn wiped me out. I barely make it to the big plaza surrounding City Hall. The Christmas tree and Ferris wheel are still up from the winter village, and people are walking around casually watching the light show projections against the old building. There's laughter and squeals from the ice rink. My eyes burn when I see families all together, sharing cups of hot cocoa—moms and dads who stay together, brothers and sisters who get along—and it only makes me madder.

I'm so busy staring, I don't notice a certain curly-haired girl drop her phone and sneakily break away from her parents.

"Farrah, is it really you?" Arzu body-slams me and crushes me with a huge hug. "Omgomgomg you're here and not kidnapped by international spies!"

"Why would international spies want me?" I ask, too shell-shocked to say anything else.

"How am I supposed to know!" She lets go to hit my arm before folding me into another tear-filled hug. "You're the one who disappeared, you jerk! And what's with this *hideous* outfit you're wearing?"

I don't know if it's the angry bubbles or losing the ring again or being around a brother who lies to me, or all those things wrapped up in one, but a little something that was broken in the court starts to get fixed when Arzu hugs me.

"I thought I'd never see you again," I wail into her arms. "There's so much that's happened, but I c-can't—"

I hug Arzu tight, too afraid to let her go in case this is a dream.

And then I cry and cry and cry.

"It's okay," she whispers into my hair. "It's all going to

be okay." She nervously glances at her parents, who are busy window-shopping in the winter market. "Let me tell my parents the good news. We can go to your house and explain everything—"

"You can't tell them anything." I shake my head. "It's . . . dangerous if they get involved."

"Dangerous like activating Mission Omega Protocol dangerous?" Arzu lowers her voice.

"Yeah. Exactly." I sniffle while grabbing her hand to initiate our secret handshake when a plan is in motion. "I just gotta do one thing first before I come over."

"Say no more." Arzu gives me a small, worried smile. "The meeting spot will be secured. You can explain everything to me then. Just don't take too long this time, okay?"

"Okay."

MISSION OMEGA PROTOCOL IS CODE FOR WHEN ARZU AND I need to discuss ultrasensitive information without our parents knowing what we're talking about (because they *always* try to snoop on our talks). Which means to get ultimate privacy, one of us has to sneak out and hide in the other person's basement, preferably with flashlights and snacks.

Now that I've cooled down and the voice is quiet, I first try looking for Yaseen and Idris. The mall is closed now, and after walking around Center City, I realize it wasn't the best idea to leave them by themselves in the middle of a human city they know nothing about.

"Maybe I overreacted a little bit," I grumble to myself when I remember the last words I said to Yaseen. But knowing Idris, they'll be able to find me soon enough. Plus, they can't go to the Realm Beneath without me or the ring anyway, so with that small thought in mind, I finally make my way over to Arzu's house. I just hope they don't crash in before I have a chance to let Arzu know what's going on.

Arzu's back door is conveniently propped open when I arrive. The first thing I do is drop all my stuff and melt into the warmth. I breathe in the familiar smells of lamb and rice.

"Took you long enough. I was getting worried." Arzu pops out of a lair of blankets and chairs. She darts out to close the back door, freezing for a second when we hear footsteps above us and a flush. "That's just my dad. He's gone to the bathroom, like, ten times today. Hopefully there won't be an eleventh."

"That is so gross."

"I know, adults really are." Arzu sighs before burrowing back into her fort. I immediately follow her lead and shut the hanging blanket flaps. There's a little camping lantern inside, giving just enough light (and way too many shadows across Arzu's face), but there are snacks, so many snacks. My stomach grumbles when I realize it's been a long time since I had regular human food to eat.

"Are you feeling a little bit better now?" Arzu asks cautiously.

I nod while I chomp into two packs of Fruit Roll-Ups. I'm so happy they're just regular food—no extra zings or memories or special effects. Just amazing plain sugar.

"Great, because now . . ." Arzu rolls up her sleeves and gives me a hard stare. "It's time you tell me everything. And I mean *everything*, Farrah."

The words spill out of my mouth like a waterfall. I tell her everything, even the stuff I didn't tell Idris or Yaseen. When I'm done, Arzu's jaw is hanging open like her brain got temporarily zapped.

"Are you sure you didn't hit your head too hard?" Arzu asks.

"I guess this means you never got my texts."

Arzu shakes her head.

"It's okay. I have proof." I run out to my bag and pull out Yaseen's academy uniform. With Arzu watching, I take my entire bag and stuff it into the pants pocket. Arzu's eyes widen when the bag impossibly disappears. "Believe me now?"

"That is so cool." Her face lights up in excitement. "So let me get this straight. Not only is your dad a jinn, but he's also a jinn *king*." Arzu is making the calculations in her head. "Which makes you a jinn *princess*. With an annoying prince brother and another jinn boy who is obsessed with you."

"Idris is *not* obsessed with me." I pelt Arzu with an empty candy wrapper. "It's not like that."

"Then explain why *Idris* has been following you around this entire time like a lost puppy." Arzu dodges the wrapper and scoots super close to my face. "You could have already had your magic moment and not realized it!" If there's one thing you should know about Arzu, it's that she's—what do the adults call it?—a hopeless romantic. She always thinks she'll meet her Prince Charming in the airport or on the first day of school with a song and dance. I blame all the Bollywood movies her mom made us watch when we were kids.

"So out of everything I told you, that is what you want to talk about?"

"Fine, just tell me one thing, and then I'll drop it." Arzu holds one finger up. "Is he cute?"

"No way." My ears burn in embarrassment, mostly because I owe him an apology when I see him again. "Not even a little bit."

"That's disappointing." Arzu sighs a little dramatically before plopping back onto a small pile of pillows. "You'd think if the universe throws you a curveball like this, you'd get a cute boy as a consolation prize."

"Can we focus on how I'm going to tell my mom tomorrow?" Lost or not, I still need to get back home to convince Madar to make a protection charm for me. Which means I've got to finally tell her the truth. That Padar did have a reason for leaving her behind—but would it make her feel any better to know it? I pick at my fingers. 'Cause it doesn't make *me* feel any better.

"Your mom is a tough cookie," Arzu says. "She'll be able to handle it."

"Yeah, but she isn't going to *like* it."

"Well, it beats you being kidnapped by international spies, or worse," Arzu says through a yawn. Her eyelids struggle to stay open. "At least you're back and safe."

Are we really safe?

I lie back on my own pillow bed and stare up at the circles of light from the flashlight, thinking about Idris's question. I can't tell how dangerous the journey still ahead of me is going to be. With the shadow jinn, getting to the Realm Beneath, and facing Azar, I don't think I'll be safe for a long time. So while Arzu is sleeping next to me, I make myself remember this moment in case it's the last normal sleepover I have with my best friend. I take a mental snapshot of Arzu's snoring face and store it in the little organization boxes in my head. Safe and sound next to the other snapshots.

I stay up for a long time, thinking and waiting. Every little footstep and noise outside has me on high alert for Idris and Yaseen or a shadow jinn to burst through the door, but nothing does. At least I don't have to worry about Azar popping up here. I'm glad to know he's stuck in his realm.

Before I can think any more about trapped fire jinn kings and wishes and rings, sleep gets the better of me and wins the final battle of the day.

CHAPTER FIFTEEN

PROMISES AND PLACES

I dream that I'm back at Wissahickon Valley Park.

I'm standing at the edge of the cliff, reaching out my arm, about to take a selfie with Padar. He is in his human form. The sun is just right, casting us in the prettiest golden colors I've ever seen. Right when I say, "On three!" the golden light turns fiery and it trails all along the cliff, catching fire.

The cliff transforms into my bedroom, and all my belongings are going up in smoke.

"Grab my hand," Padar shouts from the fire escape, but the fire is too thick.

"I won't be able to reach you," I cry back. "How will I get out?"

"Look around you. Your answer is there."

"Where?" All I see are my maps and trails and books and photos burning.

"I promise you're in the right place." Padar's voice fades.

I reach through the flames for him, but it is too hot.

I am too hot.

I wake up in Arzu's basement, wrapped in the fluffiest blanket ever. When I peek my head out of our fortress, I notice Arzu is gone.

"Arzu, I need a toothbrush," I whisper into the musty basement. I smell my armpit. "Ugh, and a shower." I hate to say it, but I'm missing that magical self-cleaning chest right now.

There are footsteps and chairs scraping above me, meaning her whole family is probably awake. Since my stomach is full of butterflies, I quickly dig out my tablet from the wall where Arzu left it charging and huddle back in the fort. I open a blank page and start sketching the first thing that makes me feel better. I'm a little worried Idris hasn't managed to find me yet. I wonder if something bad happened.

"Hey, save some for me, you greedy monsters." I hear Arzu's muffled yell as a stampede of giggling footsteps rains against the ceiling. That would be her younger brothers. "And don't you dare disturb me while I'm down here. I know my rights to privacy!" The basement door swings open as Arzu marches down.

The smell of syrupy pancakes peeks through just as Arzu's curly head bursts into the fort. "You're so lucky you don't have to deal with those little animals. Sometimes I dream about being an only child—"

"I technically have a brother."

"And it's proof that brothers are the worst because you can't trust them!" She goes on her tangent while handing me her plate. "Seriously, what kind of brother tries to poison his sister?"

"He was being compelled. I don't think he was going to actually do it." It's so clear now, after seeing the enchantment break, that Yaseen had no choice but to lie.

"Are you defending him?"

"No. I'm just saying King Barqan enchanted him to not be able to talk about it." I put the plate down after taking a tiny bite, because I might have had *too* many sweets last night and my teeth feel fuzzy. The blanket fort is getting cramped now with all these questions. I scuttle out.

"Not being able to talk about it is one thing. But he still had a choice whether to go through with it or not. Which means he still can't be trusted." Arzu tries to follow me out of the fort, but she trips on my tablet. "Hey, who is this cutie you're drawing?"

"Give me that." I yank the tablet from her hand and stuff it back into my backpack. I rummage around and find some spare clean clothes to change into. I can't face Madar with life-changing info smelling like whatever I smell like now, but the only clean outfit I have is the academy uniform. "Can you pretend like you're using the bathroom or something so I can get ready?"

"Don't think I won't ask you again about that drawing, but okay." Arzu gives me a thumbs-up as she stomps up the stairs and yells, "I am showering now! Please do not disturb me unless you want to scar me for life!"

I roll my eyes while shutting the door but can't help smiling.

At least I have Arzu in my corner.

ANOTHER HOUR PASSES BY, AND THERE'S STILL NO SIGN OF Idris or Yaseen.

"You sure you want to do this alone?" Arzu asks for the millionth time while I stand frozen, staring at my front door like it's going to reach out and bite me.

"Yeah, I think so." Even though I see Arzu as my sister, she's really not, and I feel this conversation is a *for family only* type of situation. Time to face the music, Farrah. I take the biggest breath ever and knock as loud as I can. I rehearse the words in my head: *Hi, Madar. I'm very sorry for worrying you but I just found out I'm a half-jinn and I need to be your someone-worth-protecting so I can travel to the Realm Beneath to make a deal with a very scary fire jinn so I can save my dad so he can explain to you why he left so we don't have to move, though now I'm not so sure if moving is a bad thing. Also sometimes the fire jinn talks in my head and I can't get him to stop. Did I mention that I'm very sorry?* Fifteen seconds go by before I knock again. And again. And again.

"Maybe they're not home?"

"That's weird. Usually my grandparents are here." I poke around in my pocket for my key. With nervous fingers, I jab my key in the door and twist the doorknob. "I'm hoooooooooome. Madar?" I call out in the narrow entryway. Because our house is so tall and narrow, I can pretty much see all the way in past the TV room and dining room and straight into the kitchen. "Bibi jan? Baba Haji? Anyone?" I drop my bag inside and peek up the stairs. "I guess no one's home." There are papers scattered everywhere. Flyers with more of my face, and dishes piled up on tables. In my whole twelve years, I've never seen the house this messy (well, except for my room, but that's the exception to the rule). *Because of me*, I think with shame, and I hurry to pile all the papers in nice and neat little stacks for my mom to come home to.

Arzu lingers in the open doorway and slowly shuts the front door. She shakes her hair free from her winter cap and hangs her winter coat on the wall rack.

"Think doing extra cleaning chores will make them less mad at me?" I've got used teacups hanging from all my fingers and tiny plates in the nook between my elbow and shoulder.

"Um. In my expert opinion?" Arzu tucks her hair behind her ears. "No. I mean, not to make you feel bad or anything, but . . ."

"I can handle it, you can tell me."

"They were really, like, really *really* sad when they couldn't find you." Arzu touches her two pointer fingers together uncomfortably. "Like, I don't think I've ever seen your grandpa cry that much. Or cry . . . ever."

"Oh."

"I'm sure it won't be as bad as you—"

The ceiling groans above us, followed by a small thump, like something got knocked to the floor. Arzu and I both freeze.

"I thought you said no one was home," she whispers.

"All the shoes are gone, so technically, yes." Which has me on red alert.

I put a finger to my lips and quietly tiptoe toward the stairs (and quickly grab the strongest coat hanger I can find, just in case). "Stay behind me," I whisper while going up the stairs. Unfortunately, our house is really old, so the floorboards creak. Very loudly.

"Did you hear that?" a muffled voice asks. "I told you not to touch that thing. Now there's white powder in my socks."

My favorite chalk bag! I gasp and race up the stairs. Right when I turn the corner, I half-laugh, half-cry. Idris is holding a stack of my books while Yaseen is furiously wiping chalk off his uniform. He's got a little remote in his hand and is accidentally pressing the buttons, changing the lights in my room from blue to red to green to yellow. Little chalk footprints are everywhere.

"What are you doing in here?" I barrel through the door and snatch the remote from Yaseen's hands. "And stop changing the lights. It's making my eyes cross." A pink glow splashes around the ceiling.

"What are we doing here? Why weren't *you* here?" Idris doesn't even look surprised as he keeps on reading through my collector's edition of the *Shahnameh*. "We've been waiting since last night for you after your meltdown."

"Oh right. That makes sense." On the inside I'm glad nothing bad happened to them. But on the outside I am very embarrassed. Horrible images flash through my head of snoopy boys going through my things and discovering embarrassing secrets. "You better not have scared my mom or grandparents, because if I find out—"

"Cool it. Your family has no idea we're here, remember?" Yaseen says in a monotone voice. He looks firmly at his shoes. "We're *invisible*."

"Also, the whole point of coming here was getting your protection charm," Idris says, upset. "Or does none of that matter when your feelings are hurt?" I feel a little guilty and awkward when Idris keeps flipping through the pages of the book. So that makes two jinn boys mad at me.

"Um, Farrah." Arzu pokes my back while peeking slightly behind me. "Please tell me there isn't a ghost in here that's making all those footprints right now." Because she's Arzu, she doesn't wait for me to reply. Instead she boldly steps out next to me and waves her arms around like she's trying to feel the air. "Ghost or not, it's rude to go through a princess's personal belongings."

"She is not a princess," Yaseen snaps in Arzu's direction, only to clam up and go a little pale. "She—uh, I—" he stammers, forgetting his train of thought.

Arzu takes a step back and gasps so loud. For a second, no one moves.

"Well, if we're revealing ourselves to every human that walks through the door . . ." Idris sighs and shuts the book. Arzu gasps again as she turns her head between both boys.

"Okay, rapid-fire intro." I put one hand on Arzu's shoulder and point with the other. "Arzu, this is Idris. Idris, this is Arzu." Then I point again. "Yaseen. Arzu. Great, everyone acquainted?"

"Whoa." Arzu looks a little dazed, as if her brain is whirring to take in all this new information. I can't really blame her. It's one thing to talk about jinn—it's something else to actually *see* them. "I need a second to process this." A little starry-eyed, she floats into the hallway mumbling, "Can't believe they're *both* cute . . ."

"That's a great idea. Maybe we should all do a little bit of processing." Idris clears his throat and sidesteps past me in a plume of chalky smoke. "And by *all,* I mean you and the unbearable complainer," he whispers before continuing into the hall and shutting my bedroom door.

"So *you're* Idris. . . ." Arzu's muffled voice floats from the hallway.

For a few minutes, Yaseen and I don't say anything. We stand awkwardly while the LED lights around my room alternate between different shades of pinks and purples. Yaseen leans against the window and, after looking around at the organized chaos of drawings, pictures, and hiking trails on my walls, surprisingly says, "The colors are cool."

"Thanks, it was my mom's idea. She's a little bit of a gamer, so."

"Gamer?" Yaseen winces while fiddling with his protection pin between his fingers.

"The video games I was talking about. The box that can take you to different worlds," I say. "Does your mom like games too?" Oh wait, that's a sore spot for him. "Sorry, you don't have to ans—"

"She did," he mumbles, still playing with his pin. "She hasn't played in a while."

I'm so shocked that he actually answered, all I can manage is a squeaky "Oh."

"Yeah," he says softly.

It gets silent and awkward again.

"So . . . ," Yaseen starts, "I think we need to talk about yesterday."

"I shouldn't have yelled at you and run away, but losing the ring again really got to me." I walk over to my desk and plop down in my spinning chair. One of my favorite stuffed animals gets squished under my butt. I grab it and crush it to my chest.

"It was hard for me too . . . for a lot of different reasons." Yaseen's face gets pinched. "This isn't easy for me to say, so just listen before you bite my head off, okay?"

I squeeze my stuffed animal tighter. "Okay."

"My whole life I've been told keeping half-humans out was for our protection. To make our world safe. Protected from the chaos humans bring with them. The same way the kings kept us safe when they removed Azar and his realm from ours. So when King Barqan came to me in the court with his mission, I couldn't say *no*."

"But what about me is dangerous?" Sure, I can be rude (and mean) sometimes, and yeah, I could clean my room better, but I'm not *bad*. Plus, if we're talking about scary, when Yaseen compelled the shop attendant, *that* was scary, and that's something all jinn can do.

"It's not you specifically," Yaseen explains quietly. "A long time ago, before I was born, there was a warning that came through King Mudhib. He had a horrible vision about the end of our world order, and it was a mixed jinn's fault. So ever since then, the jinn world separated from humans."

"But I would never do something like that!" I *like* the jinn world; I want to be part of it, not destroy it. "You believe me, right?"

"I didn't really know you then. All I knew was that you were the reason why my dad and Ahmar disappeared. I thought maybe the vision was coming true."

"I can see how you'd think that. . . ." Knowing the history behind the seven jinn kings and Azar now, I probably would have thought the same. It *did* look really bad bringing Azar's ring into the court.

"But when King Barqan cornered me in the library and told me the whole plan, it didn't feel right to me. He knew I had doubts, so . . . he compelled me to not be able to talk about his plan, just in case I had a change of heart. Don't get me wrong, I know I've been . . . rude, but I never wanted to hurt you in the way King Barqan had planned."

I gulp. "With those tablets he gave you?"

"You saw that too, huh? Yeah, he gave me these." Yaseen closes his eyes and shamefully pulls two white tablets out of his pouch. There's a symbol carved into them. "The reason why I couldn't stop his plan was because King Barqan also compelled me to stay the course. If I tried to throw away the tablets or talk about it, the magic would stop me until—"

"Until I mentioned it," I finish his sentence. That explains the weird way his words would go sludgy. "What are they?"

"They have King Maymun's symbol etched on them. He rules over the unconscious world. It's his realm of expertise. I was supposed to make you and Idris eat them, and"—Yaseen shudders at the thought—"when you fall asleep, it allows King Maymun's minions to infiltrate your dreams and take control of your body."

"That's . . . dangerous." I'm squeezing my stuffed animal so tight, fluff starts to come out of one of the worn holes in its neck. I can't imagine what that would feel like—to be controlled by someone else. If one jinn king could do that, I wonder what ancient powers the rest have.

"It's very dangerous, which is why I tried my best to

get rid of them, but every time I threw them away, they'd reappear back in my hands." Yaseen shakes his head, and his messy hair falls from his topknot into his eyes. He draws little circles with his foot. "Because I couldn't tell you, I thought if I could just take the ring from you and do this on my own, it would have been better than going through with King Barqan's plan."

I gasp in understanding. "So all the lightning bolts and trying to take the ring . . . that was to help me?"

"I mean, partly," he says. "The other part was feeling jealous that you got a wish and I didn't, but yeah, that's the truth."

Seeing Yaseen so . . . not mean makes me feel guilty about what I said back in the observatory too. He's not the only one who messed up. "I didn't mean what I said before," I blurt out. "About the school stuff and . . ." Not being good enough.

Yaseen's bright green eyes look up at me. "Yeah, you did."

"No, I—"

My bedroom door bursts open. Idris is breathing hard while pointing an ink-stained finger toward me. "I thought you told me you didn't know what a protection charm was."

I swivel around in my chair, really confused. "Because I didn't."

Arzu's head pops up over Idris's. "A protection what?"

"Then why . . ." Idris rushes over and grabs my hand, jolting me out of my chair and into the dark hallway. There are rows of pictures hanging along the walls—mostly of my family. ". . . are you wearing one here?" He jabs at a baby photo. I'm in a very embarrassing pumpkin outfit (thanks, Madar), but pinned next to my collar are two small charms. One is a small blue eye, and the other is a small gold, sparkly elephant charm.

"That's just something my family puts on babies for good luck or p—" *Protection.* "It's not a . . ." My hand reaches up to touch the photo, right where the pin is, and I feel something warm, like the softest hug, curl around my fingers. It travels up my wrist, straight toward my heart. Little tears smoosh in between my eyelashes because it feels like Madar.

It couldn't be.

Madar didn't know about Padar. She said it herself, on the car ride home when my dad disappeared! *Our life is not a fantasy; there is no magical rainbow or story or thing that will take us away from our problems.* She couldn't know the truth.

Unless . . .

My dream comes back to me. *I promise you're in the right place,* Padar's voice echoes.

I hesitantly reach for the frame and gently take it off the wall. When I turn the frame around, I hear a tinkling. Taped to the brown cardboard is the pulsing elephant pin.

"A protection charm," I whisper as Idris and Arzu crane their heads around my shoulders to look at it. Yaseen hangs back, looking uncomfortable. "But then that means . . ."

My mom knew. Which means she *lied.* My world crashes down on top of me.

"Maybe someone put it here and my mom didn't know." My stomach lurches, and I can taste the Fruit Roll-Ups coming back up. I drop the frame. "There's got to be some mistake."

"There's no mistaking that's a protection charm," says Idris. "And it's got your mom's smell all over it."

"Is someone going to fill me in on why this is bad?" groans Arzu.

Yaseen's quiet voice surprises all of us. He leans against my bedroom doorframe. "Because it means your mom knew who our dad was this whole time."

There's noise downstairs. A lock clicks. Footsteps rush in, followed by "Hurry up, my fingers are going to fall off if I stay out there any longer."

We all look at each other in surprise.

Madar is home.

CHAPTER SIXTEEN

I'M FINE

"What do we do now?" Arzu whispers nervously.

Before anyone can answer, the floor under us rumbles, softly and then really loud. It shakes so much, pictures from the wall fall onto our heads.

"Ouch!" Idris rubs a bump on the back of his neck.

"What's going on?" shouts Arzu. I quickly clasp my hands over her mouth before she gives up our spot.

"It's happening again!" Madar's panicked voice from downstairs cuts through.

"That's the third time this week," Bibi jan adds.

As soon as the rumbling starts, it ends. All four of us stare at each other with looks of horror, just as Azar's voice growls in my head, *A third king down, four to go.*

"I guess no one heard the voice again?" I whisper.

Three heads shake no.

"Another king is gone." I relay the message. "Which means we're running out of time. We need to go."

"Wait, aren't we supposed to be letting your mom know you're not, you know, missing anymore?" Arzu asks.

I glance at the protection pin on the ground. The whole point of coming back was to tell my mom the truth so we could stay where we belong. Here, in Philadelphia. But if Madar already knew, then it didn't matter if I left or not. She was *always* going to move us. She was always going to leave Padar behind, just like how he left her behind. And she was never going to give me the chance to choose. It was always her way. This makes me even sadder than before.

I can't talk, so I shake my head.

"Are you sure?"

"Just talk to your mom and get it over with. We can't afford to lose another king," Yaseen orders quietly while turning back into my room. There's a sadness that creeps around his shoulders. "Idris and I will be waiting outside your window with the cloud." When no one moves, Yaseen turns around and adds, "Idris will make sure we wait."

"Sounds like a solid plan," Idris agrees.

"Wait, what about me?" Arzu puts her hands on her hips. "You can't just leave me here with the adults."

"Trust me, you don't want to go where we're headed," Yaseen says.

"Says who? Did you even *ask* me?" Arzu walks toward Yaseen, wagging her finger. "If you think I'm going to leave my best friend alone with you two untrustworthy boys, then you'd better think again!" She quickly grabs one of my puffy jackets off the floor and follows Yaseen out the window.

"I hate to say it, but your insufferable brother is right." Idris puts a hand on my shoulder and flashes me a small smile that makes me want to grin back. "You've got this, Noorzad. I promise you'll feel better after. And if you don't, I'll endure your complaining." He slips away.

Standing all alone, I take a deep breath and go down a few stairs. My knees wobble when I see Madar sitting on the couch, her face pressed into Baba Haji's chest, with Bibi jan rubbing her back. I've never seen my mom this run-down.

"We've been searching that park for days now," Madar sobs. "What if it's too late? What if they got her too?"

"Shh, don't say such things," Bibi jan says. "She's protected, I'm sure of it. You'll see, Shamhurish will bring her back. He keeps his promises."

Time freezes when I hear my grandma say my dad's name—his true name. Somehow, knowing they *all* knew hurts more than my grandparents being left in the dark.

I get stuck on the stairwell. I want to run into my mom's arms and go back to before my twelfth birthday. I want to make ice cream with Bibi jan and spend afternoons lying on the couch, sketching on my tablet. I want everything to go back to normal, when home still felt like home, like a place where I belonged completely.

But you don't belong. Azar's voice swirls so loud in my

head. *Neither here nor there. You're worse than being in between worlds—you're nowhere.*

Very quietly, I go to where the tiny elephant pin is. I carefully take off the tape and tiptoe back down the stairs. When I'm sure no one is looking, I leave the pin and the picture on the first stair, so Madar knows. And then I decide for myself.

I don't need to be someone's worth-protecting. Not if protecting means lying.

I can protect myself.

I am indestructible, after all.

"IS ANYONE GONNA TALK ABOUT THE ELEPHANT IN THE room?" Idris whispers, a little too loud. Even though I'm sitting at the very front of the cloud, I can imagine the glare Arzu gives Idris. "What, too soon?"

"This is exactly why I had to come. Boys don't know how to handle anything correctly," Arzu grumbles. She very slowly crawls to where I am. I hear her gulp. "H-hey, princess. How are you feeling?"

"Fine."

"Well, that's great." Arzu tries to be her bubbly self, but it's too obvious the way her teeth are chattering—she's afraid of how high we are. We're gently rising higher and higher, past all the skyscrapers until we reach the airways. "So then, no need to be all doom and gloom, right? Because I'm totally not fine hovering hundreds of feet in the air on a *cloud.*"

I keep looking ahead—at the sun, the bright blue sky— and then down, at the river and skyscrapers that glitter in the distance. I wrap my arms around my knees and don't look back. I don't want to ever look back. How could I have gotten it all wrong? I thought Yaseen was the one who was hiding secrets, but he tried to tell me twice. It wasn't his fault King Barqan enchanted him. Madar doesn't even have that excuse. She was hiding the biggest secret of all. For twelve years my family took away my choice. Maybe they were trying to pro- tect me, in their own way, from the dangers of my existence, but it was *my* right to know. And they took it away.

I sniffle and wipe silent tears from my cheeks.

"Okay." Arzu scoots back and whisper-shouts at the boys, "She is not fine! Do something."

There's some shuffling and grumbling. "I thought *boys don't know how to handle anything correctly,*" mutters Yaseen. I sigh as the cloud wisps re-form around my body like a hug.

Someone shuffles their way next to me.

"For the last time, I'm—"

"You're fine, we got it." The wind pushes Yaseen's hair into his eyes as he squints at me. "I couldn't care less about your mom drama. We've got more important things to worry about. Like figuring out where the gateway to the Realm Beneath is. Since they only exist in the human world, I feel that . . . would be . . ." Yaseen says the next words like he's got a mouthful of sticky caramel. ". . . your area of expertise." He sighs. "Also . . . are we really going to do this with the human?"

I glance back at Arzu, who is holding on to the cloud for dear life. She waves a forced thumbs-up at me. "This is so great." She smiles through tears. "So great."

"Why? Does the rotten-cabbage smell bother you?" I ask.

"She actually smells like apples," Yaseen mutters with a confused expression. "Agh! That's not the point. Gateways. Any ideas?"

I recall Azar's hint. "A land destined to burn for two hundred years." The bubbles fizz, pushing the gears in my brain to figure out where that could be. This would be so much easier if I had a phone and some internet. . . . That's it. "Arzu! Please tell me you have your phone on you."

"Y-yes, I d-do." Her teeth chatter as she digs in my puffy jacket and takes out her phone. "Aren't you g-guys c-c-cold up here?"

Idris shakes his head. Yaseen just mutters, "Humans are so fragile." I realize I am also not cold, not like the first time I used the airways.

"Ignore him," I say. "Can you look up places on fire for two hundred years?"

"You g-got it." Arzu shivers while tapping frantically on her phone. Idris looks curiously over her shoulder.

"What a fascinating . . . invention. Look how it stores moments and memories. All without magic. Incredible."

"They're just pictures. It's called a search engine." Arzu keeps typing. When she's thinking really hard, a little line forms in between her eyebrows. Her curly hair bounces with the wind. "I think I got s-something."

"'Centralia'?" reads Idris. "What's that?"

"It says it was an old mining town that is almost abandoned because the underground tunnels caught fire a long time ago," Arzu says. "And scientists say there's enough coal in the ground to keep the fire going for two hundred years." She looks up and blinks her bright eyes at Yaseen and me. "Does that sound good to everyone?"

"Y-yeah," stutters Yaseen.

I hide a smirk. "Still wanna ask why we're bringing around 'the human'?"

Idris hands Arzu the jeweled pen. "Just think it and the cloud will take you."

"Whoa." Arzu's eyes grow to the size of marbles as she whips the pen around like a wand. Unfortunately, the cloud also decides to loop the loop very aggressively.

"Watch it!" Yaseen yelps. "Are you trying to kill us!"

"How was I supposed to know it was going to do that!" Arzu throws the pen at Yaseen. "That's too much power f-for me. You dr-drive." Her lips are a little blue from the cold.

"Gladly." Yaseen looks at the phone and sets the course.

Feeling bad for my friend, I scoot over to where she is and wrap my arms around her shoulders to keep her warm.

"You r-really don't feel it at all?" she asks, teeth chattering.

"No."

"It's because of the food," Idris mentions. "You've been around so much essence, it's made you more like us."

"Here." Yaseen rummages in his pouch and impossibly pulls out a full-size blanket. "It should help." He doesn't look at Arzu when she takes the blanket and wraps it around us. "We'll be up here for a while, and I really don't want to have to deal with a frozen human slowing us down."

"He sure is prickly," Arzu says while cupping her hands next to my ear.

"Would you believe it if I told you this is actually him being nice?"

"I think that means you're starting to grow on him."

"Maybe." I burrow into the blanket and watch Yaseen out of the corner of my eye. "Maybe he's growing on me too."

CHAPTER SEVENTEEN

EMERGENCY EXIT

Here's another pro tip I wish I didn't have to learn first-hand: Do you know what happens when your cloud runs out of gas? If you don't know, let me be the first to tell you. It goes something like this.

"Why is your cloud sputtering?" I sleepily ask after a nice hour-long nap. We're currently passing through a lot of farms. Arzu is still snoozing peacefully on my shoulder.

"Oh, this is not good." Idris jolts up as his foot slips through the cloud. He pats his pockets and then sheepishly laughs when Yaseen glares at him.

"Please don't tell me you forgot to bring spare jinn essence with you?" groans Yaseen when he sees the pen is nearly out of ink. The cloud shakes even more now as Yaseen tries to push it forward.

"What's all the commotion?" Arzu yawns dramatically.

"Funny story." Idris ruffles his hair with his hand. His

pants billow in the harsh wind. "I may have accidentally . . . forgotten that the cloud needed . . . a refill."

"Idris, what happens when the cloud runs out of essence?" I try to stay calm for Arzu, but I notice the cloud fluff loosens around my waist. The ride gets bumpier, and I feel my stomach swoop.

"Well, I've forgotten the technical term for it, but theoretically, when an enchanted cloud runs out of jinn essence, it just turns back into . . . a regular cloud." Idris leans next to Yaseen. "You wouldn't, by chance, happen to have a spare bottle in that handy pouch of yours?"

"No, why would I?" Yaseen is livid as we spiral faster and faster toward the ground. "I didn't exactly have time to pack!"

"WHY ARE WE FALLING?" Arzu screams as she holds on to the blanket for dear life.

"There is no need to panic," Idris says calmly as the ground gets larger and larger. "But I do suggest bracing yourself for this."

"Aren't there any emergency measures on this thing?" Arzu continues to scream as our cloud loses shape and begins to function like a normal cloud made out of air and water.

"Idris's cloud is from a hundred years ago! Before reserve tanks and emergency air chutes were installed," Yaseen screeches as the cloud dissolves and we tangle apart from each other. The wind makes my eyes water as we fall. I hold on to the blanket connecting me and Arzu together.

"I DID NOT SIGN UP FOR THIS," wails Arzu. "I CHANGE MY MIND. HOW CAN I GO BACK HOME?"

"Stop screaming in my ear!" Yaseen winces as he also grabs hold of the blanket.

"I'LL SCREAM ALL I WANT! AAAAAAAAHHHH!"

"Maybe scream about three hundred yards to the left. You see that over there?" Idris's eyes are doing that weird cloudy thing again. He's looking ahead while pointing to the left. "We gotta glide onto that soft-looking pile."

The soft-looking pile is a pile of hay. Lots and lots of hay. Horses and cows and goats are walking around. If we land even a little off course, we'll squash the animals (and ourselves).

Well, I'm pretty sure *I'll* be fine. I've never broken a bone from a fall, after all. It's Arzu I'm worried about.

"Like a star; angle your body like this." Idris twirls and glides closer to me. He holds my arm, and, still holding on to the blanket, I follow his lead.

"HOW ARE YOU SO CALM?" Arzu continues to shriek. "WE ARE FALLING TO OUR DEATH!"

"Panicking won't help either!" I wince as Arzu's fingers dig into my arm. "We've gotta think. Hold on, Yaseen! Do you have any more blankets in your pouch? We can try to parachute to soften our landing."

"A blanket is not going to—"

"DO YOU HAVE ANY BETTER SUGGESTIONS?" Arzu

cries. "Otherwise we have less than thirty seconds until we're pancakes."

"Go for it," grumbles Yaseen. He gives the pouch to Arzu, who hands it to me. I shove my hand inside and start digging around. I touch what feels like a toothbrush, some shirts, a candy bar, a prayer rug, and more shirts.

"How much stuff can this tiny thing hold?" I keep looking. "And why do you pack so many shirts?"

"Fifteen seconds, Noorzad!" warns Idris. His grip on my arm is cutting off circulation.

"I can't find anything that will work." I panic as the ground gets closer.

"It's too late!" Idris squeezes his eyes shut. "BRACE FOR IMPACT."

We spiral closer to the ground. I've never been afraid of falling before, but there's a first time for everything. At the last second I hold on to Arzu. If I hit the ground first, maybe she'll be okay.

There's a bone-crunching sound as something jerks the blanket up. My eyes fly open, and I see the ground getting farther away as we slow down and hover.

Above us, Yaseen grits his teeth while holding on to the blanket. His upper body has shape-shifted into what looks like a very large, fleshy parachute.

"I . . . really wish I didn't see that," Arzu says.

We softly touch down onto the bales of hay. As we tumble

into each other, the bone crunching returns as Yaseen transforms back into himself.

"Remind me, who said"—he gasps—"I only care about myself?" He collapses into the hay.

"That couldn't have worked any more splendidly." Idris looks oddly cheery. His white hair is standing on end. His eyes are completely white, like someone put frosting over his pupils.

"Hold on." I sit up, but the world is spinning. "Oh, I think I'm going to be—" I crawl over to a bucket and throw up.

"Wait a second. I knew there was something off about you." Yaseen unsteadily crawls over to Idris. Once he gets his balance, he stands up and grabs Idris's face. "That's why you were so calm when we were falling. I thought it was weird that you knew where to land, but your eyes prove it! You have the power of recollection and you didn't bother to tell any of us!"

"Let go of my face." Idris wiggles out of Yaseen's grasp.

"He's a wha—" Another round of nausea hits me.

"I don't care if he's Santa Claus. I am never getting on a cloud ever again." Arzu hasn't moved from her starfish position.

"He's a *recollector*. It's a rare jinn ability to see things in the past and future," says Yaseen. "It's died out from the population. Not even the jinn kings can do that." He narrows his eyes suspiciously at Idris. "But the telltale sign is the frosted eyes!"

I sit up when the world finally stops spinning. "Wait, does that mean you can tell the future, like a psychic?"

"You could have told us where to go this whole time!" shouts Yaseen.

"It doesn't work like that." Idris's eyes clear. He gets very defensive. "It's pretty much a useless talent, which is why I didn't mention it," he snaps at Yaseen. "I just happen to work very well under pressure."

"Uh-huh." Yaseen keeps his guard up as he tears off his ruined shirt. Underneath, his skin is covered with stretch marks. He digs for his pouch in the hay and gets a new shirt. "If that's the story you want to go with. But don't think I'm not watching you."

"Guys, no fighting." When the world finally stops spinning, I wipe my mouth with the back of my hand and stand on wobbly legs. A goat stands next to me and nibbles on some hay. Past a red barn, a sign reads LANCASTER FARMS.

"What are we doing in Lancaster?" I push my tangled bangs out of my eyes to get a better look. "Yaseen, you sure we were going in the right direction?"

"I'm not the human world geographer. Your guess is as good as mine." Yaseen tugs an emerald-green sweater over his head and pulls on my arm. We walk toward an open stable, away from Idris. Arzu is still lying semiconscious in the hay. "It's hard to steer against crosswinds in ancient jinn equipment like that cloud. And anyway." His voice gets even lower. "I have to ask you again, how did you and Idris become friends in the first place?"

"Why do you want to know?"

"There's something . . . off about him." Yaseen eyes Idris from a distance. "I can't put my finger on it, but I can't help feeling like he's not being entirely honest."

"Maybe he's been compelled too and can't talk about it, like you were."

"This feels different," Yaseen mutters. "I just . . . don't understand how you *forget* to bring backup essence with you when you rely on an enchanted cloud. Or why you hide a rare jinn ability. It's almost like he wanted this to happen."

"Look, I know Idris is . . . a little weird, but he's my friend. If he says his ability is useless, then it probably is." There's no way Idris would purposely put all our lives in danger like that. He's saved me more times than I can count, and that's got to mean something. "I trust him, even if he likes dark chocolate and occasionally rubs handfuls of jinn berries under his arms."

"He *what?*"

"Yeah, it was when we first got to the Qaf Mountains. He said it was to get the human smell off him," I recall. "And he was right because I didn't do it and the jinn kings sniffed me out in a second."

"Because you're half-human." Yaseen blinks very slowly. "But why would Idris . . . ?"

"Now you're being weird." I look between Yaseen and Idris by the hay pile, who is scribbling away in his notebook. "Isn't that what you would do if you came back from the human world?"

"No . . ." Yaseen trails off. "I wouldn't need to."

"Oh, well, maybe I misunderstood," I say nervously. "He was probably being extra careful."

"Maybe . . ." Yaseen fixes his hair. "But there's a difference between being extra careful and behaving strangely. Just . . . keep that in mind, okay?"

I nod, not liking the little flag of worry that's now waving in the back of my head.

IT TURNS OUT, NEARLY FALLING THIRTY THOUSAND FEET TO your death can take a lot out of a person. Or at least, a person without any conveniently magical blood.

So we decide to camp out at the farm until morning for Arzu to recover.

"Does that pouch ever get full?" I sit next to Arzu on the hay. She's curled up in a blanket, snoozing away.

"I'll let you know when it happens." Yaseen pulls out enough material to make a little tent around the hay pile. "Well, see you in the morning, and . . . keep an eye out, okay?"

"You got it." My stomach grows warm when I watch Yaseen walk away and settle next to Idris on the grass a little ways off.

It's weird, this new side to Yaseen. It's how I always imagined a brother to act. It's . . . nice to not argue for once.

I try to channel Arzu's sleepiness and count the stars to fall asleep, but Yaseen's words keep sloshing around in my head. Sure, Idris is a little smell-obsessed, and his taste in dark chocolate is questionable at best, but that doesn't mean he's hiding something. And even if he were, pretty much everyone (except Arzu) had a secret from the beginning. Maybe Idris didn't want us to treat him differently after being stuck in the ring for a hundred years. Maybe that's why he hid his ability. Being stuck in a ring could make anyone do weird things, like rub berries under their arms or . . .

. . . take a hidden entrance into a heavily guarded jinn world.

There's a difference between being extra careful and behaving strangely.

A stone drops in my stomach as I toss and turn. Because there's only one reason why Idris would know about that secret entrance.

Are we really safe . . . from the tricks of a jinn king? Idris's question pops up again, and I bolt upright. When Idris was telling me the story about Azar, I thought he was worried about being safe from the forbidden jinn king, but what if . . .

. . . he was talking about the *other* jinn kings? It's still on my mind when the sun rises.

"Good mor—whoa, did you sleep at all last night?" Arzu stretches and yawns in her blanket cocoon.

"Couldn't, 'cause someone snored all night!" I lie while crawling out of the tent. I've got to talk to Idris.

"This cursed beast nearly pooped on my foot!" Idris shrieks from across the farm. He speed-walks away from the cow and snaps his fingers to get us going. "I think I've had enough of these creatures for a lifetime. Let's go. Forward and . . ." He frowns. "Please tell me someone has directions."

"Don't look at me." Yaseen clips his pouch to a loop on his pants.

"Give me a second to wake up at least." Arzu scratches her head while climbing out of the tent. She yawns and takes her phone out of her pocket. "Let's see. The nearest town has a train station that I think can get us closer to Centralia. . . ." She trails off, suddenly getting wobbly on her feet. "Whoa, head rush."

"Maybe you should take it easy." I loop my arm in hers. Idris will have to take a back seat for now. First I've got to make sure Arzu is okay to keep going. "Yesterday was stressful for you."

Arzu gets a determined look on her face. "Aw, Farrah, don't make me feel like the weakest link." Her brows push together. "I want to help."

"And you are. You've got the navigation!"

"What good is a navigator who can't navigate?" Yaseen puts his hands on his hips and looks around at the field of cows. "Man, it smells here. . . . Wait, that's it." He stalks over to a wooden fence that herds all the cows in. He plugs his nose just as a purple aura glows around him. His eyes darken.

"Whoa . . . do you feel that?" Arzu shivers.

There's a chill in the air when Yaseen hops up on the fence, reaches over, and touches a lone grazing cow. He whispers something in its ear. Its eyes go pitch-black as it breaks through the fence and makes its way toward Arzu and me. It looks at Arzu and waits.

"Why is this zombie cow giving me creepy looks?" Arzu shrinks back.

"Since you're the weakest in the group, the creature will pick up the slack," Yaseen says, like it's the obvious choice. I can't help but giggle a little when it dawns on Arzu what the suggestion is.

"I am *not* riding on a cow." She resists as her legs buckle. Her hazel eyes get big and wide when she looks at me. "Isn't there anything else, another nifty gadget to travel on?"

"It's either the creature . . . or Idris." Yaseen rests his hand under his chin. "Don't let his twiggy arms fool you, he's strong enough to ca—"

"Help me up on the cow," Arzu grumbles.

We struggle to push her up, but once she finds a comfortable position, Yaseen compels the cow, *"Walk, creature."* His purple aura lessens when Arzu pulls out her phone and gives instructions.

"So how does this phone know our location without ingesting any jinn essence?" Yaseen is weirdly very into the map.

While Arzu explains the idea of GPS, I slow down and let them get farther ahead. Idris pokes his head back, noticing. He slows down so we're walking side by side.

"Can I ask you something?" Little nervous bubbles roil in my stomach when Idris raises a confused eyebrow.

"What is troubling you, Noorzad?"

"Well . . ." I'm not sure how to start. "Remember when we escaped from the shadow jinn that first time?"

"You mean the first time I saved your life?"

"I didn't need—" Okay, fine. Maybe I needed a *little* help. "Anyway, after that, when we got to the Qaf Mountains, there's something that doesn't really add up."

"What is it?"

I hold my hands together and look down at my feet. It's now or never, Farrah. "How did you know about that secret entrance?" I peek up at him. "And how did you know it would lead to the garden, and why was the first thing you did rubbing *yourself* with the berry bushes and not me?"

"Because I needed to get the human smell off me," Idris explains, confused. "I told you this already."

"I know. . . ." I twirl my thumbs together. "But it doesn't explain the entrance. An entrance that had to exist for at least a hundred years, and the only reason why someone would know it was there is if . . ."

They had something to hide. Like a jinn mixed with mortal blood.

"Spit it out, Noorzad." Idris's face goes stony. "What is it you're trying to ask me?"

"Are you hiding that you're not all jinn?" I keep my voice low. "Because that's the only reason why you'd know about that secret entrance and how to disguise yourself. And why Yaseen thinks you're being weird."

"So your brother put you up to this."

"No, I'm putting you up to this. As your friend, I'm asking you. Are you like me too?"

Idris doesn't say anything, but something in the way his face gets twitchy and sad says *yes*.

"Why didn't you tell me?" I ask, hurt. "Instead of making me feel like I was the odd one out. We could have helped each other."

"Because you wouldn't understand." Idris's face goes blank as he walks ahead.

"Like I wouldn't understand that you didn't feel safe around the seven jinn kings?" I cup my hands around my mouth and shout at him. "Or that I wouldn't understand that you're a recollector? Are you really lost, or is that something else I wouldn't understand?"

Idris doesn't answer. He speeds up to get farther away from me. I watch him, tears stinging in my eyes, as he walks past Arzu and Yaseen and takes his spot at the front of the line. Leaving me all alone and wondering what I wouldn't understand.

After a long while Arzu turns around. "Hey, slowpoke. Do you need a turn on the cow? It's actually not that bad." Yaseen compels the cow to slow down so I can catch up.

"No thanks."

"So it seems humans have come up with one invention that isn't useless." Yaseen is angling Arzu's phone in every direction—up, down, side to side, spinning around in circles—watching with wonder when the little blinking pin readjusts to his new location. "How does it know?"

"If you spent more time down here, you'll find out we've got way cooler inventions than GPS." I want to roll my eyes, but Yaseen glances up at me with a conflicted frown.

"That might not be . . ." He stops and gasps when the phone buzzes. "It went away."

"Because we reached our destination. Finally! I can get off this gassy cow!" Arzu holds out her hands to steady herself as she climbs down, only to lose her balance and fall.

"Stop trying to break yourself!" Yaseen darts a helping hand out without thinking and catches her.

"Thank you, that was really nice," Arzu says in Yaseen's arms. Horror dawns on his face when he recognizes what he did. Yaseen shudders and lets go of her. He tries to wipe his hands on his green sweater. "I will never get this cursed human smell off me."

"Look at you," I say, impressed. "You've finally gotten over your phobia of touching humans."

Arzu laughs when Yaseen rubs his hands all over the cow,

who farts at just the wrong . . . or right time. This makes Arzu laugh more.

"*Ugh, leave us alone, creature,*" Yaseen compels, a little too loud. The cow moos in response and trots away.

"You know, you should really stop compelling creatures down here," Idris calls out from down the road. We've reached a small town. There are signs for a train and some small shops a little ways down. "How can the son of a judge break so many rules?"

"You're one to talk," Yaseen mumbles.

"What was that?" Idris cups his ear.

"Maybe it's a family trait," Yaseen says a little louder. He pulls out a towel from his pouch and starts vigorously wiping his hands. Of course, they turn out sparkly clean (with a hint of lemon scent). I know Yaseen wasn't directing the word *family* at me, but a little part of me does smile at it. Because if he asked me, I would definitely agree. We are a family of rule breakers.

And secret keepers. My mood sours when I think about Madar again. Did she assume I wouldn't understand, like Idris?

"I hope you've got another lead, navigator, because I don't trust the rule guard to get us somewhere without us falling to our deaths," taunts Yaseen.

"Hey, I take *personal offense* to that," Idris retorts.

"Tell me I'm wrong." Yaseen reconsiders. "Actually, Farrah, tell me I'm right."

"Why would she take *your* side?" Idris asks, but it's unsure.

"I wish I had some popcorn right about now." Arzu's head bobs back and forth like a tennis ball watching the arguing. "This is so much better than watching my mom's Turkish dramas."

"I—"

Feelings splash onto me like buckets. One splash makes me sad because Idris didn't trust me enough to share he's mixed with human blood too. Another splash is relieved Arzu wasn't hurt too bad and is acting like her normal self. And then there's the biggest splash: Yaseen called me Farrah instead of *half-human* (which feels like warm sunshine finally peeking through a month of dark, cloudy weather). It slipped out so quickly, I don't think he noticed.

It is too many splashes at once.

Instead of answering, I make myself *remember* these feelings. Remember the way the glowing sun washes over Idris's shoulders and shines on Yaseen's exasperated face. Remember Arzu's social commentary.

And when I feel like I've remembered enough, I pack all the feelings away into the nearly full boxes in my head. Then, with the feelings safely tucked away, I say, "Actually, I do have a plan. But it's going to require a little bit of rule-breaking."

CHAPTER EIGHTEEN

IT'S NEVER TOO LATE FOR AN APOLOGY

"**Y**ou want us to what?" Idris whisper-shouts.

We're sitting inside the train station on a bench by a coffee shop. The overhead announcer is rattling off train schedules and departure delays. Luckily, the restrooms were well stocked, so we were able to get the farm smell off us. I'm biting into a croissant from the coffee shop. ("Looks like I do have some money after all," Arzu chides.)

"Technically, we won't be breaking too many rules. Since the humans can only see Arzu and me," I say through chomps. "All you need to do is distract the conductor when he checks the tickets to enter the train. And then it'll be smooth sailing to Centralia."

"I told you, *compelling* is illegal—"

"I think you owe me one," I say a little quietly, still stinging from what he said before. "Unless you think that's something else I don't understand."

The air gets tight when Yaseen looks between us. "Trouble in friendship land?"

"That's an understatement." Arzu—after somehow finding herself actual popcorn—is shoveling it into her mouth in fascination.

Idris goes silent, shoving his hands into his pockets. "I think I liked it better when you two had problems."

I don't know why, but one of the boxes in my head shakes loose and spills out the hurt from Idris's words. Maybe I tried to pack away too many things at once, but I can't get it back in.

"I need to wash my hands." I stand up abruptly and speed-walk to the bathroom.

"Now you've done it." Arzu's voice trails behind me. "And here I thought Yaseen was supposed to be the mean one."

"Hey!"

I push open the bathroom door and stomp my way over to the sinks. My bangs tickle my eyes, making them water even more. I shake the bangs out of my face, but that also rustles the little boxes inside my head free until everything is one big confusing mess. I blink very fast while looking at my reflection. At my eyes that look like Madar's—big and wide and sad.

I'm splashing water on my face, mad at so many things—but mostly mad at myself for being so sensitive. So what if my friend hides stuff from me and doesn't want me to get along with my brother. It shouldn't bother me this much.

The bathroom door swings open.

It's Arzu.

"I'll be out in a sec." I march over to rip off a piece of paper towel from the wall dispenser.

"No rush," she says gently, "but the train leaves in ten minutes."

"Okay."

"I showed Yaseen how to buy tickets from the counter, so he compelled the adults to give us four tickets."

"He *what?*"

"I think he's starting to come around, you know. Though I wish he could have warned me about the . . . shape-shifting. Said it helps with convincing the adults. I dunno. Personally, I think he does it to show off." Arzu fiddles with a strand of her curls. "We thought it'd be easier this way since it seems like you've got a lot on your mind."

"I'm fine. I could have gotten my way in on my own—"

"I know you're, like, really tough and all," Arzu interrupts. "It's okay to rely on us. You don't have to keep all of it inside, you know. The stuff with your mom and dad . . ."

Nope. This conversation is not happening. My head is too messy to talk about this.

"You're right, I am tough. And I'm feeling much better." Moms lie. Dads lie. Brothers lie. Friends lie. *Everyone* lies. It's something I've just gotta get over. I throw away the towel, plant my hands on Arzu's shoulders, and push her forward. "So thanks for the talk, but we've got a train to catch. Let's go."

Arzu sighs. "Whatever you say."

We slip into the train just as it starts to pull away from the station.

I sink into the fluffy seats and watch the sun go down. Arzu sits next to me, and Yaseen sits across from Arzu. Idris finds a seat all the way in the front of the car and stares moodily out the window with his arms crossed. Every now and then his eyes go cloudy while he scribbles in his notebook. Now that I know it's not a normal jinn thing, I want to know what he's trying to see.

I prop my legs up in the empty seat across from me.

"Watch your feet." Yaseen swats my shoes when they get too close to him. "I just cleaned this blanket." He's dug out a bright-blue-and-white blanket, a refilling mug of something that smells like butter and honey, and a book written in Arabic.

Arzu is snapping photos of the sunset, right until her phone blinks off. "Oh rats. I've run out of charge." She sighs and sinks back into her seat. "Now what will we do?"

"There's a thing called silence," says Yaseen.

"What are you reading?" Arzu says in not silence.

"Something not for humans."

"Like?"

I expect Yaseen to say, *Like none of your business,* but instead he surprises me.

"It's *Jinn Law 101.* I have midterms next month, and the

last thing I need is to . . . fall behind." He frowns while trying to concentrate on the words.

"Oh, if you need help studying, Farrah is a literal genius, like, *amazing* at studying." Arzu lights up. "She's got the top grades in our class. Our teacher even thinks she could skip a grade if she wanted."

"Arzu." I want to shove a huge chunk of chocolate in her mouth to get her to stop talking. "I'm not that smart. Just regular like everyone else."

"It's okay. I already know you're smart," Yaseen mumbles while flipping over pages. "You don't have to hide it to make me feel better."

"I'm not . . ."

"I noticed you like to do that. Say things sometimes to make someone else feel better, but you don't really mean it." Yaseen closes his book. "Like when I said you should talk to your mom, I bet you didn't. I bet that's something you wanted all of us to believe, which is why you've been so defensive about it."

"I—"

"Wait, you didn't talk to your mom?" Arzu whispers. "That explains why you're so mopey—"

"Why does this *matter?*" I lie back in my seat and cover my face with my arms.

"Because you've got someone who has the time to listen to you." This, somehow, really matters to Yaseen. "You know how hard it is to just keep up with school when your dad doesn't even notice if you're failing or not? Baba is so distracted overseeing the Supreme Court and working out other jinn's problems, he doesn't have time for mine." Yaseen tugs at his eyebrow (which is nearly half gone). "At least you've got a mom who cares."

"I think this is my cue to visit the snack car, so if you'll just excuse me." Arzu climbs over my legs and quickly goes through the car doors.

There's a prickly feeling in my throat when Yaseen doesn't say anything else. "My mom doesn't care. If she really cared about me, she wouldn't have made me feel so silly for believing in the magic of jinn and faeries and dragons and—" My throat stings too much to say any more. Because that's where the hurt is. All this time, Madar and Baba Haji made me feel *small* and silly for getting lost in Padar's stories, for wanting to believe in impossible things—to believe that I too could do the impossible one day.

Yaseen doesn't say anything.

"If my mom really cared, she wouldn't have made me feel like I had to shrink myself to make her life easier. She should have just told me the truth."

"And tell you what?" Yaseen angrily flips through the pages of his book. He points at a few lines. "That under jinn law, the discovery of any half-jinn born after 1923 is considered illegal and punishable by exile or death? If you don't get why keeping this big secret from the rest of us to keep you safe doesn't show that your mom cares about you, then I don't know what to tell you."

"Why does it bother you so much what I think about my mom?"

"Because . . ." Yaseen rubs his pointed ears and runs his hands through his hair. "It just does, okay?" He glares out the window, watching the tracks roll by. "It just does," he says even lower.

I can practically feel the wall that goes up when Yaseen looks out the window. I want to know more about his mom and why it's so hard for him to talk about her when it's obvious he loves her a lot. Maybe his parents got divorced; maybe that's why he doesn't like to talk about it.

Whatever it is, I know it's his story to tell. So I drop it and say, "Your mom must be a really great mom for you to protect her so much."

Yaseen doesn't say anything. He just chews on his lip and tries to take a sip of his drink, but the cup shudders and cracks. "Great, another thing that's run out of jinn essence." He throws his cup and book into his pouch. He sighs. "You know who I'm really dreading facing when we get back to the City of Jewels?"

I shake my head.

"King Barqan," he says. "He's going to fail me out of second year for sure now. I think I'm going to break a record. Oldest second-year at the academy."

"He can't do that."

"He will. It's what kings like him do," he replies. "They all do it when you disappoint them. All the kings. They've got this expectation of us at the academy to be exceptional. I can hear their voices now. *There goes the prince to the judicial throne who can't get past Jinn Law 101.*"

"Then he's a jerk," I say quietly. Passengers are snoozing in their seats. "And I'm a jerk for making you feel not good enough. I really didn't mean the bad things I said to you from before."

Yaseen shrugs. Even though we had a bumpy start, in the end, Yaseen did admit to King Barqan's plan *and* he saved all our lives when he didn't have to.

Lifesaving I never said thank you for. I get really red in embarrassment. Idris wasn't kidding—I have *terrible* manners.

"And I'm sorry for not thanking you when you saved our lives." I curl my legs under me. "I know how much it hurts when you have to shape-shift—"

"It doesn't hurt that much—"

"Well, it looks like it. You could have just saved yourself."

"Yeah, I could have. But we're all in this together now," he mumbles quietly. "It would have been wrong to just save myself."

"When we save our dad, remind me to tell him you said this. He could learn a little bit from you. Maybe he could learn from the both of us. To be better."

If Yaseen could change, who's to say Padar couldn't get better too?

Yaseen doesn't say anything. He just looks out the window and watches the towns go by. His body deflates, little by little. But after a minute, he says to himself, "You don't know our dad like I do. If he hasn't gotten better by now, he never will."

I want to ask him why but don't. Instead, I end up watching out the window with him, just in case he's putting tough feelings in boxes too.

CHAPTER NINETEEN

IT'S LIKE RIDING A BIKE

"How are these metal . . . tangles going to get us to the gateway faster?" Yaseen complains as we're walking down a long, winding street. The train dropped us off at the nearest town, but Centralia is still a little far away by foot.

"They're bicycles," I say while swinging one leg over the seat. Arzu stands on the little spokes on the wheels and holds on to my shoulders. "You just balance like this and pedal. Easy." I demonstrate by riding in a big circle around Yaseen and Idris.

"I don't know about this." Idris looks at the pink bike suspiciously. "Looks . . . very unstable."

"Just try it!" Arzu shouts.

"Also, your bikes have training wheels, so all you need to do is pedal." I thought the boys would be a little more adventurous. It took way too much convincing to get Yaseen to compel a family at the train station to give us their bikes ("Why do I even bother," Idris had mumbled), but I love riding bikes and feeling the wind in my hair. It makes me feel like I can outrace the boxes of feelings that won't stay put.

"I'm only doing this for the sake of the jinn world!" Yaseen wobbles as the sparkly purple streamers rustle in the wind. His knees come up to his waist and nearly bump into his chin. I have to stop myself from laughing. Idris is no better.

"Let's get a move on, slowpokes!" cheers Arzu.

We ride along the winding road. Small wisps of steam come up from little wells in the forest as we follow the signs for Centralia. I wonder if tiny pari might live behind the wells. I hear faeries like to hide in stone.

It feels like we're marching toward the finish line of our adventure. Shadows twist around the trees that dot the street. Suddenly, the road veers, and we cut right into a bumpy and cracked concrete road. The shadows have me on high alert. I keep an eye out for red, glowing eyes.

If Azar's hint leads us to a true gateway, then we need to be extra careful. There's no telling what tricks he has up his sleeve, but I know we'll be ready.

"There have to be more effective ways to get around," Idris huffs to himself. After the train ride, Idris's mood plummeted. He's avoided looking at me since we deboarded. "I can think of ten things that require less energy."

"Like what?" I ask.

"Explaining it will only take more energy," he puffs while

pedaling. With laser focus, he speeds up so he's side by side with Yaseen.

"Remind me next time to come prepared." Yaseen breathes through his nose. "This would have been so much easier if we had another cloud. Or some bottled jinn essence!"

"Well, I hope there isn't a next ti—" Idris narrows his eyes when he sees huge mounds of dirt blocking the road. Above the dirt a barrier twists and shimmers. "What the—?" Lightning flashes against the dark boundary, warning us to stay away. "Keep your guard up. I don't like the smell of this place."

"What is that?" I hit the brakes, nearly knocking Arzu over. The bike skids a few feet away from the barrier.

"Hey, careful how you're driving!"

"I think we've found our entrance." Yaseen hops off the bike and throws a rock through the barrier. It sizzles and disintegrates. A ripple goes through the entire force field, extending past the road and into the trees. "Yep. Looks like our shadow friends set up shop here. Which means we are definitely on the right track."

"Wonderful," Idris says under his breath. "Another step closer to *you-know-who*."

I shiver as we walk nearer to the barrier and shy away from the slithering shadow jinn watching from the treetops. "Why aren't they attacking us, then?" I think about my shadow puppet, the hungry look in her eyes.

"Probably because their boss told them not to." Idris jumps off his bike and stares down the boundary.

"Are we supposed to go through that wall of death?" Arzu shivers into her jacket. She huddles closer to me. "Do you think there's another way around?"

"If there is, we'll find a way through." I squeeze Arzu's hand. "I promise."

Yaseen wanders off the road and into the grass, throwing rocks against the swirling darkness. Each time, the barrier ripples and more lightning flashes. He looks up at me and shakes his head. "No way around. One of us has to test it," he says while walking back. "We can put it up to a vote."

"I'll do it," Idris volunteers.

"*You?*" Yaseen raises an eyebrow.

"Yes, me." Idris rubs his shoulder and hesitantly clears his throat. "No point in delaying the obvious." He takes a deep breath and squeezes his eyes shut. "I'll run fast, like ripping off a bandage."

"Wait, you don't have to go firs—"

"Better to face pain quickly than avoid it, Noorzad," Idris mutters. Without warning, he runs right into the barrier. "It only hurts a little bit!" His voice cuts off as darkness swallows him.

"Well, if Idris can do it, then I guess it should be fine. . . ." Yaseen trails off.

"Um, I'm not sure if I can . . . I mean"—Arzu gulps and

looks at the crackling force field with wide eyes—"it's not gonna do anything . . . bad to me, is it?"

"I'm not sure." Yaseen squints against the barrier. "I've never felt a barrier this strong before. It's blocking everything. I can't even see through it to the other side."

"And that's supposed to make us feel better?" It's one thing for Idris, Yaseen, and me to go through, but what will it do to Arzu?

"I guess we'll find out." Arzu tries to put on a brave face, but her knees wobble.

"No way," I say. "We can't put Arzu through the barrier without protection. . . ." Like a protection charm. "That's it." A light bulb goes off in my head. "Arzu, stay here. I know what to do."

"Great, and I'll just . . . continue to babysit," mutters Yaseen.

I take a deep breath and face down the scary barrier. It feels like the longer I look at it, the bigger it gets. The fear of dark places swirls around in my head, making me freeze, but I push the thoughts out. *Arzu is worth protecting.* Plus, I'm indestructible. How bad could it be? I make a run for it, yelling the second the barrier touches my skin. *I'd do anything to keep her safe!* It feels like I'm being stung by a thousand yellow jackets, but I keep going. I hold my best friend in my heart and push past the pain. My feet trek through the barrier as I fight with gravity to move ahead. Something light glows in my chest. My eyes burn as I continue forward and finally make it to the other side, falling onto my knees.

"It only hurts a *little*?" I gasp and chuck a rock at Idris, who is sweating profusely. I am so glad I didn't make Arzu go through this with me. There is *no way* she'd make it.

"I felt it was the kinder thing to do. It got you through it, right?" Idris pushes his sticky hair out of his face. "Wow, it's hot in here."

"Honestly, there's only one kindness I need from you." I march toward him and hold out my hand. "Give me the materials you got for the protection charm."

"Why?"

"Because I *need* them. Now," I say, near tears. "And if you were ever my friend, you'd do this for me."

Idris looks taken aback. "Noorzad, of course I was always your friend."

"It doesn't seem like it."

"I—" Idris looks down at his shoes. "I was afraid, okay?"

"Afraid of what?"

"Of jinn finding out. I'm not the son of a powerful jinn king. My existence won't get excused like yours," Idris says. "I'm only one-fourth human, so it's easy for me to stay under the radar. And I didn't want you—or anyone—to know, because then it truly means . . ." He gets really small at this. "I failed."

"Failed what? Your wish?"

Idris shakes his head. "I failed my family. I thought by concealing who I was, I could hide the truth of everything I'd lost. . . ." When Idris finally catches my gaze, I believe him. You can't fake the way his face looks like it's about to split in two. A hundred years is a short time for jinn, but it's a lifetime for humans. A lifetime Idris didn't get to see.

"It's true, then, that you really can't remember them?"

"I wouldn't lie about that, Noorzad," Idris says. "I was trapped for a hundred years. If I remembered, do you think I'd choose to spend another moment away from whoever is still here?"

So he is really lost. Not only in his hometown but in the world. I wonder how it feels, to be all alone. "What is it like? To be lost?"

"Awful. When I was in the ring, I thought I was in a dream of eternal darkness and couldn't wake up. Everything was blurry and unclear. I couldn't remember why I was there in the first place." Idris scrunches his nose. "But when I got out, the darkness never went away. And that made it worse because all I want to do is wake up and be found, to remember them, but how can you wake up from reality?"

"I'm not sure." My heart hurts for Idris. "But thank you for telling me. That was really brave."

"Wish I didn't have to be brave." Idris fiddles with his notebook at his waist.

"Well, I'm still glad you told me." This doesn't fix our friendship, but it makes a tiny difference. I don't know what it's like to be him or know what he's lost. "And I can forgive you for lying now . . . in exchange for those protection charm books."

"I didn't bring any books."

"WHAT!" I nearly lose my balance when Idris waves his hands frantically to explain himself.

"I mean, I didn't need to bring them with me. The instructions are annoyingly simple. All you need to do is pick something—it can be anything—that means something between you and the person you want to protect. Once you have that, you just write a symbol that bonds you together, and— okay, so this is the hard part—you have to mean it, with everything you have."

I blink. "And that's it?"

"You have to think of what's most important to you, and it has to be true."

"How do I know what that is?"

"Search deep down and you'll find your answer." Idris gives me a knowing look. "You can't lie to your own heart, you know. Once you have that, you have to one hundred percent give it away. For your someone-worth-protecting. But I'm not sure why I'm explaining this to you when—"

"Thanks, Idris!" I turn around and brace myself to enter the barrier for a second time. I don't think—I leap right in. Spoiler alert: it feels just as bad as the first time. I nearly pass out when Arzu and Yaseen pop back into view. I fall on my hands and knees, breathing way too hard.

"Farrah, are you okay?" Arzu rushes over and drops down beside me. Her worried hazel eyes swallow her face when she shakes my arms.

"Indestructible, remember?" I roll up my sleeve and show her the marks that go away instantly.

"Whoa. That's incredible." She taps my arm to double-check I'm really all right. Her touch feels like the warmest, fuzziest, safest hug ever, and that's how I know there's no turning back. Whatever I'm going to give up, it's not more important than my best friend in the whole world.

"What's the most special thing you have on you?"

"I didn't bring any stuff with me, just your jacket from your room." She pats the puffy jacket and finds a secret pocket. Inside is a crumpled piece of paper—a note she had written me in class. "I didn't know you saved this."

"I didn't either." I must have forgotten. Arzu and I have tons of notes (that my mom usually throws away). She brings the paper closer and we squint, trying to read our scribbles.

"It's all smudged." Arzu's brow furrows.

"It doesn't matter what it says. It matters that you're the one I can tell all my secrets to." I hold my hands on top of hers and wish it with all my heart, like Idris said—wish that she'll always be around to tell my secrets to, because even the toughest, most indestructible people need a best friend.

"Well, duh," Arzu says, "but you don't need to death-grip my hands so hard to tell me that."

Yaseen hangs back when I groan in frustration and

squeeze my eyes shut. Why isn't anything happening? Shouldn't there be a whirl or a bang or a sparkle? Where is the magic?

Footsteps ruin my train of thought. Yaseen holds out a pen.

"You need the right symbol," he says quietly.

"Symbol for what?"

"For the protection charm. Here, let me do it." I hand Yaseen the note. He writes a combo of looping letters before handing it back to me with a curt nod.

"I don't need—" Arzu starts.

"I know you don't need it, but you will always be my someone-worth-protecting. Charm or no charm. It's gonna happen." When my fingers touch the paper, there's a buzzing energy, like when I first entered the court. It flows and ripples from my fingertips to my shoulders and down to the tips of my toes.

The whispers curl around my ears and circle rapidly around Arzu and me, creating a whirlwind—a shield against the outside world. It circles around our hearts, searching for what's most important to give up. I wonder if it will take away my perfect grades, or my rock-climbing gear, or my love of video games. That would suck, but losing Arzu would suck more. *Not enough.* The magic keeps searching. *To protect is to leap without looking, to give without hesitation.* I look at my best friend and see myself staring back in her eyes. The energy gets faster, louder when Arzu smiles and raises a hand.

"Can't make a promise like that without our special hand-shake to seal the deal."

The energy transfers from me to her when our hands meet again and searches my heart one more time. What is leaping without looking to me? I close my eyes, think about how I ran right back into that barrier for Arzu. When I'm honest with myself, I know it immediately. I'd give all my strength to get her through this barrier, no questions asked. A bright flash of warm gold bursts from our hands and showers us in sparkling stars, causing us to fall backward.

"Whoa." Arzu sits up, her hair standing on end. "Did you feel that?"

"Yeah." I groan, rubbing my elbow. It weirdly stings.

"You okay, Farrah?" Yaseen offers me a helping hand.

"I'll live. As long as it worked."

"You bet it worked!" Arzu is jumping up with glee. "Look at how pretty it is." She shows me the glittering pin in her hand—it's a teeny-tiny bird (a simurgh, to be specific). "It's . . . perfect." She pins it on proudly and shakes out her shoulders. "It also feels weirdly tingly."

"You get used to it." Yaseen glances up at the red glowing eyes of shadow jinn around the barrier. "Whiiiich is great timing because those guys have been multiplying a little too fast for my liking."

"Everyone ready?"

Arzu and Yaseen nod as we face down the swirling darkness of the barrier.

"Let's do this."

"FOR THE SAKE OF OUR WORLD!" Yaseen shouts as he races through the barrier. "HOLY OUCH!"

"WHY DOES IT FEEL LIKE BEES!" Arzu yelps as we hit the boundary at the same time.

This third time feels the worst; it knocks the air from my chest, and I struggle to move through the sludge. My feet get stuck when the stinging is too much. It all hurts too much. Everything burns. My cheeks, my lungs, my arms, even my ankles.

I fall to my knees. It's too hard to breathe. I'm . . . not going to make it. Out of the corner of my eye, I can barely see the swooping shadow jinn, looming closer. Waiting like vultures.

"Come on, slowpoke." Arzu grits her teeth while grabbing my arm. Her pin glows and flows around her, like she's got the golden feathers of the simurgh safeguarding her. "Best friends protect each other, right?" We run and make it through together. Idris rushes from the edge of the barrier, jogging toward us.

"I never want to do that again." Yaseen gasps and takes huge gulps of air. "How did you do that three times?"

"'Cause she's—" Arzu gasps when I collapse on the ground. "What's wrong?!"

"Can't"—I wheeze—"breathe." I roll onto my back. Everything hurts—even my bones hurt.

"Noorzad," Idris says softly. "Your cheek."

"I—I have a cut." My hand flies to the spot where my face stings the most. I sit up immediately. "It's not healing." I check the rest of my body, and there are little scratches and cuts and bruises everywhere. I count the seconds, but they don't heal. Oh no. *No no no.*

"The charm," Idris mutters. "It's got to be the charm."

"I— It's fine," I say when Arzu paces back and forth. Her jacket is tied around her waist, and she looks weirdly energized after crossing through the barrier of pain.

"It's most definitely not fine. I stole your power! Look at you!" Arzu nervously bites her cuticles. "We're through the barrier now. How can we change it back? Here, take the charm. I don't need it." She hands me her pin, but I shake my head.

"The charm is a one-way deal. Once you make it, there's no getting back what you lost," says Yaseen.

"And I'd do it again if I had to, so don't worry about it." I flash Arzu an uneasy smile as I try to stand. "I just need . . . a second."

"If you say so . . ."

I don't hear the end of Arzu's sentence. Sound doesn't travel the way it's supposed to here. Move five steps and everything gets super muffled and warped by the barrier. Even though it hurts, I keep walking. The blacktop street continues in front of me. It's filled with layers of spray-painted, shimmering graffiti that trails all the way down past what I can see. There are little cracks with steam pouring out of them. *Just put one foot in front of the other, Farrah.* The pain will go away if you push hard enough.

The problem is, it doesn't.

The pain gets *worse.*

"AARGHHHH!" I shout as loud as I can. How can I be strong without my power? I'm used to being the best, the fastest, the strongest—invincible. I look at my hands. Now I'm weak on the outside *and* inside.

I didn't think the charm would take all my power—my super strength and super healing. I close my hands into fists and look up at the trees filled with shadow jinn. The red jeweled eyes of my shadow reflection blink through the branches.

Who am I if I'm not indestructible?

Suddenly, the ground rumbles and shakes again, causing the street beneath me to groan and split. Huge fissures of fire and steam rise up. I scream when the road splits, nearly melting my shoes. I roll out of the way just in time to see the ground get swallowed up by the hole.

Four jinn kings down, the whispers chant, *three to go.*

I run back to my friends. "That's another jinn king down," I say. "It feels like the rumbles get worse the more kings we lose."

"We've got to— Whoa." Yaseen's eyes get as wide as saucers when he sees the fiery road in front of us. "Do you guys feel that?"

"Yeah." Something terrible is slithering through the

air—some ancient energy I can't explain, other than it feels very, very dark. "Almost like it's . . . the gateway we've been looking for."

"I guess an exiled all-powerful jinn can have some intense feelings?"

I nod. Now I get why none of the other jinn kings wanted to come down here personally. I wouldn't want to face Azar's wrath either . . . especially if I were the one responsible for imprisoning him in the first place. "At least it's deserted. If people lived here, I don't think they'd survive."

"There are some humans who live here." Idris looks like he jumped in a pool. He is fanning himself very aggressively. He's taken off his shirt and tied it around his waist. "I can definitely smell them."

We walk carefully, avoiding the cracks as we enter the town.

"You see." Idris points at an old home, but it doesn't look solid. (It looks like a hologram.) There's a man on the porch, rocking back and forth in a chair. A shadow jinn swirls near him, pushing the chair forward. "The humans are here, but not here."

"How is that possible?" asks Arzu.

I walk to where the ghostly mailbox is and wave. "Hello, sir! I'm lost and looking for directions!" The man doesn't notice me. He just continues to rock.

"Jinn essence can do more than enchant clouds and refill cups." Yaseen pulls out the mini spear from his back pocket and activates it so the light from the tip shines a better path for us. "Use enough of it and you can lay realms on top of one another. Like here. Visible and invisible all in one space."

"Like another dimension?" I ask.

"Not exactly," replies Yaseen. "This is really advanced Essence Theory stuff, so I haven't learned the proper concepts yet."

Arzu walks very close to me. "Are you okay?" she whispers.

"Never better." I wince and wipe sweat off my forehead.

"Farrah, seriously, I'm worr—"

"I'm *fine*." I break away from Arzu and walk a little faster. I don't look back, and I hope she gets the hint.

Up ahead there is a clearing. Another man—a very solid-looking man wearing an elaborate robe and holding a walking stick—is standing at a fork in the road.

I distract myself from the throbbing of my cheek by asking, "If jinn and humans can live in the same place at once, like this, then why don't they?" I rub the little hairs on my arm as my shadow jinn's beady red eyes continue to watch from the trees and rooftops. The rest of the puppets march silently in the wake of the glow from Yaseen's spear.

"One, it's illegal, but no one here cares about that," Idris chimes in. "And two, it would take a lot of essence to keep that up. Like, it would drain and kill all the jinn living in the Qaf Mountains. It's just not . . . worth it."

"Which is why"—Yaseen leans close as we all huddle together—"we need to be on our guard, because somehow

I don't think Azar cares about whether something is good or bad."

And you think the jinn world cares about good and bad? Azar's voice swirls around my shoulders and taps along my spine. *You think they're always right in dealing with the ethics of mortals and immortals? You think it's right what they've done to you?*

"Keep out of my head," I whisper to the voice.

I'm only allowed in because you let me, the voice says. *Because a part of you is mad at the jinn kings too, particularly your father.*

"That's not true!" I shout, holding my head.

"You are not fine, Farrah!" Arzu rushes over to me. "What's going on?"

If you don't want me in your head, all you have to do is push me out, Azar's voice says. *But if you do, then you'll never know your true potential. Don't you want to know why the jinn kings fear you?*

Now Idris and Yaseen are next to me too, their eyes big and worried.

I hesitate. "How could they fear someone so weak? I've lost my power," I barely whisper.

Have you? Azar asks.

"Don't let him get to you, Noorzad," Idris encourages me.

"If Azar is messing with your head, it means we're close." Yaseen squints down the road. The robed man ahead of us stops moving. His walking stick stills in his hand. Something gold glints on his pinkie.

"The ring! The shadow jinn must have dropped it." I point. "Hey! Sir! Please wait a minute." I run, full speed ahead, not caring about the sting in my ankle or cheek. Not when the ring is close enough to grab.

"Noorzad, stop!" Idris is suprisingly fast when he needs to be (or I'm slow). He grabs my wrist and pulls me back.

"Why?" I struggle to break free.

"Because there is no man," he says.

Huh? "But he's right there." I look again.

"Guys, I'm getting a doubly bad feeling," Arzu whispers.

"Ditto." Yaseen's spear shakes in his hands.

The man turns slowly. A crown gleams on his head. Peeking through his shaggy long hair, a golden eye glints. He nods, smiles. *The bad feeling has only just begun, dear children,* the voice roars in my head.

Then the entire world around us goes up in blue flames.

Now the fun can finally begin, Farrah Noorzad.

CHAPTER TWENTY

AND THE ANSWER IS . . .

Who are you?" I shout through the ring of fire. Yaseen, Idris, Arzu, and I make a circle, with our backs together and our elbows locked.

Who I am, the whispers twirl, *will not gain the answers you seek.*

"Why don't you talk like a normal person!" The flames grow higher and then suddenly go dark. The shadow jinn line up in rows on both sides of the man. They are an army of shapeless blobs with shiny red eyes and frozen smiles.

"Why are they all lined up like that?" whispers Yaseen. His lightning spear sparks.

"Wish I knew." My eyes are glued on the ring dangling between two of the man's fingers.

Four gems glow in the dark.

Ask the real question your mind seeks. The man smiles

wider, but it's hard to get a good look at him. Scary shadows slash across his forehead, covering most of his face.

"I want the ring back now!" I shout. "I'm tired of these shadow jinn games." That's what this has to be, right? This is just another puppet talking. The seven jinn kings banished Azar, so his true form is imprisoned in the Realm Beneath the Unseen. He can't walk here. It's probably a shadow jinn he's using to talk through.

Clever girl. The man continues to smile, one eye gold, the other red. *But that's not a question. Try again.*

"I can see the ring." Yaseen squints. "But I can't see who is holding it."

"Can't all jinn see each other?" Arzu asks.

"Yes, but . . ." Idris trails off. His eyes go completely white, and I think he's using his power. There's a rustling of the boxes in my head, like someone is taking little peeks and making a mess of the careful order of my mind. "I see him," he whispers to me. "Through your memories."

My whole body goes cold.

I don't like that *at all.*

"I thought you said your power was useless," I say quietly to him. "Stay out of my head."

"I was just trying to help—"

"I said *stay out.*"

"Now is not the time for whispering." Yaseen makes a mean face at where he thinks the man is. "Farrah, what is he saying?" Smoke and ash swirl around us as the fire burns.

"To ask him a question." I try to ignore my worry that Idris is poking around in my memories . . . and that he's done it before. "'Ask the real question your mind seeks,' whatever that means."

"Well, I have lots of questions, but I don't think that's what he means," Yaseen mumbles.

I take a step away from our circle, coughing on fresh clouds of smoke, and get closer to the man and his army of shadow jinn. His crown is tilted to the side of his head. His dark red robe trimmed with gold embroidery trails behind him and fuses with the smoke, so it's hard to know where his clothes end and the shadow begins. It's almost like they are one. He looks just as scary, just as all-powerful, as the jinn kings when I first met them in the court.

You don't want your friends to know who I am. His voice slithers in my head. *That's why you don't want that quarter-human poking around in your memories.*

"How can I convince you to give me that ring?" I point directly at him to help the others look in the right direction.

You can only deny the truth for so long, but who am I to deny a game. The puppet man's smile gets even wider. *Ask and you shall receive. Give and take. Question and answer. There is a cost for answers, for wishes and dealings. For things that do not yet belong to you. What am I asking of you?*

I relay his message to the group.

"He could get to the point," Idris mutters.

"Who is this man?" Arzu asks.

"I was *hoping* a guardian to the Realm Beneath." Yaseen looks increasingly distressed. "But I've never felt jinn power this ancient before. . . ."

"You don't think it's . . ." Arzu trails off.

"Don't say his name here." Yaseen gets very scared. "Whether he is or not doesn't matter. Names give more power than you think."

The man's smile gets even bigger.

"He can *hear* you." I grit my teeth and wipe my sweaty bangs from my forehead. "I don't know what you're asking!" My head is overflowing with too much stuff, too many feelings crowded and pushed aside; there isn't room to think. Give and take. Ask and receive. "Um, a trade. You want a trade!" Just like when the ring of fate took Idris, took my dad.

Very good, the whispers chatter as the shadow jinn nod and clap. I don't see the puppet that looks like me. *An answer for an object. Now listen well, for J'll only say this once. Are you ready?*

I nod.

This should be easy for a clever girl like you. The man plays with strands of his hair and says, *Jf you drop me, J am sure to crack, but give me a smile—*

"And I'll always smile back. What am I?" I repeat the rest of the message to my friends. Arzu is deep in thought.

"I'll be honest—I'm not good at wordplay," Idris admits.

"Always smiles back . . . ," Arzu mutters. "That's not very original. Taking a line from a Goldfish commercial."

"What smiles back at you but also cracks . . . ?" Yaseen rubs his hands over his forehead.

"I've got it!" Idris exclaims. "It's eggs."

"Eggs?" Yaseen and I say at the same time.

"Yes, because when you crack them, they resemble smiles."

Yaseen throws me a look that says, *Is this guy serious?* "Idris! And here I was impressed at your trivia knowledge. . . . The answer is obviously a reflector."

"A what?" I ask.

"A reflector." He digs in his pouch and pulls out a small and shimmery triangular object. It looks very delicate. "See?" He angles it so it hits what little light is around us, and a shimmering reflection of me pops up, 3D and all. I take a step back in awe and look at myself. I smile and my reflection smiles back.

"So it's like a mirror," Arzu pops in, also impressed by the reflection.

"A reflector," Yaseen corrects her. He turns to where he thinks the man is and opens his mouth. "My answer is re—"

"Wait!" I nearly tackle him and cover his mouth with my hands. His reflector drops to the ground and cracks. It's definitely way more delicate than I thought. "I'm sorry, I didn't mean—"

"Don't look at it. Don't touch it." Yaseen kicks the reflector with his foot.

"Why?"

The reflector answers instead. It starts to spark, and through the crack a swirl of energy rises up like a firework for twenty seconds before stopping.

"That's why. Now you can touch it." Yaseen pockets his broken reflector.

"That's too complicated. The answer has to be something simple, like a mirror," Arzu rationalizes.

"Yes, exactly!" It makes perfect sense.

Yaseen snorts. "The answer is most definitely not a mirror."

"And why not?"

"Do you have one on you?"

I feel around in my pockets. "No . . ."

"Well, have you ever seen a jinn in a mirror?" Yaseen rolls his eyes. "Have you seen a single mirror in the jinn world?"

"I—" Actually, I haven't. My brow furrows.

"We don't use them, because they are a human invention that doesn't work on us." Yaseen is getting more annoyed. "So we should go with my answer."

"Maybe if we were in the jinn world, but we're not. A mirror is the answer. It shows your reflection in the same way water does."

"So then why can't the answer be water?" asks Yaseen.

"Because water doesn't crack."

"It does if it's *frozen*."

The man's face lights up as we bicker.

"Eggs is still a viable option," Idris interjects.

"IT'S NOT EGGS!" Yaseen and I shout at the same time.

"I was just trying to lighten the mood." Idris looks miffed.

Ticktock goes the clock, the whispers say. *When the sun expires, the deal is off.*

"But it's already dark!" I glance at the setting sun. The moon twinkles through the barrier. "Guys, we don't have much time. Let's put it up to a vote, and we'll go with whichever answer wins. I'm voting for mirror. Yaseen?"

"Reflector," he huffs, and raises his spear higher to keep an eye on the shadow jinn.

"Idris?"

"Well, if those are the only two options . . . reflector," he mumbles.

That just leaves Arzu. We all stare at her expectantly.

"I mean, obviously I'm going to choose mirror."

"Come on!" Yaseen rubs his face and walks in a big circle. The sun is getting lower. "Why can't you just listen to me?"

"Because Farrah is—"

"Supersmart, I get it, but only about human stuff. When it comes to the jinn stuff, you've got to trust me."

I'm getting way too frustrated. The bubbles pile up in my stomach as the sun sinks lower. Everything is on the line. If we don't answer now, it'll be too late. I've lost my invincibility, but I can make up for it with my smarts. With Yaseen and Arzu bickering, I make the decision. I march toward the puppet man and stare down his army of shadow jinn. I don't flinch at the fire as it swirls around my ankles. It burns, but I keep a brave face.

Do you have an answer? The man spreads his arms wide. *I am waiting.*

"Hey, Noorzad, what are you doing there . . . ?" Idris looks alarmed.

"You better not be doing what I think you're doing!" Yaseen gasps and makes a beeline for me.

"Don't leave me behind," Arzu yells, chasing after Yaseen.

He cups his hands around his mouth, and we all shout at the same time—

"THE ANSWER IS MIRROR!" I exclaim.

"REFLECTOR!" shouts Yaseen.

"EGGS!" screeches Idris.

Arzu doesn't get a chance to answer. She trips over her shoelaces and knocks into Yaseen, who knocks into me. We go tumbling onto the hot floor. I am so sweaty, the dirt immediately sticks to my clothes.

"What are you doing?" I try to move Yaseen off me just as the sun is fully set.

"What am I doing? What are *you* doing?" Yaseen studies me with a look of betrayal. "We hadn't settled on a vote!"

"So what!" Anger bubbles and bursts in my stomach. "You were taking too long to realize I was right!"

"Oh, because you're always right. I knew you didn't mean it when you said you were sorr—"

The man's laughter cuts into our arguing. It is a booming, enormous sound.

We all freeze.

"Please tell me I'm not the only one who hears that. . . ." Arzu rushes closer to me. We both look at the man at the same time . . . only, he doesn't quite look like a man anymore. He has grown extremely tall and wide, towering over us.

"Oh my god—" Yaseen scrambles backward on his elbows and knees. He crab-walks away from the man's growing shadow.

"I liked it better when I couldn't see him," Arzu shrieks as she stumbles and trips.

"Wrong answer for the ring," his voice booms. "Now it's time to pay up, little ones." The sound splits the ground, creating fissures between all four of us. I jump up and immediately run to a tree and start climbing as high as I can, away from the shifting ground.

"Guys, grab hold of something and climb!" I shout, fear taking over.

"Now we know why he didn't open his mouth before!" Idris follows suit and tries to latch on to a tree, but a shadow jinn grabs his ankle and drags him down into one of the fissures. "Help me!"

"Idris!" I shout to him, but the ground shakes again, and I lose my grip on the tree. I fall backward.

"Yaaa!" Yaseen runs and jumps, slashing forward through the shadow jinn who come closer to us. "We answered your stupid riddle; now give us what's ours before we take it from you!"

"Brave for one so naive." The giant man is full of glee as he pockets the ring. "You failed to answer my question, so now it's your turn to pay the price. Three wrong answers mean three admissions to the Realm Beneath the Unseen."

"This is the gateway?" I shout as the entire street beneath us is swallowed whole—trees and trash cans and all.

Darkness falls as gravity pushes us down a gaping dark abyss.

"Noorzad, grab my hand!" Idris reaches out for me. We are falling too fast, spinning too far away from each other. *Where's Arzu?* I want to yell, but something cold pulls me deeper into the darkness. A shadow jinn wraps around Idris and pulls him down too.

Arzu. Yaseen. I see his glowing spear above me. Soon enough the darkness snuffs it out too.

In the blink of an eye I see the sky of Centralia, and then in another blink it's gone.

It's your lucky day, the whispers laugh. *Don't have too much fun now.*

CHAPTER TWENTY-ONE

WELCOME TO THE REALM BENEATH THE UNSEEN

O f all the ways I thought the Realm Beneath could look, I didn't imagine the Qaf Mountains stuck in a domed snow globe. That's a twist I didn't see coming.

"Why does this keep happening to us?" Yaseen woozily sits up and clutches his head. "Oh, bad idea. Do not sit up after falling . . . however far we fell."

"Really far." I groan because everything hurts. *Everything.* Muscles I didn't know I had are yelling, *No more falling, please!* I blink the stars out of my eyes and roll over, coughing, on my stomach. I hate the way I feel—weak and vulnerable and small. I don't feel like me at all. It's like I'm in a stranger's body, but I put on a brave face because I can't let Arzu see how much I'm hurting. I already feel bad—I don't need her to feel bad too. "Arzu, we're gonna need a whole month to recover from all these emergency falls."

There's no response.

That shakes me out of my pity party. "Arzu?" I try to move my head to look around, but it just makes me dizzier. Tears of frustration leak out of my eyes as I count to three. *One, two, three, up!* I manage to sit up . . . and I'm already exhausted. I hold my head in my hands and take a deep breath. I thought disappointing others was the worst feeling out there. No one talks about what it feels like to be disappointed in yourself.

Spoiler alert: it stinks.

"I—I don't see her." Yaseen holds out his hands for balance. He's trying and failing at standing. (He reminds me of a baby deer learning to walk for the first time.) To be honest, it makes me feel a little better that he's struggling too. He looks up and grimaces. "That's a lot of darkness." Above us, instead of a night sky with clouds and stars, there's a domed wall of black glass blocking all light.

"She has to be here." This is really bad. I promised Arzu she'd be okay, gave up my strength to protect her. She's got to be around here somewhere. What was the point of giving up what makes me *me* if she's not okay? "Look harder because I can't move yet."

"What is this place?" Idris flops onto his hands and knees, coughing.

The boys' lack of progress is too frustrating. *Up, Farrah, up.* I force myself onto my feet and take a good look around. The scenery resembles the Qaf Mountains, from the way the jeweled mountains glitter against the dome to the clear floor, only it's so polished, I can see my fuzzy reflection. With each step I take into the mirror city, more fires light up my path. Fires in all colors—red, orange, blue, green, yellow—burn brightly. "Whoa."

The city morphs and twists. The streets with shops and cafés clear, leaving a fancy red-and-gold archway in front of me instead. Come to think of it, everything is red and gold here.

"I'm h-home?" Yaseen woozily walks through the entryway and into a huge garden. In the center is a bubbling fountain—well, it would be bubbling if the liquid weren't frozen in place. I swallow back a bad feeling when I see the stagnant liquid—"Is that *blood*?" Idris gasps—spurting from the top of the fountain. A sculpture of a winged jinn holds a sword up in the air, and from the sword's tip, "water" spews out in a frozen arc back into the pool of the fountain.

"Oh, I wish I hadn't seen this." Idris turns green as he covers his mouth.

"Don't get distracted. We need to find Arzu." No matter where I look, there's no sign of her. I pinch my cheeks and focus. *Think, Farrah*. Come on, why isn't she— I gasp. "Wait. *Three* wrong answers. Arzu didn't answer the riddle." Which means . . .

"Maybe she didn't get sucked down here." Yaseen is breathing hard as he holds his side and hobbles past the fountain and deeper into the garden. "For your friend's sake, I hope that's true."

I hope so too.

Yaseen pauses when he gets to black iron gates and studies the house in the distance. I can see four domes on it. Yaseen points to the balcony all the way to the left. "That's where my room is. When I was a kid, Baba and I would sit there and talk about the latest kite-fighting matches and cases he had scheduled for the day." Yaseen groans and slides against the gates.

"Are you okay?" I crouch next to him. He's sweating really bad. We both are.

"Never been better," he grits out, but I see how he tries to hide his upper leg. "Wish I had some of that super healing of yours right about now."

I wince at his comment and try to touch his leg. He yelps. "I think the bone might be broken."

"It's not broken." He moves his hands to where his leg is hurt. "It's just a cut. I'll be fine. See?" Yaseen grimaces as his cut begins to shape-shift and the skin fuses back together. "Good as"—he wheezes—"new."

"I really didn't need to see that either." Idris hurries ahead with his hands over his mouth and disappears into the entrance of Yaseen's house. "Why are there no trash receptacles for emergency vomiting? Who designed this purgatory?"

"Idris, we shouldn't split up!"

"Sorry, Noorzad. It's an emergency!"

I chase after him and trip over a long Persian rug in the entry hall. In a flash Idris is gone. Again. A little warning flag waves in my head, but I try to shrug it off. Even though he never told us he could peek into our minds . . .

. . . and purposely gave wrong answers during riddles.

I shake my head. Idris is my first friend in the jinn world; I've got to believe there's good in him. Sure, I've been the one to force the truth out of him, but he probably has some serious trust issues. I would too if I had been trapped for a hundred years in a ring.

"Let me guess, Idris is gone too?" Yaseen glances around with a frown. "I hate to say I told you so, but—"

"He's my friend. I've got to trust him, okay?"

Yaseen sighs. "I wish I had your loyalty."

"You said this was your house?" I change the topic. I wrap my scratched fingers together and take a look around. "It's . . ." Nicer than anything I've seen before. The domed ceilings are so high, they make me dizzy when I look up. Art hangs on almost every wall, and in spots that aren't cluttered with paintings, there are plenty of vases, weapons, and other items I can't name but that are most likely worth more than my house and Arzu's house combined.

There aren't any mirrors, though, I notice begrudgingly.

Feeling a little less tired, I continue exploring. I find myself in front of a stained-glass window that has a lamp displayed next to it. I walk toward it, almost in a trance, as if it's calling to me. I should lift the glass and pick it up—

"Don't touch that," Yaseen warns, pushing the glass case down. "A lot of these items are highly confidential and extremely dangerous."

"What is it?"

"Something you shouldn't be touching. This lamp was enchanted by King Suleiman. One touch and you're stuck in there forever."

"That's really cool." I want to know more about it.

"It's not cool, it's dangerous," says Yaseen. "Nothing that has the power to trap jinn is cool. When the human king died, his power source and this lamp were taken into jinn possession to make sure no human would ever have that kind of power again. It's just *one* example of why we keep our world separate."

"You can't blame all humans for one person's actions," I murmur, suddenly reminded of the rule that kept me apart from Yaseen and the rest of the jinn world. "We're not all the same."

"I know that now," Yaseen says. "But it's hard to . . . let go of all the bad stuff I was taught. I . . ." His voice trails off as he takes out a little handkerchief from his pouch and wipes my fingerprints off the glass. "I was wrong about you."

"I was wrong about you too," I say. "You're not as annoying as I thought."

Yaseen smiles. "What a relief."

I want to ask Yaseen more questions about his house, but something weird catches my attention.

"We don't have any shadows." Even though there are floating fireballs lining all the walls, there aren't any shadows moving around. Actually, nothing really moves at all. "It's like everything except us is stuck or frozen." To prove my point, I march over to the nearest archway and tug at a red Persian rug mounted on the wall.

"Hey, careful with that!" Yaseen flinches, waiting for the rug to fall, but it doesn't. It stays floating in midair.

"How is that possible?" He examines his house with narrowed eyes. Carefully, he pushes a vase with one finger, and it does the same thing. "Why does the Realm Beneath look like an upside-down version of home?"

"Maybe . . ." I think about the puppet man with his growing smile and piece it together. "It's a riddle."

"Another one?" Yaseen's right eyebrow is nearly gone from the tugging, but that doesn't stop him from finding new hairs to pull as he quietly walks down the halls, making a handful of turns through diverging crossways. "Then that means we still haven't found the real gateway. There's another test we have to pass." Yaseen sighs. "I'm getting tired of all these tests." He stops short in front of a surprisingly empty (and very cobwebby) hall. There's an elegant set of doors.

"But what could it be?" I ask.

"I—" Yaseen doesn't talk, or move, or even breathe. He just stands frozen with his hand out in the air, like he's afraid to open the doors.

"What is it?" I come around and wave a hand in front of his face.

"I can't do it," he whispers.

"Go in there?" I point at the doors. "Why, what's so scary about this room?"

Without warning, the doors swing open, inviting us to explore. I walk inside the room. It's big and bright and *empty*. The wall on the left is all window, where I can see the prettiest garden just beyond the glass. The only item in the room is one lonely stand, with a single flower blooming.

"I've seen this flower before," I mumble. I reach out to touch it but stop short, afraid I might accidentally break it. It looks very fragile. The red petals curve up. Long stamens grow past the petals, reminding me of little spider legs. I wonder why the house would have this kind of room. It reminds me of a quiet place for quiet thoughts.

Yaseen is still standing in the doorway, knees shaking. "I'm sorry. I can't do it." A tear slips down his cheek before he turns around and runs away.

"Yaseen, wait!" What happened? Did I do something wrong?

He runs up a staircase. I follow him as he goes headfirst into a dark hall. Big portraits of serious-looking jinn hang in neat rows. I hesitate when the space starts to shrink, getting smaller and darker. Yaseen has disappeared, just like Idris.

"Hey, don't leave me alone up here," I whisper, backing away from the glowing pictures. It doesn't matter how far I walk; their eyes follow me. It's when I see Padar's and Yaseen's regal faces that I realize what this hallway is.

"It's a family tree. . . ." I shrink back when I look at Padar's photo. His dark eyes burn into me, and I can't seem to move. It reminds me that I never knew my dad, not really, not in the ways that matter. The cut on my cheek stings, opening new waves of feelings and hurts I was able to outrun by being the smartest, the fastest, the toughest, the best.

By being indestructible.

Only, now I'm not.

And if I'm not those things, then what am I?

Who am I?

I sink down and stare at my hands—both human and jinn and scarred and hurt.

And alone.

"This isn't real," I remind myself. "It's a test. None of it's real. Azar's just messing with us."

Sitting alone, in the dark, away from my mom, and my grandparents, and my best friend—it feels like the worst nightmare ever. Is this what it would be like, to live in Padar's world? In a big, cold house, full of old relics, that still feels empty because there's no mom or dad home.

Suddenly, Yaseen's anger makes sense.

I study Padar's photo for one more second before shutting it into a box in my head.

Then I get up to find my brother because I think I've figured out exactly where we are.

CHAPTER TWENTY-TWO

IF I NEVER HAVE TO SOLVE ANOTHER RIDDLE

I headbutt Idris as I'm running back down the stairs. "Ooof!" Stars dazzle in front of my eyes. I am *not* used to everything hurting so much.

"Watch where you're going," I moan, and clutch my head.

"Sorry, Noorzad. I got a little lost in this place." Idris keeps me steady. "Rooms twist and vanish. When I ran in, I couldn't find my way back to you guys."

I sigh in relief. *See, it wasn't on purpose.* "It's okay. I know how to get out of here. Azar is playing a trick on us—well, actually, it's another riddle, but I'm sure of the answer this time. We just need to—"

The ground shakes and knocks us over. I cover my head with my arms, convinced that the earthquake will rip the ground in two and send Padar's belongings crashing on top of us. Then, as quickly as it started, it ends.

Five jinn kings down, the whispers remind me. *Two to go.*

"AZAR, COME OUT NOW!" roars Yaseen as he suddenly pops into view. He's angrily walking from one room to another. "I'm tired of your riddles. Let us out of here now!"

"Quick, before we lose track of him," I say.

"Somehow, I don't think we could lose him even if we tried." Idris winces and covers his ears. "What's got him so mad?"

Yaseen's rage is a force bouncing and barreling through the house.

"It's the riddle," I explain. "I'm pretty sure Azar wants us to figure out where we are. And I think we're in a nightmare."

"Clearly, it's his nightmare."

Yaseen rips open curtains and steps into the inner gardens, shouting curses that would make my teacher's head spin. By the time we catch up to him, he's kicking the fountain, shouting, "It's my nightmare! There! Now stop playing with us and show yourself!" Nothing happens. The flames floating above us grow a little bit larger, but the feeling that we're stuck in a dark snow globe doesn't go away.

I trudge up next to Yaseen, trying to get rid of the cottony, scratchy feeling in my throat when I say, "It's *both* of our nightmares. Azar is showing me what I'm afraid of the most." My voice wobbles, but I know I've got to say it. "That even with a wish, I'll never be good enough. No matter how hard I try, I'll still be alone."

"*I'm* the one who's not good enough." Yaseen puts a hand on my shoulder. His wide green eyes are glassy. "Baba cared so much to keep you hidden from the rest of us, he risked unearthing a forbidden object to help you. He's never done anything like that for me. Not even when—" He breathes deep. "You think because I lived in the same house as Baba, I never felt lonely. But ever since"—he chokes a little—"ever since my mom . . . went away, this place is lonelier than ever. And I don't think the empty feeling will ever leave."

I don't know what to say, so I stare at the tiny jeweled flower pinned to his shirt, and understanding clicks into place—why Yaseen couldn't go into that room, why he got so mad when I didn't talk to my mom, why our dad going missing turned him into a ball of anger, why there wasn't one personal photo in his room at school, why he never talks about his mom.

I'm the one who has so much more to wish for.

I don't think there's anything I can say to make Yaseen's hurt go away. Just like how there aren't enough words to make my hurt go away. But maybe we don't need words.

I hug Yaseen as tight as I can, to let him know I might never understand what it's like to lose a mom, but he doesn't have to go through it alone.

Yaseen hugs me back.

"I'm sorry," he says. "For being so mean to you."

"I'm sorry," I say. "For being so mean to you too." When Yaseen pulls away, I ask, "Ready to answer the riddle?"

"I thought you'd never ask." Yaseen cups his mouth with

his hands. "The answer is, it's both of our nightmares. Now let us out!"

The world around us is as still as ever.

"Are we missing something?" I ask, squinting at the garden.

"Knowing Azar, he might have a few more tricks up his sleeve." Yaseen takes off his shoes and his shirt. He hands them to me. "But so do I. Stay here. If he's hiding, I'll find him. We don't have time to waste."

"What are you—"

His bones start to crunch and shift. I shut my eyes until the bone breaking stops.

"You could warn me, you know," I say. Clutching Yaseen's belongings in my hands, I watch him transform into a very oddly shaped bird. His wings flap as he goes higher and soars across the dome, searching for his prey.

While his jinn power is cool, I don't think I'll ever get used to the shape-shifting.

"Idris, do you know how to play tic-tac-toe?" I sigh and turn on my heel. "Might be a while before Yaseen gets back."

But Idris is gone.

"Idris? Did you wander off again?" I peer around the hedges to where he was last standing. "Hellooo?"

There's a trail of footprints in the grass, leading straight into a maze of hedges.

I'm about to follow the footprints when something feels

weird in my head . . . like someone is peeking into the mess of boxes in my mind.

When they realize I notice, they abruptly go away.

I get a really bad feeling again, and this time I can't ignore it.

CHAPTER TWENTY-THREE

BREAKING FRIEND CODE

A person's mind is the most private of places, and no one (like a certain recollector) should ever open up and read someone's personal memories without permission, especially since there's no way I can put a lock on my head, or a sign that reads KEEP OUT, I MEAN IT!

Idris has broken friend code for the last time, and I can't continue making excuses for him.

I slowly walk toward the hedge maze and keep glancing at the footsteps in the grass. Too bad the bread-crumb trail of stepped-on grass ends at the entrance of the maze. There's a fork, and I remember learning you should always turn right when dealing with a maze, so I do. I hurry down, feeling like someone shoved a bowl of ice water on my head. It's a dead end. "Shoot." I double back, go left, run down the maze— another dead end.

That doesn't make any sense. I spin around and head back to the fork and look up.

In the middle of the hedge is a handprint.

I press it.

Bright red flames curl around my hand. The flames are cold, like ice cubes or liquid nitrogen.

"We need one of these back home," I mutter when the hedge splits in two, revealing another path into a large clearing. There are benches and prayer mats and little bookshelves filled with books covered in ink. In the corner of the hedge room are materials for making kites—tissue paper, string, bamboo sticks—but they're all torn in half. There are puddles of ink everywhere. In the center of it all is Idris, who is writing very quickly in a notebook.

Around his feet are open notebooks with pages of scribbles and ink splotches and faceless drawings. Idris is so busy, he doesn't notice me. His eyes are completely white and sad—so very sad.

Because he peeked in my head, I don't feel bad when I pick up one of the papers and read:

> I woke up today after what feels like a long, dreamless sleep. The world didn't wait for me while I was gone. . . . No one did. I try to remember what I lost, but it's like the ring took more than time from me.

The Qaf Mountains are not the same. No mixed jinn live here anymore. No matter how much I try to recollect, I can't find them in my memories. I can't see their faces, remember their names. It's like they've been erased.

Tears smudge the next line.

Or they're dead. And it's all the jinn kings' fault.

I shiver when I read *dead* and *jinn kings' fault*. That definitely sounds strange and suspicious. . . .

"What are you doing?"

"What are *you* doing?" I glance from the pages to Idris. "What's with all the papers?"

Idris doesn't say anything.

I crunch up the papers in my fist and let out my worries again. "I thought we were friends—"

"We are—"

"So then why do you keep reading my mind when I've told you not to?"

"Because you wouldn't understand." Idris's eyes clear as he begs, "Please don't make me tell you."

Red alert. *You wouldn't understand* sounds a lot like *none of your business*. Something really doesn't feel right when

Idris gets up and takes a worried step toward me. I step back. "What are you so afraid to tell me?"

"You don't want to know, because if you did . . ." Idris rubs his hands through his messy white hair. Streaks of ink have dried in it, causing some of his hair to stick up. He wipes his cheeks. "You wouldn't want to be my friend anymore."

Alarm bells go off in my head as I take a closer look around. Somehow I don't think this scene has anything to do with Yaseen or me. One of the brightly colored kites reminds me of the kite Baba Haji stored in our basement.

When I was really little (before Baba Haji got arthritis in his knee), we'd go out to the park. I'd watch Baba Haji run and throw the kite up, letting out string until it flew up, up, up. When it found its place, Baba Haji would hand me the spool of string. *When I need more string, you unspool it, okay, janem?* he would say.

I sniffle a little and find myself missing him.

I wonder if Idris has a similar memory . . . or if that's the problem.

I gasp.

"I don't know why I didn't realize it sooner. What you really meant when you said you failed. The real reason why you hid being mixed too." The gears in my brain are turning when Idris laughs nervously. "Why you'd tag along to help me save my dad."

I remember the way Idris was sprawled across the café table back at the City of Jewels. How he gave me that book, but he had to have known I wouldn't be able to read it. How he slowed down when the ring dropped from our cloud. How he told me to not confront Yaseen about King Barqan's plan. How he said looking for the ring wasn't important. How he "forgot" jinn essence. How he hid the instructions to make a protection charm. How he gave wrong and confusing answers to riddles. How he got mad when Yaseen and I started to get along. How he'd peek into my head, even when I said to stop. All the little mistakes along the way that added up to so many delays . . .

Yaseen was right.

It wasn't only the shadow jinn that were wasting our time.

"It's not what you think."

"You don't want to help me save my dad or the other jinn kings," I say slowly, now understanding all the papers and chaos around me. "You didn't tag along to help me stop my wish. You *want* my wish to happen. You want the jinn kings locked away. You . . ."

"I knew you wouldn't understand," he says very quietly.

I wait for the angry bubbles to come and zip through my head so I can tell Idris how messed up his actions are. The bubbles don't come, though. "The truth," I say, "once and for all, Idris. Now."

"You want the truth? Here it is. Just because one of the kings is your dad doesn't mean he deserves to be saved," Idris starts. "You don't know what it was like when the seven kings banded together and created new laws, new rules that exiled anyone with human blood. Over a ridiculous *prophecy*. My world changed overnight. My home became a place where I was no longer welcome. And I don't know if it's because I spent so much time in that ring—it's all so fuzzy in my head—but what I do remember is the feeling that everything was a ticking time bomb for us.

"Since I'm just a quarter human, I could have hidden under the radar with the rest of my jinn family, but then I'd miss my human family. Time works differently for jinn. They don't grow old and weak, not in the same way mixed jinn do. I will one day, but . . ." He scrunches his face and squeezes his eyes shut, like he's trying really hard to remember. "Why should I have to choose between worlds? I didn't want to miss a minute of time with either. It wasn't . . . It wasn't fair. It isn't fair. I had to do *something* to fix it."

"That's why you wished on the ring."

He nods.

But just like me, he didn't know that wishes had a price, and in the end Idris did lose more than a minute. He lost a *century*.

"Maybe they're still out there. You don't know for sure—"

"If they were, then why can't I recollect anything about them? Why are their faces so fuzzy in my mind? Why can't I remember them?" he whispers. "Instead of being with my family, I'm stuck here, protecting you."

I wince because that stings, but it also slots in the missing piece to our riddle, why the gateway hasn't appeared.

"Being here is your nightmare too," I realize. "You knew it but didn't tell us. You wanted to let the clock tick until the wish completed. You wanted revenge."

"I wanted *justice* . . . but I never meant—I didn't think it'd get this bad." Idris's mouth twitches and wobbles. He's fighting against the prickly feeling that happens right before you cry. I know because I do the same thing when there's a big emotion I don't want to feel. He looks like he needs a hug, but I have one more question.

"Were you ever my friend?"

"I've been your friend this whole time." Idris throws his hands in the air. "Okay, maybe not the *whole* time, but I was the one who convinced Yaseen to calm down after that explosion you two had. If it weren't for me, he would have gone straight to the Realm Beneath by himself. I never wanted you or your annoying brother to get hurt. I never wanted us to make it to Azar's kingdom in the first place! I just wanted fairness for my family. So what if I wanted the wish to go through. So what if the jinn kings are stuck in that cursed ring forever. It's what they deserve. If you were me, you would do the same."

Would I?

If I had to choose between worlds, could I pick just one? Maybe before I was spirited away to the Qaf Mountains, before I got to know Yaseen and see his school and want to know what it would feel like to be a royal student too . . .

I don't know if I'd want to choose.

I think I would want both, but both isn't possible.

Something moves above us. Flying in a small circle is Yaseen.

"Please don't tell your brother," Idris pleads. "Let me be the one who tells him first."

Yaseen spots us before I can answer. He swoops down and crash-lands in the hedge. I plug my ears when his bones crunch back into place. He looks really, really tired.

"I need the longest nap of my life after this," Yaseen mumbles sleepily. "It was a waste of time. I searched everywhere, but there's no way out."

"Actually, there is." Idris awkwardly clears his throat. "But first, there's something I need to tell you." Idris looks hesitantly at me. I keep my eyes on the ground and walk away. I don't know if I can listen to Idris twice.

"What is it?" asks Yaseen.

Idris traces circles in the grass with his foot before glancing at Yaseen. "There's something you need to know, and then you'll understand why I have to continue on this mission with you."

CHAPTER TWENTY–FOUR

WHEN IDRIS FINALLY TELLS THE TRUTH

"**I KNEW IT.**"

Yaseen would have sprung to his feet and thrown his finger in Idris's face if he'd had the energy. So instead he settles for shouting.

"DIDN'T I TELL YOU HE SMELLED WEIRD?"

"This isn't helping me feel any better," I grumble.

"There's one last tidbit of information I need to share. . . ."

Yaseen rubs his face in his hands. "There's *more*?"

Whatever it is, it can't be any worse than knowing he wants my dad and the remaining jinn kings locked away.

"When your dad got sucked into the ring and I was spit out, there was a moment when he . . ." Idris gulps now, looking very nervous. "He might have made me your familiar, Noorzad."

Yaseen chokes for a second before he says, "You have got to be kidding me. Why would he do that?"

"Am I going to regret asking what that is?"

"Our dad, as a jinn king, in really dire circumstances, can bind jinn to other jinn, for protection," explains Yaseen. "Which sounds like something he'd do because he was literally in danger, but the irony is, he picked *him*."

"When you say *bind,* you mean . . ."

"He's stuck to you. Where you go, he goes, until whatever started the danger is gone."

I stare down Idris, suddenly feeling very, very silly for not noticing all the times he randomly left and very reluctantly came back. I don't know how my friendship with Idris can ever be the same after this. "Anything else you'd like to share?"

"No, that's all, I swear. I'd eat a truth tart to prove it." Idris holds his breath, waiting for our reactions.

"I know he's your friend, Farrah." Yaseen shakily gets up and takes out another shirt from his pouch. "But I don't want him on our mission anymore."

"He's not my friend, and we don't have a choice. It's like you said, he's *stuck* with me," I say quietly, while stealthily swiping at my eyes. A friend wouldn't pretend the way Idris pretended. Yaseen didn't have a choice when he kept his secret from me. Idris *did*. He always had a choice. And that hurts the most. "Anyways, when the danger is gone, the bond will be broken, so all we have to do is keep moving forward." Because Idris's betrayal hurts so much, I focus on the only thing left to do.

"The answer to your riddle," I shout out to the sky, knowing Azar is listening, "is that it's all three nightmares wrapped up in one!"

Instantly the hedge maze comes alive. Time resumes. The bushes rustle as bright flames erupt and grow higher around us. A breeze sweeps through my hair just as a metal doorway encased in fire appears in the center of the maze. It grows five, ten, fifteen, twenty feet tall, pushing waves of heat into our faces.

Congratulations, the whispers rumble. *You may proceed.*

THIS IS IT. THE DOOR TO THE REALM BENEATH IS FINALLY here. I take a big breath and walk toward it. It's time for this wish to end.

"Noorzad, wait a moment." Idris tentatively catches up so he's next to me. "Can we—"

"No, you listen." I stare at the doorway. It glitters with rubies and gold. Steam wafts from the metal as it melts and re-forms over and over again against the fire. "Our friendship doesn't exist anymore. I'm going to undo my wish, and then you'll be free. I'm sorry about your family. I really am, but you made a choice, so now it's time for me to make mine. You can stop pretending to care."

"But—"

"Can you stand?" I help a very pale and tired Yaseen up

and hook my arm under his elbows. His protection charm glows and pulses, moving in his veins like he's got gold running through them. In a few seconds, he looks a lot healthier.

"Thanks, Mama," he says to the pin. He clears his throat and says louder, "So long as there isn't a mountain of shadow jinn waiting for us, I should be fine."

We walk slowly toward the door.

Are you ready? a voice asks from behind the door.

I nod. "Ready."

Ask and you shall receive, the whispers welcome us as the grand, scalding door swings wide open. Beyond the door is a large spiral ruby staircase that goes down farther than I can see. Floating beyond the stairs are levels in the Realm Beneath—they resemble flaming cities that go on forever. I understand why the jinn kings locked Azar's realm away. It's enormous.

"Think we'll make it out of here alive?" Yaseen gulps.

"That is the hope." Idris's knees knock together while peering down the stairs. "Yaseen, remember what you said about being fine?"

"Yeah?"

"Don't look down."

We look down. Below is an army of shadow jinn, waiting and bobbing like an ocean of terror.

"I . . . should have seen that coming," Yaseen groans as he stands on his own. He reaches into his back pocket, but I stop him.

"Are you sure?" I'm seriously worried for him. His protection pin can't possibly guard him from an ocean of puppets. One wrong move and it'll be all over.

"It's not about being sure, and if you haven't noticed, you're not looking so tough either." Yaseen studies the cut on my cheek before steeling himself to unleash the lightning spear. "But just in case this is the last time we can say it, I'm glad I got to meet you," he says to me. "I'm glad to know that I was so wrong about half-humans . . . and, Idris?"

"Yeah?"

"Don't get in the way, or else."

The sea of shadow jinn roar as Yaseen takes one step down the ruby stairs, then another. I grip my fists, and say to myself, *Be brave, be brave, be brave.* Superpower or not, I've got to do this. Not only for Padar but for Yaseen.

"Let's do this!" I say, charging down the steps. There's no energy bursting and fizzing in my fingers or toes, but I don't let that stop me. I tumble and knock down the first row of shadow jinn that stand in our way.

Yaseen takes down three more shadow jinn as they rise from the stairs—each a mirror of Yaseen's determined face. My knees really hurt from the tumble, but I keep going. So far there's no sign of my shadow jinn, but I know she'll show up soon. I race down past Yaseen just as two shadow jinn pop up in front of me. Their red eyes gleam hungrily at me as they lunge. Too bad no one told them about the girl from Philadelphia who races against the moon and leaps from buildings to protect the people she cares about. Even when she's scared and small and vulnerable. *Especially* when she's scared. I front-roll toward them. They scatter and jump up in confusion, right when Idris yells, "Now!" and Yaseen unleashes a huge arc of lightning right at them.

"Take that, shadow puppets!" Yaseen laughs before he charges ahead again.

Rinse and repeat. I leap and block down the swirling staircase, wincing at each bump and bruise.

"You've got to take it easy," Idris warns. "You're not indestructible anymore, remember?"

"I can handle it—don't worry about me," I shout, and wipe sheets of sweat from my face.

"That's the problem, I do worry about you," Idris says.

"Stop lying, Idris!" My hair is basically glued to my forehead now the lower we go. Each stair gets harder to run down, and my legs are getting tired, but no matter how hard I try, I can't outrun the hurt in my heart or the fear that I trusted the wrong person.

"I'm not lying!" Idris bats away another shadow jinn as Yaseen sweeps through with his spear.

"I can see the bottom," Yaseen shouts. He points. Below us there's a glittering throne surrounded by a huge sprawling castle. Lying in the center of the throne is a crown and the ring. Five gems glow, no, wait—

The ground rumbles and the staircase crumbles, little by

little. A huge crack beelines for my feet, and I dodge a chunk of melted rubies right before it crashes on my head. My elbows skid against the rough stone and I cry because wow, it *hurts.*

Six jinn kings down, Azar's voice roars, *one to go.*

One to go.

"No!" I slap the floor of the shaking staircase, frustrated with my bleeding elbows and legs that are too slow. I'm so dizzy, I can't find my balance. The unstable staircase doesn't help. Shadow jinn are getting knocked off and screeching as they fall far below.

"It's gonna collapse," yells Idris when Yaseen loses his footing and lurches forward, tripping toward the center of the spiral. He braces himself, but it's too late—he falls.

"Yaseen!" I call after him, scrambling to jump in and save him.

"Noorzad, you can't keep fighting like this." Idris blocks me. He kneels down and says, "Get on. If I run fast enough, there's a chance we can catch him."

"I can do it myself."

"You can't," says Idris. "Please, for this last time, let me help you."

"How do I know you're not tricking me?" The staircase cracks even more as I try to keep my balance.

"Because two wrongs don't make a right. Just because the jinn kings hurt me doesn't make it right for me to hurt you too. I'm sorry it took me this long to realize that," he says. "So what do you say? Will you let me help you, for real this time?"

Yaseen doesn't have time for me to think. I say, "Okay," and hold on to Idris's back. His arms hook behind my knees as he stands up.

"Hold on, it's gonna be a bumpy ride!" Idris runs like he's never run before. He dodges chunks of breaking stairs moments before impact. We're gaining on Yaseen, but we're still too far. Unfortunately, Idris loses his balance, and we end up tumbling off the staircase too.

"This is the part where you hold on as tight as you can!" Idris grits his teeth. His eyes are watery but determined as he squeezes himself into a ball around me so he's the one who hits the ground first. But I know Idris is not indestructible. He's going to break. The burning wind swirls around us as we plummet all the way down.

"We're not gonna survive this!"

"Maybe I won't." Idris squeezes me tight and says, "But you will survive, Noorzad. You just gotta believe it's all gonna be okay." Then he closes his teary eyes, scared but ready for the impact. He whispers, "It's all gonna be okay."

"You're gonna be okay too!" I shut my eyes and hug Idris tight, and I wish with all my heart that it's true.

I wait for the part where we slam into the floor of the Realm Beneath, but it never comes.

"Now, where's the fun in cleaning up your guts moments before you get to admire my kingdom for what it really is?"

Azar's voice booms as we drop into a bubble of fire. It feels weirdly like landing in a pool full of Jell-O. That's as gross as it sounds. All three of us are staring at each other as we slowly sink through the sludge and lightly touch down at the bottom of the stairs. The Jell-O disappears.

The moment our feet touch the ground, it stops shaking.

Idris lets go of me and laugh-cries. "I thought I was a goner."

"We're not out of the woods yet." Yaseen lifts a shaking hand.

A gold throne looms over us—and the giant exiled fire jinn sitting with his crown crooked on his head. His dark eyes—one gold, one red—glitter through the fire behind him as he spins the ring of fate round and round on a string.

"Well then, little ones." His voice shakes the entire realm. He leans forward, his sharp, pointy teeth on display as he smiles. "I hear someone has an issue with their wish."

I gulp as I stand in front of the exiled fire jinn king. The jinn who is my only hope at saving Padar, myself, Yaseen, and the future of the jinn world as we know it.

Whatever happens from here, there's no turning back now.

CHAPTER TWENTY-FIVE

THE LAST TRADE

It's time to make things right.

"My name is Farrah Noorzad," I say, "and I'm not leaving until you free the six jinn kings from that ring."

"Oh." Azar kicks his feet up and stretches his arms wide. "And if I don't want to humor the request of a mortal?"

"Then you'll have to face an immortal instead," Yaseen growls right next to me. He's about to pounce, but a riptide of fire pushes him back.

"Ah, ah. I would be careful if I were you, little ones," says Azar. "Wouldn't want to accidentally hurt an innocent now, would you?" He moves just a little bit to the side of his throne. Behind his massive shoulder is a floating, glowing orb of fire with a curly-haired girl sleeping inside.

"Arzu! You let her go! She isn't a part of this," I shout.

Her pin glows on her shirt, pulsing as something golden wraps around her, keeping her safe. *For now,* I worry.

"Just let our dad go and cancel the wish. You made the ring; you should be able to stop it from happening," says Yaseen.

"Ah, there is the fatal flaw." Azar brings his massive face closer toward us. I can see my reflection in his golden eye. "As much as it flatters me that you think I can snap my fingers and alter fate to my whim, I'm afraid that is something I cannot do so easily."

"What do you mean?" I ask.

Azar continues to stare at us. He lifts his wrists and nods at the chains of fire I hadn't noticed until now. "You think if I could rearrange fate to my will, I would still be here? Chained to an everlasting nightmare—a nightmare *your father* had a hand in—where my only purpose in this immortal life is to watch time go on from this prison? You think that sounds like *fun* to me?"

"Well, no." I glance at Yaseen, who looks just as bewildered as I am.

Idris, surprisingly (or unsurprisingly), is not next to me.

"All magic, even mine, operates under a set of rules," Azar continues while examining his ring. He holds it up, and it glints against the levels of his kingdom that float above us. "While it has taken me an eternity to get the interior design of this place just right, sometimes I do grow bored. Hence, this ring. It's great fun to see the wishes and whims of mortals. It reminds me of what it was like to be young and naive." At this, Azar gets a wistful and far-off look. "When once upon a time, I used to be young and naive and good . . ."

"Why am I getting a feeling there's a *but* coming?" Yaseen nudges my shoulder. He's looking around for an exit plan and freezes when he sees something. "Does Idris have a death wish?" he whispers urgently.

Because Azar is caught up in his monologue, he doesn't notice Idris slowly climbing up the back of the throne. Oh no. His eyes are on the ring.

"He better not be doing what I think he's doing," Yaseen grits through a smile. "Just when we thought we had one jinn to worry about. . . . What do we do?"

You gotta believe it's all gonna be okay.

"Just follow my lead." I take a steady breath and say out loud, "So it must be a lot of fun when you get visitors, then?" I gulp and take a step closer, choosing to distract Azar. The fire jinn laughs.

"Not as many as I'd like," he says. "Not many souls are brave enough to make the trip here."

"You've got to give me credit, then." I nervously watch as Idris gets higher up. "Enough credit to give me another chance to save my dad."

"Save your—" Azar shakes his head, and the strangest thing happens. He begins to shrink from evil giant jinn to tall human adult. He adjusts his crown to sit square against his long black hair and rubs the seven chains on his wrists.

Curiously, Idris keeps climbing higher, passing the ring . . . *Where is he going?*

Azar walks toward me, and a dark blood-red aura glows off him as his eyes dig into mine.

Why would you want to save a father who upholds the rules? Azar's voice whispers in my head. *No, who created the rules to keep half-humans like you out of his world?*

"Whatever he's saying to you, don't listen to it," warns Yaseen.

Case in point. Azar rolls his eyes. *Look what your father and his friends did to me. They kept us both out of their world. Why would you want to save a jinn like that?* His voice grows louder. *When even your own brother agrees with your father? You think a few days together is going to undo a lifetime of teachings? You think he'd fight for you to join his world? Maybe his heart has softened toward you, but what about other mixed jinn?*

I take a few steps backward, nearly tripping over myself.

"You're just trying to confuse me! They banished you because you wanted to take over the world!" I shake my head.

Oh, little one. Don't you know there are always two sides to every story? Don't you want to know mine?

"I'm not listening to you!"

Admit I'm telling you a truth you don't want to hear. Consider this. Do you think your father would really bring you my ring all on his own? Azar bends down and opens his palm. The ring hovers and twirls. There's only one jewel left to be lit. One last chance to save Padar before he and the other jinn kings are trapped in there forever. *Why would your father give you the chance to change what has always been done?*

"What are you saying?" Azar's words make me feel like I've inhaled salty ocean water. "You're saying *you* made my dad bring me the ring?"

"My dad would never fall for your tricks!" shouts Yaseen. "Never!"

Azar just smiles a knowing smile before closing his palm and snatching the ring away.

"I guess you'll never find out, little ones," he says out loud. "Since you'll be gone when this wish completes."

The ground starts to tremble, and I look at Azar with wide, worried eyes.

"Gone?" Yaseen asks.

"Oh, you mean you haven't figured that part out yet?" Azar chuckles. "And here I thought you two were intelligent."

Yaseen winces at the jab, but it makes me remember something.

What a waste, the shadow jinn said. *This time next week there won't even be a soul to steal.*

"I thought the jinn kings would only be stuck in the ring. . . ."

"Of course they'll be stuck." Azar goes on to fill in the holes. "But who is to say they don't disappear a little bit earlier in the timeline, before, you know, say a certain treaty was established?"

Yaseen nearly collapses in horror. "That's not possible. You wouldn't—"

"You're right. *I* didn't. Your lovely sister did." Azar smirks. "It's just pure happenstance that I get to delight in watching their world turn upside down."

I look at Azar in alarm. "But if the jinn kings are disappearing from a hundred years ago, w-what will happen to us?" I stare at Yaseen, who is thinking the same thing.

If the jinn kings aren't around to create the treaty, that means Padar will never meet Madar, will probably never meet Yaseen's mom, will never put Idris on course to search for the ring.

It will change *everything*.

"Will I still be me?" I whisper to Yaseen. "Will you still be you? Will either of us actually exist in a world where our dad *doesn't* make the rules?"

"Finally, an interesting question." Azar adjusts his robes as he solemnly looks up at his kingdom. His shadow jinn crowd against the ruined spiral staircase, blinking and watching. Waiting. I wonder if he talks to them the way he talks to me.

"Well?" I try to blink back tears. I can't believe I never thought of this until now. I can't imagine a world where Madar, Bibi jan, and Baba Haji aren't my family. A world where Arzu isn't my best friend. How could they live their lives without a single memory of me?

"Farrah Noorzad, you are the most interesting girl I've

ever met," Azar says. "You've risked your life to save a world that does not want you. You gave up an incredible power to protect a life that is bound to perish, if not today, one day. You trusted those who have deceived you, hoping for the good to shine through. And because of that, I will give you this answer. You should know, to change one's fate requires a heart's truest wish. It is an incredible feat of magic, and your heart has already answered. But to change a mortal's fate twice? It's nearly impossible. It's never been done before."

Yaseen looks worriedly at me. My heart sinks when I say, "So it's impossible." I look at my hands, my bruised, hurting hands, and make fists. Is the jinn world right? Maybe half-humans really are dangerous. Maybe it is for the best if I don't exist. For everyone.

"I said it's *nearly* impossible." Azar sighs, bouncing the ring on his palm. "But the rules are the rules. A mortal can only wish upon the ring once. Seems a pity, though. I suppose once your wish goes through, perhaps the other mortal girl will wish for you back." He grins. "I wonder what chaos that would cause."

My head snaps up when Yaseen and I both say, "Arzu!" just as Idris leaps and holds on to Arzu's flaming bubble, jostling her awake. Her hazel eyes sleepily blink open.

"Oh." Azar spins to look at Idris. "Now, how did you get all the way up there?"

The ground shakes harder than before. It catches Idris off guard. "Argh, I'm slipping!" Arzu's bubble pops, dropping them both to the ground.

"Oh no, it's the last earthquake!" Yaseen races toward Arzu and Idris just as they are swallowed up by a wave of shadow jinn.

"Well, that settles this visit. I've seen everything I needed to see. It seems you are not the one I seek." Azar bows with a flourish. "It was a pleasure to meet you, Farrah Noorzad." He laughs at my last name, like it's a joke. "It seems even your divine light cannot battle my eternal dark." He throws the ring up as my jinn puppet finally appears. She catches it. When she looks at me, her eyes are uncertain and defeated.

More shadow jinn pile onto Yaseen as he reaches the throne.

I think for a second to chase after her, but there are three someones who need me right now. I hesitate, feeling small in the face of so much darkness. Who am I without my strength?

Can I really do this?

I'm about to find out.

"Hold on, guys, I'm coming!" I battle my way past the shadow jinn and push them off me. The only good thing is, they're not very coordinated on unstable ground. The bad thing is, neither am I. I topple over Yaseen. "Where's Idris and Arzu?"

"They got dragged somewhere, but I don't know. It all

happened so fast." Yaseen is woozy on his feet. He can barely dodge the shadow jinn. I do the first thing I can think of. When you can't go right, left, or down, sometimes the only way out is up.

"Climb now!" I shout. My arms and legs scream when I try to dyno up the throne. *Please, please, please. For Arzu.* I keep climbing. *For Idris, who chose me over revenge.* It can't end like this. Not when there's so much that needs fixing. Yaseen scrambles up with me, and we climb all the way to the top.

"Do you see them?" I yell against the roar of the ground crunching and fire growing.

"No, I don't. . . ." Yaseen shudders. "What if . . . What if they took them over?" Like what almost happened at the observation deck. The shadow jinn who wanted their own free will, even if it meant stealing it from us. "There's so many of them. I think we lost, Farrah."

"Don't say that!"

"AAH! MY HANDS," Yaseen shrieks. "THEY'RE DIS-APPEARING."

Yaseen and I study each other. I can see through his transparent head. He's fading away. My hands are starting to blur too.

Think, Farrah. Think. I look frantically as the shadow jinn slowly climb their way up. The throne shakes and I hold on tight—but my fingers slip through, like they're not there anymore. No! There must be a way. There—

"Azar, wait!" I shout as loud as my voice will go.

I think of hidden meanings, tricks within riddles, and turns of phrase. I think about the one thing Azar loves to do. The hidden answer in between the lines.

"Asking for another wish isn't the answer, and you know that," I bargain, hoping I'm right. "Because what you want is a trade, so how about this: tell me a riddle, and I'll make you a trade you absolutely cannot refuse. If I answer correctly, you change the rule and let me have another chance at a wish. And if I answer incorrectly, then . . . you can keep the version of me that will exist when the wish goes through, but you leave my friends alone. You're not allowed to keep their souls, just mine. Those are the rules."

"You what?" Yaseen tries to kick a shadow jinn, but his translucent foot goes through it. It seems the shadow jinn can't touch us anymore. "You take that back right now."

It's too late. Azar's grin grows ever wider as he whispers, *How exciting, you figured it out. I do love a good wager. So let's have ourselves a trade, little one.*

CHAPTER TWENTY-SIX

THE CHOICE IS YOURS

Yaseen is immediately encased in another fire Jell-O bubble as he floats away from me. "Hey, let me out!" The bubble flashes and he freezes, hitting the pause button on his fading.

From somewhere far below, Idris is unconscious in another bubble. So is Arzu. They're okay! My heart gives a flutter. They all float next to Azar, who grows larger and larger, in true final-boss form.

"I said I'd make a deal, not my friends. What are you going to do with them?" I keep looking between my friends and Azar. The ground doesn't stop shaking, and I am on pins and needles trying to figure out how much longer I have before I disappear too.

"Think of it as an insurance policy." Azar floats up next to me. "After all, a boring deal is almost as bad as . . . well, a bad deal." He laughs at his own joke.

"Stop stalling!"

"Have it your way." Azar snaps his fingers. My shadow puppet drops the ring into the palm of his hand. She floats closer to me, looking nearly invisible too. "Final riddle. Answer me this, Farrah Noorzad, and I will use all my awesome power to grant you one last wish on this ring, but only if you answer correctly. Are you ready?"

"Yes."

What he says next surprises me.

"Why is your father worth saving?" Azar asks.

"I—huh." I blink at him. "That's not a riddle. It's just a question."

"You're right, it does seem a little anticlimactic, so why don't we up the ante a little." The ring floats in the palm of Azar's hand. I count six glowing gems before the ring starts to spin, faster and faster. Little specks of dust and lightning funnel out of the ring right in front of me. After a few seconds a glowing figure stands a few feet away.

Dark hair. Brown eyes. Eyebrows that furrow together, looking suspiciously like a unibrow.

It's . . . my dad.

"Padar? Is it really you?" I take a small step forward, too scared to blink in case he disappears again.

"Farrah?" My dad rubs his eyes sleepily. "What is this? Where is this?"

"It's—"

"Ah, ah, ah." Azar wags his finger. "The clock is ticking,

and you've still got a question to answer, little one. Remember, if this ring lights up, it doesn't matter what you say. Even so, I am extremely curious to hear your answer, as I'm sure your father is eager to know if you value his life. So I'll ask you again, in front of our audience: *Why is your father worth saving?*"

This is the trick, isn't it?

"I have to answer in front of my dad." I look on with wide eyes. But how?

"Farrah jan, please." Padar's weak voice cuts through. "I—I don't know what's going on, but I need you to be strong. This evil jinn, he tricked me. I don't know how, but he got into my head, so I need you to listen very carefully on how to handle this—"

"What do you mean, he tricked you?" Uh-oh. My stomach is flopping uncomfortably when Padar looks at me with weary eyes. His weary brown eyes. His human eyes.

"He enchanted me to give you that box." Padar takes another step closer and falls to his knees. He's covered in those white glowing scars. He's still bound to the ring . . . the gift he never meant to give me.

"He . . . tricked you?"

"Yes. Exactly."

Azar only smirks.

Azar was telling the truth. Padar never wanted to change my fate. He never intended to bring me into his world. He wanted to keep me out.

"You were never going to tell me about my heritage, were you?" I squeeze my fists so tight to keep myself from falling down and crying on the ground next to him. This whole time I was holding out hope for my dad to be better than this. "You were always going to keep me a secret from the rest of the jinn world." *Be brave, be brave, be brave.* This is the only time I have to ask the questions I've been avoiding. "Were you ever going to tell me about Yaseen, or the other jinn kings, or the Qaf Mountains, or the City of Jewels, or Al-Qalam Academy?"

"How do you know all that?" is all Padar asks.

Red alert. Red alert. Red alert.

"Farrah, tell me." Padar sounds irritated now. "How do you know all this?"

"That's your answer?" I mumble back.

I wish my dad would say, *I'm so sorry for lying to you* and *I was waiting for when you were older* and *I made a mistake, but I can show you now.* I wish he would say anything else, but he doesn't. He doesn't even show me his true form.

Even after all my questions—the questions that I've hidden in boxes to protect myself—he doesn't choose me. After I've gone through this adventure and risked my life to save his, he still *doesn't choose me.*

Is he worth saving? Azar asks again in my head.

"I don't know!" I shout. I'm so confused. He should be because he's my dad, but what does it mean to be a dad when he's never around? When he lies to keep his own life comfortable? When he hurts the hearts of the people he's supposed to protect? When he hurts me?

No, I think. *He's not worth saving. . . .*

But then I think about Idris, who lost his family, and how much it hurts him to know that while I found the rest of my family, his is still gone. It hurt him, but Idris chose to help me instead of seeking his own revenge.

There are also the other jinn kings to think about. Saving my dad means saving all of them. Is King Barqan, even though he blackmailed Yaseen to slip nightmare tablets into our food, worth saving? Or King Maymun, who was ready to control Idris and me based off our blood? Or the other jinn kings, who might not have agreed to their plan but still let it happen?

I don't know. I crouch and curl into myself, feeling the weakest I've ever been. My see-through arms don't block anything, so I end up staring at Azar's curious face.

"Well?" he asks. "Time is ticking."

"Farrah, *please,*" my dad pleads.

I look at Yaseen, who is frozen in his bubble and slowly disappearing too. *I'm glad to know that I was so wrong about half-humans.*

Isn't Yaseen worth saving?

And then Arzu, who will be trapped here forever when I disappear. *Come on, slowpoke. Best friends protect each other, right?*

Isn't Arzu worth saving?

And lastly Idris, who chose us over his sadness. *Because two wrongs don't make a right.*

Isn't Idris worth saving?

And what about me? I watch my shoes and ankles and calves get more transparent. Aren't the memories with my mom and grandparents worth saving? Even though our life hasn't been the easiest, it's still *ours.*

Aren't all our lives worthy of a second chance?

Maybe it isn't all about Padar. I stand up tall, with my hands still in fists. I squeeze them tight, even though it hurts, and stare down Azar because I can't look at my dad. I don't know if there's a specific reason why Padar is worth saving—maybe there isn't one. We're all in danger because Padar chose to keep my existence secret, but I also had the best adventure of my life, with my best friend, a new friend, and a newfound brother because of his decision.

And maybe that's the point.

"Time is up." Azar spins the ring again, and my dad instantly slumps over before vanishing back into the ring. "Do you have an answer?"

"I do." A little light glows in my heart when I say, "Your question is wrong."

"Is that so?" Azar looks taken aback, but his eyes are shining with renewed curiosity at my heart. "And why is that?"

"Because it's never been only about my dad." The light in my heart pulses and fizzes in waves. It spreads all the way to my fingers and toes. It feels different from when I used to be invincible. Whatever it is, it burns bright, and it feels a lot like being brave. My shadow puppet smiles as she glows too. "It's about all of us. It's about the ways we're all connected to each other. So because your question is wrong, there is no answer—there's only a choice. *Your* choice."

"Is it, now?" Azar leans in close, his giant form crouched over me. His eyes gleam in hunger as he stares at the light. His smile only gets wider, happier. "Are you sure?"

I gulp and let the light within guide me. It feels a lot like Madar's encouraging voice. *Go on, janem.*

"I might have thought there wasn't a choice when I made my wish, but now I know I was wrong. I didn't need a wish to find my dad; I just needed to choose it. I chose to find him. I chose to cross oceans and protect my friends and come here, the one place even the jinn kings are afraid to go.

"You told me yourself, you used to be good," I say with a wobbly voice. "Well, now's your chance to prove it!"

The light explodes around me the moment the whispers wind and curl around my heart, repeating over and over again, *Correct, correct, correct.* The seventh jewel begins to glow.

A deal is a deal is a deal.

The ground splits Azar's throne as the ring erupts from his hand. It spins faster and faster and faster. Azar welcomes the light growing brighter around me. "Now, that's the true power I've been searching for. *Finally,*" he says, right as energy explodes from the ring.

All at once, the trapped jinn kings appear, before being thrust up and away. All the color comes back to my hands and feet. I'm solid again. *This is your chance to make it all right, janem.* I hear Madar's sweet voice pushing me forward. With all my strength I race against the chaos toward Azar's throne.

A storm swirls around me as I grab the ring. A familiar voice asks, *What is your heart's truest wish?*

This time I don't have to think about it. I climb up the broken throne and then leap, letting the storm of the ring envelop me as I collide with Azar. My hand bumps into one of the chains on his wrist. The bubbles around Yaseen, Idris, and Arzu pop, freeing them as they tumble to safety.

"You go, sis!"

"Come on, Farrah, go!"

"Told you it was all gonna be okay, Noorzad!"

Their voices barely reach me, but it's enough.

I now know my heart's truest wish. I never needed a ring to change my fate—I already did it, with the help of some friends. Now we'll take destiny into our own hands, and I'll never be afraid of where it will lead me ever again.

For the last time, I bring the ring to my glowing heart and say, "I wish for the ring of fate's threads to be clipped from now on!" The ring explodes in dazzling light as the wind starts to suck me in, just like it did Padar.

A wish is a wish is a wish, the whispers roar loud in my head. *And now your fate is yours.*

Surprisingly, Azar's giant hand opens. The fire jinn king

smiles wide and pushes me away, keeping the ring for himself. I free-fall toward the ground. "Until we meet again, curious Farrah Noorzad. Destiny has so much in store for us now that you've discovered your true power. I look forward to the day our paths cross again."

In a flash he is swallowed by the ring.

One fate for another, it says one last time. *Your wish has been granted.*

"Gotcha!" I land on a giant bird's back before I reach the ground. Its golden feathers tickle my nose. I hold on as tight as I can. Arzu's warm hand pulls me up so I'm sitting behind her. Idris piles on, and I'm sandwiched between them.

Arzu looks like she's flooded with gilded light. Behind us the flashing image of the simurgh roars, its ghostly vision pushing us up and up and up.

"I don't know what's going on, but it's totally awesome!" Arzu screams. The bird we're on swoops and makes a big circular arc, avoiding all the falling debris. The walls of the Realm Beneath shake as Azar laughs from inside the ring.

"Hold on tight," Idris says while curling his arms around me. "This is gonna be a bumpy ride."

"Yaseen?" I see his familiar eyes in the bird as he winks. "You look like a real bird. I think you're getting better at this." Nerves bubble up in me as we soar higher and higher. Past the crumbling walls, we zoom toward the slowly closing gateway. *True power.* Azar's words rattle in my head. What did he mean by that?

I only take a quick second to look behind me. My shadow reflection stands quietly as the world around her crumbles, but she doesn't seem sad. Not at all. She waves. *Until next time.*

"Faster, quickly." Idris nudges Yaseen's sides.

"Do that again and I will drop you," Yaseen groans as he flaps his wings and narrowly gets us through the gates. They close with a thud and blaze brightly in goodbye. We're back in the dark snow-globe world.

"Boys, really? You're gonna start arguing now?" Arzu is death-gripping Yaseen's feathers as we spiral.

"He started it," Yaseen mumbles. He takes us up, but not before the holographic vision of the simurgh roars again and zooms past us, growing into the size of thirty large birds, breaking the barrier of the snow globe. Its body shimmers and turns into a golden glittery shower as we fly through and into the cool night air of Centralia.

"Thank you," I whisper, and hug Arzu tight. Her protection charm stops glowing, but the tiny simurgh pin smiles, just a little bit.

"I can't believe it." Idris throws his fists into the air. "We did it!"

We whoop and twirl into the sparkling night sky.

"Land incoming," Yaseen warns. He slows down and gently touches ground. We tumble onto the smoking road. Laughing as we go. I don't even mind the bone crunching this time as Yaseen changes back.

I lie on my back—completely sore and dizzy and burnt—and stare up at the starry sky.

"We did it," I breathe quietly, and then louder. "We're still us!"

Yaseen throws on a shirt. "And now I will be taking the world's longest nap ever. Thank you."

"You deserve it." Arzu pats his back a little too hard. Yaseen winces. "Sorry, I guess I don't know my own strength." She laughs.

"Ha ha." Yaseen rolls his eyes. Then he glances at me. "Where to next, sis?"

I glance back at him. "Back to where it all started."

Wissahickon Valley Park.

To see our dad.

"Don't expect me to carry you freeloaders all the way there." Yaseen yawns and twists his back left and right. His protection charm feeds a green glow in his veins.

"That won't be necessary." Idris shakes two bottles in his hand. They look like they have exploding fireworks inside. "I may have borrowed some jinn essence from our generous friends down in the Realm Beneath."

"THANK GOD." Yaseen dramatically bows down to Idris. "I cannot stand human transportation. Finally, we're back to civilization."

Arzu helps me up from the ground and throws a not-so-gentle arm around me.

"Ow!" I say. "When did you get so strong?"

"Funny, I was going to ask you the same thing," Arzu says back.

I blink in surprise. "Do you have amnesia? I'm not strong anymore."

"You sure about that?" Arzu asks. "You looked pretty darn strong to me back there when you risked your entire soul to save us. I don't think I could do that, even with a protection charm."

"Yeah," I say. "I think you're right." I don't know how much of the last riddle my friends saw, but being vulnerable and asking the tough questions in front of my dad was the bravest I've ever been. And I'm so proud of myself for finally being strong enough to ask. Who'd have thought I'd have to lose my physical strength to do it?

"Of course I'm right," Arzu laughs. "I'm always right."

I roll my eyes. "Don't let that go to your head. Ready to leave this burning town, everyone?"

"I thought you'd never ask." Idris unleashes one of the bottles, and a storm cloud waits for us to get in. "Oh, this one is *fancy*."

Arzu wails. "Not another cloud, you can't make me!"

As the sun rises I don't have the energy to listen to Arzu and Idris argue the merits of cloud transportation. I'm just so happy to finally be going home.

CHAPTER TWENTY-SEVEN

FAMILY REUNION

————— ◈ —————

At the edge of a cliff in Wissahickon Valley Park, a very confused Padar is wandering around.

"Baba!" Yaseen rips through the trail and makes a beeline for our dad.

"Yaseen?" Padar looks shocked when Yaseen wraps his arms around him. "What are you doing here? How did you get here?"

"With a little help from friends." He gestures to me and Idris and Arzu. I shyly make my way to where they are, but Idris and Arzu hang back.

"It's your moment," Arzu urges, and stays in the trees. "Plus, I've got my own ride home."

"I thought you'd rather eat rotten eggs than endure my driving," says Idris.

"We all have to make sacrifices," Arzu says solemnly.

"You guys sure?" I ask, feeling a little nervous.

"Not really, but if I'm gone any longer, I think my parents are going to have a conniption." Arzu smiles. "I'll see you back home, slowpoke." She walks down the trail to where the cloud is waiting.

Idris nods. "It's been a pleasure, Noorzad. Now that the danger is gone"—he hesitates—"I hope you have a happy family reunion."

"Thanks. Um. Did you guys actually see the last riddle play out?"

"No. Couldn't see a thing out of those . . . slime cages we were in. It's all a blur, if I'm being honest," Idris sheepishly replies. "But I'm sure it must have been epic."

"It was. . . ." I trail off.

"Well . . ." Idris stands awkwardly. "That's that, I suppose." He turns around to follow Arzu.

"Wait." I hold on to his arm. I'm not in a rush to see my dad right now. "I-is the bond really broken?"

"Yeah, I feel . . . different. Free, in a way that's hard to explain."

"Where will you go?"

"After I drop off your annoying friend? I dunno." Idris shrugs and puts his hands behind his head. "Why d'you ask?"

"No reason." I dig a little circle in the dirt. "I just thought, if you wanted to stick around, maybe we could do something about finding your family. If, you know, you wanted my help."

Idris doesn't say anything for a second. When I look up, there are big tears splashing down his face. "You mean it?"

"Yeah, I do."

"Even after everything?"

"Don't make me change my mind, Idris."

"A deal is a deal, then, Noorzad." He smiles, and his small wave is the last thing I see before he vanishes down the trail too. I wave back, hopeful for a second chance at being friends.

But now it's time to face the music. My heart is beating so fast as I turn around and walk toward the cliff. I see my dad for the first time in his true image—as Shamhurish the jinn king, not Padar the human dad.

"I can explain." He bends down on his knees so he's at eye level with us. He scans the patchwork of cuts and bruises on my arms. He has a worried expression. I wonder if he remembers what happened in Azar's kingdom.

"You don't have to." Yaseen throws an arm around my shoulders ("Ouch!" "Sorry, I keep forgetting you're not indestructible anymore!") and says, "We know everything. And so do the rest of the jinn kings. So maybe you might need to do some explaining *there*. . . ."

"The other jinn kings know?" Padar looks aghast.

"They weren't too happy when I showed up to let them know you were trapped in the ring of fate, so I would probably tread a little lightly there," I add. Yaseen nods in agreement.

"You *went* to the Supreme Court?" Padar looks like his head is about to explode. "I need to sit down for a moment. Or an eternity." He sighs and takes both of our hands in his. "I know I owe you time for answers, but for now I'm glad you're both okay." He hugs us. Old Farrah would have loved this moment, but New Farrah is still hurt over how differently my dad is handling the situation when he knows Yaseen is involved.

Yaseen senses something is wrong when I don't hug my dad back.

I clear my throat because I'm done avoiding sensitive subjects. "I need to tell you something." I think about second chances and choices, and hope I'm right when I say, "Things can't go back to how they used to be, now that I know who I am."

"I'm not sure that will be possible." Padar has a pained expression on his face that makes my insides twist. Yaseen squeezes my hand (lightly) in support. "I will see what I can do. But you know the rul—"

"The rules are there are no more rules," Yaseen cuts in.

"It's not that simple, my son." Padar sighs big and heavy. "There is so much more to our ruling than you know."

"So tell us!"

"Now is not the time." Padar gets up and shakes his head.

"Does this have to do with my true power?" I blurt out.

Padar goes still. "Who told you that?" he asks very quietly.

The truth will always catch you, an old warning whispers. *Can't you see why they're afraid of you now?*

The way Padar is staring at me, I decide to keep this truth to myself. It's clear he doesn't remember what happened in the Realm Beneath. Whatever this power is . . . I don't think my dad wanted me to know.

"There is much to do indeed." Padar sighs. "We'll talk about this another time. For now let's get Farrah home. I'm sure her mother is worried sick."

Padar rummages in his pack and takes out a bottle the color of sunshine. It glows so bright, I can barely look at it. He gently places it in my hands.

"What is this?" The bottle is hot to the touch, and it feels like it's vibrating. "Hey, wait, we're not going together?" Padar pulls out another vial from his pack and releases it. It's an enchanted cloud. He gestures for Yaseen to get on.

"It's an Ever-Place solution," Padar explains. "You splash it on an item—a tree, door, rock, it doesn't matter—and it will turn into a portal. All you have to do is whisper where you want to go, and it will take you there. Once. Understood?"

"Yeah." I look down at the ground. I guess it's back to reality.

"Good. Yaseen, come on." Padar sighs as he heaves himself up on his cloud. "It seems I've got a lot of damage control to do back home."

"No." Yaseen stands next to me and swallows hard. "We started this adventure together; it's only fair that we finish it together too." He bravely holds my hand, but I can tell it scares him to not listen to his dad.

"Thanks," I whisper, feeling a little better.

"Anytime," he whispers back.

Even though the future is going to be messy and compli-cated, I'm glad to have a brother in my corner. "On a scale of one to ten, how bad do you think it's gonna be when I get back home?"

"Oh, definitely essence meltdown bad." Yaseen nods to himself. "I wouldn't want to be you when you face your mom."

"Hey!"

"All I'm saying is, you should have listened to me."

Padar gives in and bottles up his cloud. "Just this once, okay?" He holds out his hand for the bottle. I give it to him with a shy smile on my face. He splashes the solution against the biggest tree he can find. It moves like sunlight shining through a window and coats the entire tree until it glows. "Are you ready?"

"Yes!"

We all hold hands, Padar, Yaseen, and me.

Everything isn't perfect, but at least it's a start to a better beginning.

"Let's go!"

We jump through the sunshine, ready to face whatever will meet us on the other side.

Philadelphia winks a *hello* when the Ever-Place solution drops us off on the roof of my rowhome. I take a deep breath and hold in the crisp smell of home.

"Hello, City Hall!" I jump up and wave at the glowing yellow clock. Yaseen is staring at the city in awe as I run to the other side of the roof and breathlessly say, "Hello, Arzu's house. Hello, Philly. Hello, twinkling fairy lights. Hello, propped-open emergency door—"

Wait.

The door is only propped open when someone is up here.

"Farrah, is that really you?" Madar peeks out from the slightly ajar door. Inside the stairwell is a folding chair, a blanket, and my favorite blue chalk bag. She runs out the second she sees me.

"Madar!" I meet her halfway and hug her tight. She swings me around and around as I cry into her shoulder. "I'm so sorry I left you alone. I'm s—"

"No, I'm sorry." Madar sets me down, her eyes full of happy tears as she wipes away my soot-covered hair. "I should have told you the truth about who you are." We sink onto our knees. The moonlight shimmers against Madar's messy bun and highlights the dark circles around her eyes. "I never wanted to make you feel like I was ashamed of who you were. I jus—"

"You were trying to protect me," I say.

She nods and wipes away her tears. Then she reaches into her pocket and pulls out something small and broken—the glittering elephant pin. "When the pin shattered, I thought the worst had happened to you."

I cup the fragmented pieces in my hand, confused. "What would make the pin break?"

"I can answer that question, if I may." Padar walks into

view. I see Yaseen sitting back by the fairy lights, giving us space.

"Shams," Madar breathes.

Padar averts his gaze, a worried expression on his face. He clears his throat. "A protection charm can only be broken in one way," he says. "You can either give or receive a protection charm, but you can never have both. The second you do, one breaks. It's either protect or be protected."

"You made a protection charm?" Madar looks surprised.

"I did." Suddenly, I feel bad for breaking Madar's pin (even if it was an accident) because Madar had to give up something she held most dear. "Does that mean . . . whatever you gave up comes back to you?"

At that Madar looks up at Padar with an unsure expression. "Somehow I don't think it works that way, janem."

Padar studies Madar for a second too long, and I wonder what exactly my mom gave up to protect me.

Madar is the first one to look away. "But that doesn't matter anymore." She cups my face in her hands and brings our noses close. "I would do it all over again because you are my light against the dark, janem. Without you I am forever lost." Madar kisses my forehead and quietly says, "Thank you, Shams, for bringing her back."

When there's no response, I turn to search for my dad, only there's an empty spot where he was standing. I notice Yaseen is gone too, and that makes me a little sad.

Madar wraps herself tighter in her cardigan as she looks

up at the sky, at the cloud gently floating away. "Goodbye, Shams," she whispers.

I walk over to where Yaseen was and notice a crumpled piece of paper.

Don't be a stranger, sis. The Qaf Mountains are gonna be boring without you.

I smile and hold the note to my heart. Then I run back to Madar.

"Ready to see everyone?" Madar asks as our footsteps bounce down the stairs.

"More than ever."

As I enter the bright lights of my home, I know I didn't get the happily-ever-after ending I wanted, but something tells me this adventure hasn't ended yet.

There's still the jinn kings to face (I'm pretty sure King Barqan will stir up some trouble once he realizes his plan didn't exactly work out), and I've got school to deal with, and I'm certain Azar will have some trick up his sleeve, but that's okay.

I'll be okay.

Because I'm not alone anymore. I've got a whole group of friends and family behind me.

And I'm never going to let them go.

That's a promise.

A NEW BEGINNING

In a burning kingdom, buried deep within another realm, a golden ring of fate waits.

Its jewels gleam in the fire as it sits, suspended between the air and a ruined throne.

A girl—not quite shadow, not quite light—stands in front of the ring. She closes her eyes and wishes with all her heart for a choice, but the ring does not whisper; it does not glow; it does not answer.

A soul, she recalls, *is required.*

So instead of wishing, the shadow girl grabs the ring, squeezes it with all her might, and remembers the girl she wants to be—the girl who nearly brought an entire kingdom to ruin with her light.

A light that the shadow girl stole a piece of.

A light that now glows within the shadow girl's heart.

When the girl has had enough of wishing and remembering, she opens her eyes and lets go of the ring. One by one each gem glows. Then the unexpected happens.

The ring becomes undone and shatters, unleashing the waiting fire jinn king.

"Well done, my dear puppet." The fire king rubs his wrists as his power seeps back into his kingdom. The seven chains, imprisoning him to this realm, hold painfully against his skin . . . except, there is one chain in the link that is different. It is the chain the curious half-human girl touched. He stares in awe at the ruined link as wisps of foggy darkness seep from the crack. "So it's true." A crooked smile wraps around his wicked face as his ruined throne rebuilds itself, piece by piece. "She is the one."

The shadow girl follows the jinn king as he walks across his kingdom of fire. The king flicks his wrist. The shadow girl's light fades, and once it does, so does she, until she is nothing more than a pool of darkness, indistinguishable from all the rest.

"Now the fun can really begin." Azar laughs as he approaches an orb encased in fire. He peers within it and stares at the reflection of a half-human girl looking up at a starry night sky. "All thanks to you, little one."

AUTHOR'S NOTE

The world of *Farrah Noorzad and the Ring of Fate* delves into the wondrous land of jinn as Farrah journeys to save her distant father, who is one of seven great jinn kings. Much like Farrah, I was obsessed with the idea of legendary creatures, especially jinn. In recent years, jinn have entered Western storytelling, but unlike many other legendary beings, jinn are essential to Islamic belief. Because of this, I grew up with so many stories about the hauntings of the invisible jinn. I was the kid at school who daydreamed about what the jinn world was like and how I could get there. I especially latched on to the idea that jinn are just like humans—fully formed beings, capable of free will, with their own families, histories, and ways of life. The only difference being, well, that jinn have magical abilities and humans do not (which is supremely unfair, in my opinion). It was from this lifetime of childlike musing and wondering *What if our two worlds could collide?* that this story was born.

Ultimately, *Farrah Noorzad and the Ring of Fate* is a work of fiction inspired by pre-Islamic, Islamic, and Persian elements. Knowing the complicated history behind jinn, both their pre-Islamic and Islamic roots, I recognize that there is no way to untangle the delicate threads between them. With this in mind, I depicted the existing and imagined jinn in this story to the best of my ability, with the limited information available to me in the English language. Where I found holes, I filled them with my own imaginary creations as I built the jinn world. This story is intended to be read solely as a work of fiction.

But if you find yourself, as I do, enchanted by these mystical (and slightly treacherous) beings, I encourage you to learn more about them. Here is a good place to start:

Lebling, Robert. *Legends of the Fire Spirits: Jinn and Genies from Arabia to Zanzibar.* Berkeley, CA: Counterpoint, 2010.

ACKNOWLEDGMENTS

The making of a book is a magical affair, filled with so many wonderful people. Before Farrah Noorzad was a character in a book, she was an idea that lived in my head—an idea of the person I would have liked to be. And if it weren't for the help of the following people, Farrah's story never would have made it out of my head and into readers' hands.

To my wonderful agent, Elana Roth Parker, for signing this story so many years ago and for walking me through the long and difficult journey of publication. This book wouldn't exist if it weren't for your enthusiasm, practical advice, and support in allowing me to put this story aside until I was ready to work on it. Your patience gave me the time and space I needed away from the story to truly see its beating heart. I cannot thank you enough for guiding me through this process.

Thank you to editor extraordinaire Liesa Abrams for

reading the early pages and having a vision for what this book could be. In an industry where kindness is in short supply, I am so thankful to have your gentle support and patience through the many rounds of edits. There is a fragility to writing—especially when life, as it often does, gets in the way of deadlines—but you always prioritized the person before the book, and for that I am grateful. Thank you for giving me the time I needed to heal from grief.

The publication process for *Farrah Noorzad and the Ring of Fate* was definitely a team effort, and, wow, is the team behind this book incredible. Many thanks to Emily Harburg, for your insight and character questions that always had me on my toes. To the entire Labyrinth Road and RHCB team—Barbara Bakowski, Rebecca Vitkus, Katrina Damkoehler, Michelle Crowe, Natalia Dextre, Catherine O'Mara, Michelle Campbell, Mike Rich, and Sarah Lawrenson—this book would not exist without you. Thank you for your hard work and dedication to making books for children. So many thanks to Raidah Shah Idil and Azra Rahim on your thoughtful early reads. Your advice was invaluable and contributed to making Farrah's story so much better.

Behind every writer is a great writing community. Special thanks to June CL Tan, Swati Teerdhala, Roseanne A. Brown, Kat Cho, Rebecca Kuss, Emily Berge-Thielmann, Alexa Donne, Nora Elghazzawi, Zohra Saed, Zareena Aslami, Leila Nadir, Nadia Hashimi, Dana Nuenighoff, and Laura Pohl. I am so lucky to know all of you.

As always, thank you to my mother, who has read everything I have ever written—the good, the bad, and the "could be better." I would not be the writer I am without you and your support. Thank you for choosing me and my brother, even when it meant having to put your dreams and your life on hold. To my brother, Aman, thank you for listening to all my scattered ideas over the years. Also, sorry for always making you watch me play *Kingdom Hearts* when we were kids (but also not sorry, because us sitting together on Saturday mornings and experiencing Sora's story for the first time is the most treasured memory of my childhood).

Speaking of childhood, there were many moments when I felt like I was drowning in the dark. During the hardest years, a few beacons of light saved me when I couldn't see a way out. I am a firm believer that stories and people are what save us. The stories within *Kingdom Hearts, Inuyasha,* and *Spirited Away* were the second beacon. The first was my very first friend and my very best friend, Arzu. When my world became dark and scary, you were my sunshine; you were the hand that kept me from drowning all those years ago. You used to always tell me, "Cousins by blood, but sisters by love." What I would give to hear you say that again. If magical wishing rings were real, I'd venture into any realm, battle every power-hungry jinn to get the chance to wish you back into my world. I wish we could have stayed in those sunny, sweet days of our girlhood forever. Safe, together, and never alone. I wish, I wish, I wish.

But most of all, I wish I could have told you one last time that I love you more than you know and that my world is a whole lot emptier, darker, and scarier without you in it.

If you're reading this during a time when your world is also dark and scary, I hope Farrah's story and the magic within the world of the jinn allow you to escape. Please know that one day you too will find your light.

Until then, I hope you continue to discover the stories that guide you there.

GET LOST
IN A STORY

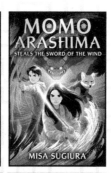

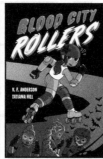

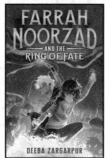

1575b